MARK MANNOCK

ECHO BLUE

A Nicholas Sharp Thriller (Book 6)

For Dad
Anthony Nigel Mannock

Contents

Chapter 1

The deepening veil of water seeped across his mask. One by one, the tropical morning clouds, in all their gray moodiness, disappeared from view. Teddy Best arched his body, rolled over and began stroking and kicking his way downward. As an experienced diver, Teddy understood what he had to do, but was uncomfortably aware that time may not be on his side. Unusually for him, a troubling sense of doubt gnawed away in the back of his mind.

Something felt different.

Within seconds, Teddy succumbed to the familiar serenity of his underwater sanctuary. The warm tropical water enveloped him as he pushed towards the ocean floor. It didn't take long for the sea to turn murky, limiting his vision. This was unsurprising. Very little recreational diving took place in Guyana's coastal waters. The country's coastline formed a river basin, receiving runoff from the multiple rivers that wound down from the Acarai, Imataka, Kanuku and Pakaraima ranges. The murky sea caused by the discharge stretched several miles out from the coast. Teddy reached for the flashlight jammed into his belt. The beam of light would help, but like headlights in a deep fog, there were limitations.

Teddy's expectations weren't high. The chances of his

mission succeeding remained small, yet he had to try. He had little information to act on. The previous day, Pedro, an old friend of Teddy's, had been fishing in this exact spot. When he hauled on his line, Pedro told him it had seemed heavy, like a deadweight rather than a fish. When he eventually wound the line up alongside his boat, what he saw surprised the fisherman. He described it as some sort of flexible hose bound at each end to a metal connector. His friend added they resembled plumbing connectors but were somehow different. They appeared more complex and oddly shaped. To his dismay, as Pedro extended his hand to seize the object, his craft collided with the peak of a swell. The line bashed against the gunnel before the hose slipped from Pedro's grip, disappearing into the depths below.

The fisherman had thought little more of the incident, but he'd considered it enough to log his GPS position. Anglers were often fixated on mapping out spots to recall productive fishing locations. Pedro was no different, so it took no great effort.

That evening at Skippers, their favorite watering hole in Georgetown, Pedro told his tale to Teddy. Teddy had grown accustomed to feigning interest in his friend's fishing stories. As a committed environmentalist and vegan, fishing wasn't one of their common bonds. That changed as Pedro described what he'd almost caught. Teddy leaned forward, put his Banks beer on the table and asked Pedro to repeat the description slowly and carefully.

As he listened, lines of concern crept across Teddy's forehead. He wasn't an expert, but his experience in the environmental movement provided him with some knowledge spanning a variety of fields. One of these was underwater demolition. From the description, Teddy grew certain that Pedro had hooked a subaquatic detonation cord.

There were others in Teddy's organization, Crimson Wave, that would know more. When Teddy excused himself from the table and walked out into the balmy night air, Pedro appeared surprised at the urgency of his manner. The detonation cord on its own was no big deal, but the fact Pedro found it within ten miles of the Reardon 3 offshore oil platform, not to mention two hundred yards away from the pipeline that lead to it, made it a very big deal. Huge.

Snapping his thoughts back to the present, Teddy continued to plow on down through the water, his beam scanning the way ahead. A brief glance at the dive computer on his wrist told him he'd just passed one hundred and thirty feet. That meant he would need to allow time for decompression stops on his ascent to the surface. Calculation noted.

A few minutes later, the ocean floor rose out of the murkiness. Teddy changed direction and swam along parallel to the seabed. He planned to find the pipeline and then perform a grid search. As small as the chance seemed, he had to locate the detonation cord, if that's what the device turned out to be. The authorities would require proof, not an angler's tale.

In the dim light Teddy almost collided with the algae covered marine pipe. Over a yard thick and encased in concrete, the pipe lay half submerged in a trench within the ocean floor. If Teddy's supposition was correct, any explosive charge would probably be attached to the line where it bridged an underwater valley. The point of maximum exposure.

For a moment, it worried Teddy how easily he channeled

the thought process of an eco-terrorist. He supposed it came with the territory. He'd spent much of his life protecting the environment. Aware of the apathy that many had displayed toward environmentalism, even some of his friends, Teddy progressed to a more radical approach. The Crimson Wave group didn't hesitate to act aggressively when required, to do what needed to be done. That suited Teddy Best just fine.

The deepness caused most of the color to disappear from the undersea world surrounding him. Occasionally, a blue hue appeared before being swallowed up by the cloudy water. For around fifty yards, Teddy grappled his way along the pipeline. He shone his flashlight alternately across and along the pipe and the seabed, hoping to find some evidence of sabotage.

If it was there.

Eventually, Teddy began the grid search, covering the area between the pipeline and his boat above. He knew his colleague in the boat would check his own watch and monitor the waves for Teddy's air bubbles. Although it would be an arduous task in today's unsettled water, Teddy had faith in his buddy watching above.

The flashlight beam exposed nothing but an undulating seabed. Sea urchins and fish of all shapes appeared and vanished. It would be easy for Teddy to become distracted, but time didn't permit that luxury.

Frustratingly, the exploration was proving unsuccessful. He glanced despondently at the dive computer on his wrist. The calculated time limit at this maximum operational depth had almost expired. In order to leave enough oxygen/nitrogen mix in his cylinder for decompression on the way up, Teddy would have to begin his ascent to the surface soon. Yet with so much at stake, he needed to do something. A blown oil pipeline this close to the shore would be an environmental disaster of gigantic proportions. Teddy Best wouldn't let that happen. He'd push his time out. It would be worth the risk.

A few minutes later, Teddy knew it was a lost cause. Crestfallen, he looked up into the hazy water above. After one last sweep of the beam over the ocean floor, he again glanced upward. Wait, what was that? He retraced the beam's path. A small metallic reflection hovered about two feet above the sand and rock. Teddy kicked hard, his arms forging ahead.

A minute later, he lunged forward, grasping at the object. His flashlight exposing the outline and detail of his find, he examined it carefully. He'd been right. No doubt remained. He'd located a detonation cord.

Damn.

Teddy pulled on the cord; it wouldn't budge. His beam aimed at the surrounding rocks, Teddy saw the other end lodged in a crevice. He pulled harder. Still no movement. He stretched down to the rock and tried to wrestle it aside. Nothing. He pulled again. It didn't give an inch. Teddy then rested the flashlight on the seabed, grabbed the rock with both hands and planted a finned foot on either side of it. With all his strength, he attempted to haul the rock upward. Again, it refused to move.

Aware that over exertion at depth may upset the oxygen/nitrogen balance in his system, Teddy hesitated.

A second later, Teddy Best ignored his own warning.

Once more, he reached down, this time applying all his effort to moving the rock sideways. He yanked hard, the muscles in his body tensing. The rock edged a quarter of an inch to the right. Encouraged, Teddy inhaled deeply and directed all his strength into one last attempt.

Pain racked his arms, but he didn't give up. Abruptly, the rock loosened and slid across. Teddy let it go while reaching forward to grab the end of the cord. He yanked it frantically.

Now he held all the proof he needed in his hands.

Unexpectedly, like a thunderbolt, a wave of nausea hit the diver. His body tried to react, but Teddy fought against it. He couldn't throw up, not down here. Clutching the detonation cord tightly, he pushed up towards the surface. The nausea came and went in disorientating rushes, but Teddy surged upwards.

As he kicked hard to propel himself toward the waves above, Teddy sensed the strength in his legs wane. He refocused his effort, yet still seemed to struggle. Checking his oxygen mix, the dial appearing only as a fuzzy blur; he was confused. Nothing made sense.

In a brief moment of clarity, Teddy realized he was in trouble. A tsunami of panic overwhelmed him as he continued to thrust upward. Within minutes, his limbs became clumsy and out of his control. The cord slipped from his grip. Its loss didn't bother him. He couldn't really remember why he'd grabbed it, anyway.

As he passed the one hundred-and thirty-feet mark, Teddy was vaguely aware he should be doing something, but was unable to recall what. Oblivious, he pushed through the decompression point, his focus solely on moving upward. He knew he was in a bad way, but his buddy in the boat would sort him out.

If he could just make it to the surface.

Teddy saw a clear light shining through the water. It came from above the waves, not his now discarded flashlight. With a last burst of energy, Teddy clawed upwards in the direction of the light. Two feet from the top, he sensed his fist break through the water. No longer swimming, Teddy simply struggled for his life.

A sudden sensation of fresh air enveloped him. He'd made it.

Almost.

Confused, his head pounding, and his vision blurred, Teddy tried to scan the horizon. A desperate inner voice was telling him to find the boat... and his buddy. Nothing else mattered.

Splashing with fierce abandon, Teddy called out. Barely controlling his movements, he spun around in the water. Searching.

A minute later, the sea muted Teddy's cries. He barely remained conscious long enough to understand.

The boat had gone.

Chapter 2

"Are you safe?"

"Yeah, I'm safe enough. But I had to disappear." Greatrex sounded elusive. He never sounded elusive, not with me.

"Where are you?" I asked.

"Can't say, but I'm out of the country."

I stared out across the white sands of Venice Beach, softened by a classic Californian sunset. The calm view had no positive effect on my frustrated state.

"Jack, what's wrong? You know just as well as I do that you're sounding out of form. It's like someone's holding a gun to your head. Are you sure you're okay?"

"I'm fine Nicholas, and I'm really sorry, but after all we've been through, I need you to trust me."

Jack Greatrex was my best friend. It had been that way since we'd been in the Marines together. Me a Scout Sniper, Greatrex my spotter. My relationship with the man defined trust.

"Trust is not at question here, Big Fella. It's your wellbeing that's the issue," I replied.

"Look, you're right. I've got a situation on my hands, but I intend to resolve it."

A situation.

"Tell me where you are. I'll be on the next plane or whatever it takes to get there." There was an urgency in the tone of my voice. Greatrex would understand.

Silence.

Then... "No."

"Jack."

"I'm deeply sorry Nicholas, I really am. But I've given my word that I would handle this alone. Your offer is appreciated, but it's still 'no'. Now, I've gotta go."

"Hang on, wait a sec. Will you at least promise me you'll check in regularly?" I didn't want to plead, but all my senses were telling me something was dreadfully wrong in Jack Greatrex's world.

More silence.

"Yeah, I can do that, but it'll probably only be every few days. I may be offline for a bit, kinda remote."

Remote. Great. Maybe I was overreacting. Maybe not.

"Okay," I responded. "But please, if you need help, call."

"Of course, I will. But Nicholas, I've got this."

The line went dead.

As things turned out, Greatrex hadn't *'got this'* at all.

Chapter 3

JACK GREATREX

Jack Greatrex gazed across the car park. He was a large man, and the moment he set foot outside the terminal, the tropical heat hit him like a stifling tidal wave. Within two minutes, he was sweating profusely. He'd done a heap of work in hot dry climates - Iraq, Afghanistan - but the moist dampness of the tropics really sapped his energy.

The Cheddi Jagan Airport parking lot was only half full. Greatrex looked around for the red Mini Amanda said she'd be driving. He couldn't see it. He strolled further into the parking area and deeper into the debilitating heat. Who in God's name would come to Guyana by choice? The Caribbean Airlines flight from JFK had been fine, but now he was tired and probably a mite irritable. LA to New York and then straight down to here was a big ask. And he had certainly been asked.

Where was Amanda?

Behind him, tires screeched loudly. By instinct, Greatrex spun, prepared to react. A red Mini with a wide black GT stripe pounded to a halt a foot away from him. The driver's door burst open. A long mane of dark hair appeared, preceding the delicate yet determined features belonging to a very familiar face.

Amanda Best rushed around the front of the vehicle and threw herself into Greatrex's arms.

"Jack, oh Jack. I wasn't sure you'd really come. Thank you so much. I've been beside myself with worry. I don't know what to do. The authorities don't appear interested. In fact, they seem more focused on moving me on. Something's going on, and…."

Greatrex took a step back.

"It's all right Amanda. We'll figure this out. There'll be some sort of explanation." The big fella's confidence belied the depth of his concern. "Let's get in the car and go somewhere we can talk."

Greatrex hoped like all hell the vehicle had a functioning air conditioning system.

They weren't five hundred yards along the road to George-town before Greatrex began doubting the wisdom of his suggestion. Amanda's hands were shaking as she clutched the steering wheel. She looked around nervously, constantly checking the rear vision mirror.

Amanda Best was clearly a very worried woman.

"First coffee shop we come to, Amanda, all right?"

Amanda turned to Greatrex. He hadn't noticed the redness of her eyes before. He figured not much sleep had been happening in her world. Given the circumstances, who could really blame her?

Fifteen minutes later, they were seated at a rear table in the café section of a roadhouse. The place had seen better days, but the coffee was good. More to the point, a chilled airstream flowed from the air conditioner directly opposite their seats.

Greatrex reached out his hand and placed it over Amanda's.

"Now, from the beginning. Leave nothing out."

Amanda sighed wearily before she began to speak.

"You'd remember all too well that Teddy just doesn't know how to give up. When he believes he's onto something, he'll move heaven and earth."

"Yup, he was like that even back in college. When he'd start researching an issue, particularly an environmental issue, he'd shut himself inside that world until he found the answers he needed." Greatrex had known Teddy Best for a long time. Although their paths had differed, they'd kept in touch. Jack Greatrex maintained a great deal of respect for his friend.

"I'm a realist Jack. Teddy's passion and ability to obsess is as frustrating as it is attractive." Amanda paused for a moment, her eyes downcast. When she looked back up, there were tears rolling down her cheeks. "I wonder if I should be saying '*was*' instead of '*is*'?"

"Let's not jump too quickly, Amanda. Teddy has always been resourceful. Can we begin by going over the timeline?" If there was any chance of a positive outcome to be achieved, the big fella needed his friend's wife to focus on specific details rather than emotion.

Amanda drew a deep breath and flicked her dark locks back over her shoulders.

"Yes, of course, you're right. The last time I saw Teddy would have been Wednesday morning. That's over seventy-two hours ago."

"Go on."

"We'd spent the night, as we do each night, staying in our little shack down in Kingston. Teddy loves it there. It's within

12

a stone's throw of the sea. You know what he's like about being close to the water."

Greatrex nodded.

"Teddy was up at the crack of dawn. He said he was going for a dive."

"Was that unusual?"

"No, not really. Although he usually planned his dives several days in advance. He hadn't mentioned anything to me about this one."

"He wouldn't have gone out alone, would he?" asked Greatrex.

"No, he was always far too safety conscious for that. He is a professional."

Greatrex noted the use of 'is' not 'was'. Amanda held out some hope.

"So, who did he go out with?"

"Teddy has a friend, Pedro. They would catch up whenever we were in Guyana. It's an unusual pairing. Pedro is a fisherman, Teddy an environmentalist. Their bond was their love of the ocean… and their sense of humor. He told me that morning that he was heading out with Pedro. In fact, they'd been out the previous evening having a drink together at Skipper's. I was in bed when he got home, but instead of joining me, Teddy went straight to his office. I heard him making phone calls, even talking quite loudly at times. Eventually I drifted off to sleep."

Greatrex soaked in the information.

"Amanda, do you have any idea who Teddy called that night?"

"No, Jack, none. I should have got out of bed and checked on him. God, I wish I could go back and do that one small thing differently."

"I don't want to sound uncaring, Amanda, but experience tells me there is nothing to be gained by regret in situations such as this."

"Situations such as this," Amanda repeated. "You've been in a few of them, haven't you, Jack? In the Middle East and, from what I hear, stateside as well. You and Nicholas Sharp."

The woman's eyes were expectant, not accusatory.

"Where did you hear that, Amanda?"

"Teddy likes to talk, especially after a few drinks. You know, typical seafarer. You must have let a couple of things slip."

Greatrex nodded silently.

"That's probably one of the reasons I contacted you. That and your friendship with Teddy."

"I'm glad you did call Amanda. But tell me, why the secrecy? Why did you not want me to contact anyone? We could sure use some help."

Amanda looked directly into Greatrex's eyes.

"The single thing Teddy said to me, just before he left, was to tell no one where he was. To be honest, I found his words and tone unsettling."

"Did you press him further?"

"He claimed it was to protect me. He made me promise."

Greatrex looked around the roadhouse. People wandered in and out. Most of them in search of a strong coffee.

"Amanda, there are two really obvious questions I must ask, although I'm sure you would have already told me if you knew the answers."

The woman nodded.

"First, are you aware where Teddy planned to dive on Wednesday morning?"

"No, of course I would have said."

"Well, that leads me to the second question. Have you asked this Pedro if Teddy had turned up for their rendezvous."

"Again, yes, Pedro was my first port of call when Teddy didn't return that evening."

"And?"

"I came across him at Skipper's. He seemed surprised when I inquired if he'd seen Teddy. He stated that my husband was a no-show. Pedro hadn't worried about it and just assumed Teddy had changed his mind."

"You accepted that?"

"At first, yes, but after running it over in my head that night, I questioned the honesty of his answer. Reflecting back, I thought he seemed a bit nervous, on edge."

"But you didn't call the police?"

"No, I figured that most cops don't start looking for anyone for at least twenty-four hours after they were last seen. Guyana is no different. I decided to speak to Pedro again in the morning, maybe push him a little further, perhaps plead a little harder. Then I'd go to the authorities."

"What happened the next morning?" asked Greatrex.

"I'd had virtually no sleep and my gut was in a knot. When Teddy still hadn't returned, I found Pedro's address from some papers on the study desk. I was knocking on his front door by 8 a.m."

"Was he there?"

"No, his girlfriend answered. As soon as she opened the door, I knew something was wrong."

"What do you mean?"

"She looked like I felt. A total wreck."

"And you asked to see Pedro?"

Amanda paused, staring hard into her coffee cup.

"That's why I went there, so yes, I begged to see him. The girl immediately burst into tears. She finally managed to tell me the police had visited her earlier that morning." Amanda scrunched her eyes.

"And?"

"And they told her Pedro's body had been found in an alleyway halfway between Skipper's and their home. He'd been stabbed to death."

"Shit," said Greatrex.

"That's when I called you."

Chapter 4

Staring across the water, Greatrex mulled the situation over in his head.

The big fella appreciated that his old friend Teddy Best was a committed environmentalist. He admired the man for his passion and dedication. He knew Teddy flew pretty close to the flames sometimes, blurring the lines between legality, personal safety and the optimal results for his cause. He'd been arrested several times but had always managed to avoid a long-term custodial sentence. He'd also been injured from time to time, occasionally ending up in hospital. Both Greatrex and Amanda knew it was pointless trying to talk the man out of anything. Teddy just wouldn't be Teddy without his innate sense of commitment and adventure.

What was unusual was Amanda's involvement in all of this. His friend would never allow his wife's safety to be compromised. It just wasn't how he was wired. When Teddy had indicated that Amanda should keep his movements to herself for her own wellbeing, it scared her. Rightly so in Greatrex's opinion.

With Pedro's murder, this mess seemed to be getting messier.

An hour ago, he'd dropped Amanda off at their shack. The

shack was as described. A small weatherboard house with a series of haphazard add-ons. It was near the water and only a few blocks from the town center. The big fella required time to think, so he'd set himself up with a coffee and sandwich at a waterfront café. The view was stunning, but his interest in it was negligible.

Greatrex examined the possibilities. Option one, Teddy had met with some sort of foul play. If so, the outcome was unlikely to be positive. Option two, Teddy contacted a third party, possibly passing on whatever information he'd come across. But even if the interaction had required him to leave town, Teddy would tell his wife. Option three, Teddy had done a runner. Greatrex considered that scenario for less than a minute. Teddy was way too devoted to his beautiful wife to abandon her; that was, unless it was for her own safety. But if that was the case, why leave Amanda in Georgetown amid this mess?

His mind made up, Greatrex decided on three actions. First, he would speak to Pedro's girlfriend and see if he could learn more about the fisherman's murder. After that, he'd return to the shack and wade through Teddy's belongings. If he could access the contact details from his friend's network, he might get lucky and find the people Teddy spoke to the night before he disappeared.

With as much information as he could muster, Greatrex would then contact the local authorities. Between the amount of time transpired since Teddy was last seen, and Pedro's murder, they'd be forced to act.

Following the directions Amanda had provided, Greatrex drove her red Mini southward. Agricola was a low socioeconomic neighborhood, a couple of miles out of George-town. The area backed onto the Demerara River. While a few houses were well maintained, most were decaying and only providing basic shelter.

Greatrex checked the address on his cell against the number on the old timber fence. The weatherboard house looked badly in need of a coat of paint. He stepped out of the car, locking it as per Amanda's instructions. Again, the heat hit him like a sauna.

The gate swung open at his touch. He followed the narrow path, overgrown with weeds, to the front entrance. There was no doorbell or knocker. Greatrex rapped his fist on the door.

No answer.

He knocked again.

Footsteps, but the door didn't budge.

"Who is it?"

"My name is Jack Greatrex. I'm a friend of Teddy Best."

"Go away."

"Graciela, is that you?" Amanda had given Greatrex the woman's name.

"I am no one. Please leave."

"I must speak to you."

Silence, followed by a couple more footsteps. The handle turned, and the door opened an inch, a chain allowing it to move no further. Greatrex could barely make out the outline of the dark face in the shadow, but he caught the penetrating stare of a single eye.

"Go away. I will not talk to you. Leave or I shall call the police."

It wasn't the reception Jack Greatrex expected.

"Graciela, I apologize for disturbing you, and I'm so sorry for your loss. But I've come a long way to speak with you. I'm searching for my friend. I'm worried and hoping you might be able to help me."

The stare continued. Then the door closed.

Greatrex heard a metallic rattle. The handle turned, and the door swung fully open.

The woman Greatrex assumed to be Pedro's girlfriend, Graciela, appeared in the light. Her figure slight, she had wavy black hair and large brown eyes. The eyes appeared sullen and defeated.

"I am sorry you've traveled so far, but I cannot talk to you."

Her speech slurred as she spoke. A bottle of something had taken a hit today.

"It's important, and I only have a few questions. Again, I apologize for the intrusion."

Graciela leaned a shoulder against the door frame for support.

"You don't get it. I can't speak to you or anybody else. I've been told."

"Who told you?"

"The police, of course."

"Why did they say you couldn't talk to anyone?"

"You'll need to ask them that. They came early this morning, woke me up, and told me my dear Pedro had been murdered. They may as well have been giving me a speeding ticket for all they cared."

"I'm very sorry."

"Maybe you are, maybe you aren't. Either way, the cop in charge said I was to talk to nobody. He said it was a simple mugging gone wrong and it would do no good to speak of it further."

"Do you *want* to talk?" asked Greatrex.

"Maybe I do, maybe I don't. The cops told me that if I cause a fuss, they will come back. They made it pretty clear a second visit would be an unpleasant experience for me."

"Graciela, do you *want* to talk?" Greatrex repeated.

The woman paused and looked him up and down, as though making a judgement.

"Ya rass mad?"

"I'm sorry."

"Are you crazy?"

Graciela shrugged her shoulders and threw the door wide open.

"Come." She stumbled as she walked, slamming her hand against the wall.

A minute later, Greatrex sat in a worn-out vinyl armchair while the young woman slouched on a stool. Her elbow rested on a wooden dining table that had seen better years. Despite the aging furniture, the house was clean and tidy, except for the mostly empty bottle of vodka perched on the table.

"So, I must be crazy," Graciela said. "But I am also drunk. What do you want?"

"Can I get you some water?"

"Water is for tomorrow. Today that bottle is my friend," she waved an arm towards the vodka. "Ask your questions now, or it will be too late."

Greatrex believed her.

"Do you know if Pedro took Teddy diving on Wednesday morning?"

She shook her head. "I'm uncertain. They planned to go out, but that afternoon Pedro only returned to briefly change

21

clothes. We didn't talk. Sorry, I can't answer you."

"Graciela, do you have any idea what made Teddy and Pedro suddenly decide to go out on Wednesday? Teddy normally liked to plan his dives well ahead of time."

The woman took a sip of vodka.

"I may be able to help with that one. Pedro went out fishing the day before. From what he told me, it seemed like a normal trip. He caught some, he missed some. My man didn't talk a lot about his fishing. He said fish talk was for braggarts, not real fisherman. But he did mention he'd hooked something strange. Something he thought shouldn't be there, but he lost the object before he managed to bring it on board."

Something strange. Greatrex considered her words. It could have been anything from a number plate to a bit of old maritime junk.

"Would he normally tell you about any debris he pulled up from the ocean floor, I mean, if he didn't like talking about his fishing?"

"No, that was odd. I think what he caught was unusual."

"Did he describe it?"

"No."

"Did he say where he went? I mean, the exact location?"

"No."

"Graciela, this is an important question. Do you know if he spoke to Teddy about his catch?"

"They met for a drink at Skipper's on Tuesday night. That's when they made plans to go out on the water. They may have spoken about it, or it could be nothing. I don't think it was that big a deal for Pedro. He was merely curious."

"Graciela, thank you. You have helped me."

"I can't see how, but regardless, please tell no one you were here. Those two policemen scare me. Now, I just wish to grieve my beloved Pedro."

"I understand. As you say, it's probably unrelated."

Greatrex gave Graciela his cell number before letting himself out. He noted the splash of another drink being poured as he left the room.

He climbed into the car and headed back towards town, disappointed at how little he'd learned. A mugging and a disappearance, seemingly unconnected. Tragic coincidence.

But there was one thing bugging him. Why in God's name had the police been so keen to silence Graciela? Why the secrecy around a simple street mugging?

That made no sense.

Chapter 5

The sun sat low in the sky as Greatrex pulled up in Amanda's driveway. He still had a lot to do before he suggested going to the authorities. He needed Amanda's blessing to make that next move, and it was something that couldn't be undone.

As he approached the front door, Greatrex sensed something was amiss. The screen door hung off the latch. Amanda was a stickler for security. Georgetown had a high crime rate. Apparently, she and Teddy had been burgled once. She didn't want it happening again.

Greatrex eased the screen door open and pushed against the wooden front door. It swung open easily. The big fella's senses raised to full alert, he entered the house. Carefully easing down the corridor into the lounge he saw nothing unusual. There was no evidence of ransacking. He resisted the temptation to call Amanda's name in case anyone else lurked in the house, moving quietly from room to room. Everything seemed in order except for one thing. Amanda Best was nowhere to be found.

Having established there were no intruders, Greatrex called Amanda's name.

Nothing.

He edged his way to the back door, opened it, and surveyed

the small garden.

"Amanda."

No response.

Greatrex pulled out his cell and dialed Amanda's number. It rang through to the message.

The big fella retraced his steps back to the hallway. When they had arrived at the house earlier, Amanda had put her handbag on the hall stand. It was no longer there. That, and the fact there was no sign of any struggle, seemed to indicate that she hadn't been forcibly removed.

Next, he checked any possible location for a note and another check of his cell for a message. Nothing.

There was always a small chance she had slipped out to the shops and would be back any minute. The trouble being, Greatrex didn't believe that for a minute.

He made his way through a pair of glass French doors into the small room Teddy used as his study. Papers were strewn all over the room, but Greatrex knew Teddy well enough to know nothing was amiss. This was just the way his old friend worked. Chaos on the outside, smart as a whip on the inside. He sat on Teddy's desk chair, swiveling it around to scan the room. Where to begin?

Greatrex allowed himself one hour to sort through Teddy's things. That would allow time for Amanda to return home if this was all a simple misunderstanding, and also enough time for him to gather whatever evidence and information he could for the police. Either way, he decided it was time to involve the authorities.

He began with a quick glance through the piles of paper scattered over Teddy's desk. His search revealed a mixture of bills, tidal and weather information, and printouts of correspondence with several environmental groups. He'd return to those. He swung around to the large wooden bookcase to the left of the desk. There were several books whose titles suggested subjects including climate change, political activism, and positive change. Teddy the revolutionist. A number of biographies, including those of several known environmentalists were among them. No surprises there. Over the last few years, Teddy and Amanda had spent several months a year in Guyana. Their Georgetown shack was clearly set up as a semi-permanent base.

There were more papers resting in the crevices above the books. A cursory glance showed they were similar in nature to those on the desk.

Greatrex swung back to the desk. Nestled amongst the disorganized paperwork sat Teddy's laptop computer. He reached forward and pulled it toward him before opening it and pressing the on button. The device lit up but, as expected, requested a password to get past the initial page. What would Teddy's password be?

The big fella yanked his cell out of his pocket. Technology was his thing, and he wasn't about to spend the next hour trying to second guess Teddy's brain until the computer shut him out. He clicked on his cell to open his preferred password cracking app. Expecting his search for Teddy to include investigating his friend's online activities, Greatrex had brought the appropriate lead to connect his cell to a USB port on the laptop.

Six minutes later he was in, scouring through Teddy's files.

First, he accessed his friend's email accounts. Teddy had several, divided into environmental work and personal. Greatrex went to the work account first. As expected, there were emails from several sources. It quickly became clear that the greatest percentage of those emails came from a group called Crimson Wave.

Greatrex was aware of the organization. Crimson Wave was an international, well-disciplined organization who had a reputation for confronting environmental vandals on their own turf, whether that be land or sea. Film footage frequently appeared on television and social media of Crimson Wave operatives confronting loggers, oil workers on drilling rigs and whalers. The most spectacular footage Greatrex had seen was of CW ships ramming whaling vessels and throwing lines around their propellors in a bid to stop what they regarded as illegal whaling in the Antarctic Ocean. The group appeared to mostly tread the fine line between legal and illegal activities. They had frequently been in the news for overstepping that line and ending up in court, if not jail. Greatrex recalled one of the leading voices in the Crimson Wave organization was a man called Deagan Jones. Jones was as enigmatic figure as he was polarizing. People either loved him or hated him, but his followers were devoted. A qualified mariner, Jones frequently captained the ships Greatrex had seen in the film footage and really didn't know what to make of him. Egomaniac or crusader.

Clearly Teddy Best thought the latter.

Greatrex stored that information away in his mind and continued his exploration of Teddy's files.

Next, he examined Teddy's recent searches. The most recent search popped up.

Underwater explosives.

Shit.

A variety of other related searches appeared, including

underwater detonators, types of explosives and the different types of explosives effective underwater. Further down were searches relating to underwater oil pipelines. Finally, he noted several inquiries about the ruptures of the Nord Stream pipeline. It was common knowledge that over fifty yards of the Nord pipeline had been torn apart by underwater explosions. Many suspected Russia of being the architect behind the damage.

Shit. What had Teddy gotten himself into?

Greatrex sat back in the chair and took a deep breath. He couldn't help but feel any chance of finding his old friend alive slowly slipping away.

Back to work, the search continued. Greatrex clicked on Teddy's personal email account. All the usual suspects were there: bills, communications from friends, some spam. Several emails down, Greatrex's eyes stopped at a heading. *'Re: Your inquiry'*. It wasn't the heading which attracted his attention, but the sender. 'Deagan Jones'.

The big fella clicked on the email.

Dear Teddy,

Based on the description you sent me, you may well be describing part of an underwater detonating system. I would need more information to confirm this. Do you have any pictures? Also, can you tell me where the object was found? I don't need to tell a man of your experience that if it was located anywhere near an oil or gas pipeline, there could be dire consequences.

I have sent this to your private email from my own for the sake of confidentiality.

Please reply at your earliest.

Deagan.

Double shit. Greatrex held no more doubts. One man

dead, Teddy probably dead, and Amanda missing. Certain the situation had escalated and required immediate action, Greatrex would alert the authorities. The threat to Graciela from the two policemen was not enough to negate that. Neither was Amanda's concern for secrecy.

After he'd spoken to the police, Greatrex decided would make one more phone call.

Chapter 6

"I've explained it as clearly as I can Station Sergeant Persaud, but I'm not certain you're understanding the severity of the situation." Greatrex grew tired and weary. He'd been at the Guyana Police Headquarters in Kingston for over an hour. He'd explained the scenario to a police corporal, then sergeant and now station sergeant. He was getting nowhere.

"It is you who must understand, Mr. Greatrex," responded the tall, lithe officer. "Everything you have said to me is either circumstantial or unrelated. You talk of a man who is supposedly missing but may very well just be away on a business trip, a lady who might simply have gone shopping, and a tragic street murder that bears no direct relationship with the former scenarios. Do you see my point?"

Greatrex shrugged his broad shoulders in despair, but he wasn't giving up.

"What about the police officers demanding silence from the young woman in Agricola?"

Persaud sighed.

"We have only your word for that, which is in itself based on your conversation with her. Hearsay. The lady concerned has not made any complaint. Besides, that matter was dealt with by a different division, not by any of my men."

"And the possibility of an explosive device?"

"There are many bits of discarded junk in the sea, Mr. Greatrex. I think you have put two and two together and come up with a wild fisherman's tale."

"So, you'll do nothing?"

"Sir, I am listening to you, just as the two officers before me have listened to you. That should indicate we are taking on board the plausibility of these events, although, as mentioned, I believe the likelihood of a connection is remote. That being said, I will speak to my division commander…"

"Can I do that?" interrupted Greatrex.

"No sir, that is not the protocol. As I began to say, I will speak to my division commander and suggest we wait for twenty-four hours to determine whether Mrs. Best returns. I shall put a bulletin out on Mr. Best requesting officers of all divisions keep an eye out for him. In addition to that, I'll make a discreet inquiry to the division which handled the murder/mugging to see if I can ascertain the circumstances of the police visit to the lady in Agricola."

Greatrex found himself shifting from foot to foot. Not a good sign. He knew, however, given his size, any aggressive behavior in a police station would not end well for anybody.

"Now, Mr. Greatrex. You have provided me with all the necessary details. I would invite you to return to the Best's residence and stay there. You may come back here tomorrow evening when I might have some more information for you. In fact, sir, consider that more than an invitation. It's a direction. We may seem relaxed here in Guyana, but we will not stand for any amateur interference with our investigations. Is that clear?"

Greatrex stared the policeman down, but to his credit,

Station Sergeant Persaud gave as good as he got.

"Crystal Sergeant, just crystal."

Greatrex turned and marched out into the warm night air.

He'd walked from Amanda and Teddy's shack to the police station. Walking helped him think, and he had a lot to think about. He began the return trek to the house a little over a mile away. Each step took him closer to a resolution. Clearly, he could not rely on the local authorities. Although polite, and seemingly quite intelligent, Sergeant Persaud had seemed more obsessed with protocols than results.

He could jam his damn protocols.

As soon as he arrived back at the shack, Greatrex would make a call. He needed help he could count on.

The running footsteps surprised him at first, seeming to come out of nowhere. He swung around, balling his fists, ready for a fight. The moment he saw the two large figures looming toward him in the dark, Jack Greatrex knew it was a lost cause, but it wasn't the figures that worried him, it was the additional footsteps closing in from each side.

Win or lose, the big fella dived into the brawl. He launched himself at the man on the left. He was the biggest and appeared to be leading the charge. Greatrex's foot connected with his attacker's knee just as his clenched fist pounded the side of the man's jaw. His attacker grunted and stumbled. A lesser man would have collapsed. By the time he faced up to the next guy, a fist smashed into Greatrex's temple. The jolt jarred his neck, forcing him to swing around to his left. As he pivoted, he kicked his foot out behind him, feeling it strike his assailant's groin.

Good.

The first man had regained himself and charged at Greatrex

with both arms outstretched. That was a tactical mistake. The big fella grabbed an arm and yanked it. The attacker lurched forward, but as he did so, swung his right fist into Greatrex's eye. Pain shot through his head like a cannonball.

Before he could transcend the fog, another blow smashed into the back of Greatrex's head, sending him downward. The guy he'd kicked in the groin.

Greatrex stumbled forward but avoided hitting the footpath. He thrashed his arms wildly, hoping to connect with anything until he could realign himself.

Empty air.

Forcing himself upright to re-confront his two main attackers, Greatrex braced himself. Suddenly, from either side, a lightning bolt of stabbing pain cracked through his torso. The men approaching from the sides. Greatrex doubled over, his wild swings now pointless.

He felt the assailants on either side grab his arms, forcing him upright. In a burst of willpower, he managed to break his left arm free, immediately swinging it across his body as he balled his fist. The guy on his right copped the blow directly on his nose. The remaining grip on Greatrex's arm weakened. The big fella tensed, ready to make the most of his new- found freedom. Then he heard it.

Click.

The sound of a pistol slide being pulled back and released.

"Enough Mr. Greatrex."

The voice came from the original attacker. With one hand, the man rubbed his jaw. With the other, he held a Glock 19 aimed directly at Greatrex's gut.

Greatrex glowered at him, his frustration boiling.

Then the lights went out.

Chapter 7

NICHOLAS SHARP

Twenty-four hours: acceptable.

Forty-eight hours: concerning.

Seventy-two hours: immediate action required.

Over seventy-five hours had transpired since Jack Greatrex's call. If he was safe then, there was no guarantee he'd be safe now.

I needed to do something, but what? I'd tried his cell, nothing. Greatrex said he was out of the country. That left a multitude of options. What should I do, book an around the world ticket and just start asking people if they'd seen a big white bald bloke with a goatee beard who may or may not seem a little scary? Clearly not.

Greatrex's apartment. I'd begin there. I didn't like to intrude on the big fella's privacy. We shared a strong mutual respect, and I was reluctant to damage that. On the other hand, given the situation, he'd have done the same.

I descended the stairs in my Venice block, climbed into my aging XJS Jag and pulled out into the street. The drive only took a couple of minutes. Greatrex lived in an apartment on the ground floor of an old gray weatherboard house a few streets back from the beach between Santa Monica and Venice.

After using the spare key, the door swung open. To my surprise, I wasn't greeted by the usual sight of Greatrex's neat and well-organized sanctuary. The place was in disarray. The chaos wasn't the result of sloppy living. Greatrex's home had been ransacked. Books were strewn across the floor where they'd been emptied from bookshelves. The normally tidy desk was a chaotic mess. Also scattered all over the floor were the contents of every desk drawer.

Before I took another step, I withdrew the Heckler and Koch from my belt. Whoever did this may still be here. I listened but heard nothing. Methodically tracking from room to room, I searched carefully. The chaos continued throughout the apartment, but there was no sign of an intruder. Finally, I opened a door at the end of the entrance hall. It led to Greatrex's inner sanctum. On the left-hand wall, the recording gear we frequently used stood shoved to one side. The digital interface lay upside down, the bottom plate removed. These people were thorough. Professionals are thorough.

The far wall remained untouched. Not surprising, as at first glance it appeared to be a normal timber wall. I stepped forward, leaned down, and found a release latch behind the skirting board. When I pulled on it, a small gap materialized in the middle of the wall. I inserted both hands and prized the two sections apart. As the doors opened, they revealed a tech set up NASA would be envious of. An array of screens, now motionless, sat above several computers and other assorted paraphernalia beyond my limited knowledge.

To my relief, everything seemed untouched. Thank God

for Greatrex's overly developed sense of security. Maybe the professionals hadn't been so professional after all.

Normally, when confronted with a tech challenge, I'd call on the big fella. Technology was his wheelhouse. That was impossible now. On the positive side, I knew all of Greatrex's passwords, and he knew mine. It was a kind of mutual security pact. I righted an upturned chair and got to work. It didn't take long to access his main computer. I dived straight into his personal emails. In circumstances such as this, I was certain he wouldn't mind. There had to be something, anything, that would give me a hint as to his whereabouts.

Sometimes you get lucky. There it was. An itinerary from United Airlines confirming a redeye flight from LA to New York. Below it was a similar confirmation from Caribbean Airlines for a flight from JFK to Georgetown, Guyana.

Bingo!

Guyana. Why Guyana? Greatrex had never mentioned the place. To my knowledge, he'd never been there. I looked further down his inbox. One email stood out. It came from one Amanda Best, its title simply reading 'Please Help'.

I opened the contents:

Jack, please call me. Teddy has disappeared. I'm worried and I don't know who else to turn to. And Jack, this is important. You can't tell anybody about this.

Amanda.

A cell number was included in the contact details at the bottom of the email. I yanked my phone out of my pocket, looked up the dial code for Guyana, and rang the number. It went directly to message, just as Greatrex's had done earlier. I tried the big fella's number again, this time using the Guyana prefix. Still nothing.

My luck had run out.

Again, Guyana. Why Guyana? I recognized Teddy Best's name. He was an old college buddy of Greatrex, and I knew they'd remained in touch. Somewhere in the back of my mind, I recalled Teddy was some sort of environmental activist, but I didn't know much more. Greatrex had mentioned his friend was married, but I'd never met his wife. For that matter, I'd only met Teddy a couple of times.

Guyana. Shit. Where the hell was that?

Either way, it looked like I'd be taking a trip.

Chapter 8

"Police Headquarters, Young Street, Kingston, please," I instructed the cab driver.

"Sure thing. Can you pay in American dollars?"

"Yup."

"Surer thing."

A short time later, the taxi pulled up in front of a large modern building set in the midst of a small compound. Blue trimming contrasted the stark white walls. I paid the driver, grabbed my bag, and strode through the gate. The warm tropical climate didn't bother me, but I knew Greatrex would hate it. I don't know whether it was his size or the moisture in the air. Iraq's dry deserts never bothered him.

A police officer stood on duty behind the desk as I entered the reception area.

"I have an appointment with Station Sergeant Persaud," I announced.

I'd emailed the station before leaving LA and Persaud's was the name provided.

"I'm afraid Sergeant Persaud is out at the moment. He should be back shortly. Would you care to wait?"

There seemed no point in venting my frustration.

"I'll wait," I responded before taking a seat on a very

uncomfortable wooden bench.

An hour dragged past. My fatigue after over twelve hours in the air and endless airport downtime did not help my state of mind. I focused on remaining civil… and awake. Every few minutes, I'd look up at the officer behind the desk. He'd just shrug his shoulders. The dance continued.

Drowsiness had almost won the battle when I heard a voice say, "Mr. Sharp?"

A tall officer with short, cropped hair and a uniform neat as a pin stood over me.

"Yes. Station Sergeant Persaud?"

"That is correct. Please come with me."

He turned and marched through a door beside the reception desk, barely pausing to hold it open. I scrambled, snatched up my bag and followed, shaking myself awake as I went. We continued down a long corridor before making a right-hand turn into an even longer one. The sergeant marched to the end and pushed another door, at this point holding it open. His office was situated at the corner of the building with windows on two walls. Persaud was clearly a man of position.

He waved me to a chair opposite his large desk while he sat down behind it.

"You have traveled a great distance, Mr. Sharp. Now, what can I do for you?"

I leaned forward.

"Sergeant, as I mentioned in my email, I believe a friend of mine has gone missing in your city. I suspect his disappearance may be related to another one, possibly two missing people. I'm here to investigate."

Persaud sat back in his chair. "Mmm, 'investigate'. I

googled you Mr. Sharp. My understanding is that you're a professional musician. Why would such a person be investigating missing persons in my town?"

A sinking feeling rose in my gut. I'd been frustrated by bureaucrats before.

"Yes sir, I can understand your surprise, but I do have a vested interest in at least one of the unaccounted. He is a close friend."

"Ah yes, Mr. Jack Greatrex. I've met him."

I sat bolt upright.

"You met Jack? When?"

"Not two days ago. In the lobby downstairs."

At a minimum, that confirmed Greatrex's arrival in Guyana.

"May I ask the nature of the conversation?"

Persaud rubbed his hand against his chin, probably considering an appropriate response.

"Mr. Sharp, it is not our normal practice to share information regarding current investigations with outsiders."

"Sergeant, I can assure…"

The officer raised his palm to silence me.

"However, seeing as no formal investigation is underway, I'll be happy to inform you of the content of my conversation with Mr. Greatrex."

"No formal investigation?" I almost exploded from my seat.

"I suggest you listen before rushing to judgement, Mr. Sharp. Otherwise, I shall end this interview now."

"Please continue," I whispered.

Nicholas Sharp, scolded child.

"All right. Mr. Greatrex came to me with concerns similar to your own."

Sergeant Persaud explained Greatrex's predicament regarding being unable to locate Teddy Best and losing contact with Amanda Best.

"Mr. Greatrex also had a concern pertaining to a mugging that tragically turned into a street murder a few nights ago. Although the victim was an associate of Mr. Best, my inquiries found the event unrelated."

If Greatrex had concerns about something like that, I had them too.

"Now, Mr. Sharp, you must understand where things stand in these matters. I invited Mr. Greatrex to return here and meet with me twenty-four hours after our first meeting. I was here, he was not. At that point, I assumed he had located all the missing parties and saw no need for further interaction with the Guyana Police Force. Although I must say, I did find it a little rude he hadn't called."

This was a shitstorm of inaction.

"Sergeant, did it not occur to you that Jack Greatrex may have disappeared too?" I asked.

"Mr. Sharp, Georgetown is not like Los Angeles. We have crime, but it is mostly small time and largely manageable. Serial kidnappings just don't happen here. However, as a courtesy to you, I've sent an officer around to the Best's address to confirm all is well. Their home is not far from here. I should receive a response shortly. If you'd care to come back…"

"I'll wait, thanks." Look what 'coming back' had done for Greatrex.

For twenty minutes, we waited, eyeing each other off from one side of the desk to the other.

To his credit, Persaud tried to stay civil, as did I.

"Forgive me for saying this, Mr. Sharp, but you don't really seem to have the demeanor of a musician. Not the ones I've met, anyway."

I considered how much of my past to reveal. Then I thought of Greatrex.

"I have a military background."

"Ah, that might explain it. Army?"

"Marines. Sniper."

"A stark contrast to your current occupation."

"That's what I had in mind."

The jangling of the phone on the sergeant's desk put an end to our stilted conversation. He picked it up.

"Yes, all right. You checked with neighbors? Okay. Thank you."

Sergeant Persaud replaced the receiver. He leaned back in his chair, his chin resting in his hand.

"Excuse me a minute."

The sergeant stood up and walked from the room.

Ten minutes later, he returned, this time standing behind his desk.

"Mr. Sharp. It seems I've been premature sharing information with you. My officer has confirmed that both Mr. and Mrs. Best have not been sighted for several days. Nor has anyone matching Mr. Greatrex's description been seen in or near their property in the last forty-eight hours."

This wasn't the news I wanted to hear, but it *was* the news I expected.

"I've just been upstairs to speak to our divisional commander. We are beginning a preliminary investigation into the disappearances of Mr. Teddy Best, Mrs. Amanda Best and Mr. Jack Greatrex. Your American Embassy will be kept informed of the investigation's progress. As a US citizen, you may seek information from them."

I felt some element of relief, but not much.

"Can't you keep me directly informed?"

"That is not the protocol." The sergeant paused, his shoulders almost relaxing under the weight of his uniform. "I'm sorry Mr. Sharp. The matter is now out of my hands."

I didn't move an inch.

"One more thing, Mr. Sharp. I appreciate you've traveled a long way out of concern for your friend. The most productive action would be to either go back to Los Angeles and await news, or if you must, bed down in a hotel here and stay in contact with the local US diplomats."

I remained motionless.

"I insist, however, on making the situation perfectly clear. You are to take no actions of your own with regard to this investigation. Military background or not, you have no authority here. I require your word that no matter how tempted, you will not undertake any inquiries of your own."

I remained seated for a full minute, staring Station Sergeant Persaud square in the eyes.

"I wouldn't dream of it," I replied.

Pushing the chair back from under me, I rose and made my way to the door.

I hated lying to cops.

Chapter 9

After checking in to a reasonable looking hotel not far from the waterfront, I headed out to find a local bar. The 'Shipwreck' appeared like it was in full swing. Reggae music blared out onto the busy street. Georgetown may not be a tourist mecca, but locals and visitors alike seemed to know how to party.

As I passed through it, the open doorway revealed a blend of an old western saloon and a dockyard pub. I liked it, but I hadn't come to like it. Given the situation, I felt increasingly exposed. If a man as skilled as Jack Greatrex could disappear, what greater chance did I have of succeeding? I needed to even the odds. Flee or fight were my choices. I didn't intend to return home without the big fella, so that ruled out fleeing. To fight, I'd need a weapon, and I was sure as hell going to find one.

I located a free bar stool situated between a large man chatting up an attractive young woman and a skinny bloke nursing a Banks beer.

"Johnnie Walker Black, neat," I directed the barman.

"American?" he replied.

"What gave me away?"

"The accent, the neat, the top shelf brand. Most folks

around here would just order a whiskey."

At least I'd made my point. I wasn't from around here and I was well funded.

Forty minutes drifted by. The second drink tasted as good as the first, but that would be my limit. The big guy on my right had cleared off with his lady friend. He was replaced by a middle-aged white man with graying hair, a rumpled suit, and no tie. He looked like an off duty traveling sales rep.

The skinny guy on my left remained. Two more beers had disappeared down his throat in the time I'd been there.

"Busy night," I said.

"Always busy."

"You local?"

"Born and bred. What's it to you?"

His tone wasn't aggressive, more apathetic.

"I'm from the States."

"No shit, there's a surprise."

"I'm looking for some local knowledge."

"Buy a guidebook. You can get 'em at any shop."

"The information I need won't be in a guidebook."

"Another beer Ike," he ordered the bartender.

"Put it on my tab," I said. "And another Johnnie Walker for me." So much for my limit.

"You don't need to buy me a drink. If you got a question to ask, just ask it." The man turned to face me.

This was the moment.

"I want to buy a gun. A hand gun."

The man took a moment to answer.

"Do I look like an arms dealer, fella?"

"To be honest, I'm not sure what an arms dealer really looks like, but I figured there was a chance you might know someone," I replied.

He swung around on his stool, surveying the whole room.

"Take a look around. Half the people in this room know someone who trades guns. And about half of them would take your money, lead you out the back lane and relieve you of the rest of your stash. You'd get hurt at best."

"I'm pretty hard to hurt."

For the first time, the man looked uneasy.

"You a cop?"

"Do I look like a cop?"

"Hard to figure what a cop looks like. Sometimes they put a lot of effort into not looking like a cop."

Touché.

"I'm not a cop."

"Maybe C.I.A.?"

I laughed.

"Na, I don't think you are a cop. But I've been wrong before, and it cost me."

Another pause.

"You know how to use a gun?"

"Yes."

"Properly?"

"Professionally."

His eyebrows arched.

"I'm willing to pay you for your trouble." I began to reach into my jacket pocket.

"Now don't be a fool and bring out a wad of your American dollars here. Not if you want to keep them."

I removed my hand.

Pause.

I seemed to have spent a fair bit of the day waiting while

people made quick assessments of my character. Eventually, he came to a decision.

"Tell you what. I'll meet you two corners north of here in one hour. Outside the big church. I'll either have your weapon or will be with someone who can provide it. Just understand this. If you ain't being straight with me, you best walk out of here now, no consequences. If me or my friends find out later that you're full of shit, you're going to get badly hurt."

"The big church, one hour," I responded.

I reached out my hand, but he'd turned his back and headed toward the door.

I wasn't sure whether I'd got lucky or set myself up for a beating, or worse.

Given the circumstances, the risk had been necessary.

"Mister."

The barman reappeared.

"Yes."

"I overheard part of your conversation. The customer you were talking to, he's got some really nasty friends. Friends you don't want to meet. My advice would be to just go back to your hotel room and lock the door."

"Thanks for the heads up."

I slipped him some cash and sauntered outside. Reconsidering my assessment of the place, I'd say it was more old-western saloon than dockyard pub.

Nicholas Sharp at the O.K. Corral.

Chapter 10

Ninety minutes later, I headed towards the Best's house. The only place that made sense to start was to retrace what I assumed to be Greatrex's steps and hope something turned up.

An aging Beretta M9 filled one pocket and a box of 9mm NATO rounds the other. Walking into a bar and asking for a weapon was probably foolish. Sometimes necessity breeds risk, and this time it paid off. My new friend Lemmy and his colleagues had come to the party, although from my perspective, it ended up being quite an expensive get together.

The directions on my phone made it easy to locate the Best's shack, although it was well past midnight by the time I got there. Having taken enough risks already, I positioned myself down the road to survey the area. As soon as I turned the final corner into their street, I noted my tactic had paid off.

Directly in front of the house sat a Guyana Police Force pickup, its blue sides and white top gleaming under the streetlight. A uniformed officer in the cabin slouched against the door, occasionally glancing at the Best residence. Clearly, Station Sergeant Persaud had been as good as his word and some sort of investigation had begun.

An obstacle to overcome, the cop's presence would make it

harder for me to get inside and have a look around. I opted to wait and consider my options.

As a trained sniper, waiting formed a crucial part of my craft. Although it had been some time since I'd been a Marine, some skills don't evaporate. Just after 1 a.m. I counted my blessings. I barely noticed it at first, but about one hundred yards past the cop car, a shadow moved. Not a windblown bush, not an animal. The sharpness of movement belonged to a human. I focused on the spot. The longer I looked, the more I saw. It seemed to be a single man, lurking behind the trunk of an old kapok tree. When he craned his head around the tree's mass, he appeared to be fixated on the Best residence.

The night just got more interesting.

Waiting and more waiting.

The question now was who had been inside the house and who hadn't? I presumed the police had been through the place. It would have been a routine part of their investigation. I wondered what they'd taken away. Would anything be left in the house that could help me locate Greatrex? Then I considered the figure in the shadows. Had he been through the property? Possibly? If so, why did he remain? Perhaps he hadn't been able to action a search because of the police guard?

A lot of questions, not enough answers.

Another hour passed by. The street remained quiet. The cop in the pickup looked weary. From my spot hidden behind a corner fence, I noted his shoulders slump from time to time. Probably dozing and then shaking himself awake.

The black shadow showed no such fatigue.

I needed to do something, or we'd all still be sitting here at dawn.

Doubling back up the road that crossed the Best's street, I headed east at the next opportunity. After a quick glance at the map on my cell, I made a wide arc of the Best's house before heading north. I again doubled back to a street that ran east-west, parallel to theirs but one block behind it.

Now moving more cautiously, and clinging to the shadows, I half crept along the sidewalk until I judged my position to be roughly behind the Best's place. Between me and their back fence was another aging shack with a driveway running past the house to an old garage in the rear western corner.

I waited five minutes to confirm there was no movement from within before leaping the front gate and padding down toward the garage. Then, skirting the outbuilding, I reached a six-foot wooden fence. I peered over the top. The backyard that revealed itself was one down from the Best's. I yanked myself up and over before landing soundlessly on the lush tropical grass.

At the side fence, I eyeballed the Best's backyard. No sign of movement. With both hands on the top rail, I prepared to launch myself over when a sharp stabbing pain in my lower back stopped me dead.

"Not tonight, brother."

I froze.

"Turn around, slowly."

I turned around, slowly.

The moonlight revealed a giant of a man with dark skin, a thick neck and a grin featuring a row of teeth that spoke of too many bar fights. A glint of steel drew my attention to the enormous knife in his right hand.

"Now, here's how this will play out. We're both going to climb that fence you just came over. After that, we'll walk down that driveway where you'll meet some friends I'm about to call. Remember, my blade will never be more than six inches from your back."

He smiled with a nervous energy. Nervous energy was better than calm confidence, at least from my point of view.

"Nod if you understand."

I nodded.

I understood all right, and I didn't like the plan at all.

"Move."

I stepped toward the fence.

"Hands on the rail."

He was really micromanaging this.

I placed my hand on the top rail, my back turned to him.

I sensed the man take a step forward, keeping his knife within easy stabbing distance of my spine. Now or never. Pushing hard against the solid fence, I lunged out with a rearward kick with both legs. I'd either make contact or get cut. A grunt of pain filled the night air. Fortunately, his not mine. A fraction of a second later my hands, now released from their grip on the fence, clasped together to perform a king hit across his jaw.

He went down.

I kicked the knife free from his faltering hand as I stamped my foot down on the man's head. Another grunt, then silence. He was out cold.

Sometimes speed and surprise beats strength and a blade.

I didn't have time to consider where my attacker had come from, but I did search his pockets, finding a car key and a cell phone. The phone looked to be a basic model sold at most US Walmart stores, likely a burner. Nothing else. I pocketed them both. Common sense would have indicated a tactical retreat would be in order. Instead, I moved forward, over the side fence and into the Best's back yard.

I'd probably have less than ten minutes before the guy regained consciousness and alerted his colleagues, so speed was crucial. I bolted toward the back door, slamming into it on the run. It opened easily.

The pitch blackness didn't help. With the cop and shadow man stationed out front, I couldn't turn on any lights. The flashlight app on my cell would provide a dim glow under the palm of my hand. I'd have to risk at least that. The small house only took a minute and a half to cover. The final room was the one I wanted. Desk, bookcase and a spot for a laptop computer. But the laptop wasn't there.

Unsurprising.

I scurried through the papers on the desk, looking for anything remotely useful. Bills, personal letters, nothing else. Three more minutes transpired.

Then I had a thought. No computer, but maybe a … printer.

There it sat on the bottom shelf of the bookcase. Even in the shadowy light, it was clear there were no papers in the out tray. I crawled over to it, keeping my phone's beam and my silhouette below the window line. Nothing sat on the floor in front of the device. Books were jammed against the printer's right-hand side, but a small space lay between the device and the left side of the bookcase.

I slid my fingers into the nook. Nothing.

Finally, I reached into the crack between the shelf and the floorboards. Less than an inch. My fingers touched something towards the rear of the space. Paper. I niggled at it, slowly working it into the grasp of my fingertips, and then my palm. Finally, I extracted it. One sheet.

I shone the light on it, not expecting much. There was a picture of a device I couldn't identify, but no written explanation. I shoved it into my pocket.

Seven minutes since I entered the house. Time to go.

As I leaped the side fence, the man I'd taken out had begun to groan. I sprang over the second fence but was more circumspect as I stole down the driveway beside the house. I didn't want to bump into any of the groaning thug's friends.

Five minutes later, I'd made it far enough to feel confident of my escape.

Then I changed my mind.

Chapter 11

Perhaps the exhaustion had slowed my thinking. Maybe I was just dim.

Every feeble lead I had in the search for Jack Greatrex was centered around that house. To walk away now would be a backward step, and I may not find another way forward. I needed to pick an option and run with it.

I chose the shadow man.

It had been my plan to rent a car the following day. If I had a vehicle now, I'd wait until the shadow man had finished his shift and follow him. The remaining alternative was to surprise him and beat the information out of him. Despite what happens in movies, effective interrogation usually takes time and resources. I had neither.

I decided to return to the front of the Best's house. I'd come up behind the shadow man. Perhaps I'd be able to follow him on foot or even steal a car.

Then it hit me. I could just find the vehicle that belonged to the keys in my pocket. I pulled them out and studied them under a streetlight. Toyota. Not much help. The style of the remote key told me it would probably be a late model. A little help.

The car wouldn't be too far from where I'd subdued the

groaning thug. Him calling for backup wasn't an option. I had his cell. Although, any moment he might appear on the street, groggy and furious. I needed to be quick.

I ran back along the road. Caution be damned. I saw at least a dozen cars under the streetlights. Nissan, Mitsubishi, an older Toyota. I kept running. Honda, Jeep, then at the end of the street, almost on the corner, a late model, black Toyota Prado. I flicked the key as I bolted toward it. The lights flashed.

Bingo.

"Hey, asshole."

The groaning thug had awakened, his footsteps closing in.

"Shitface, don't even think about it."

I yanked the driver's door open, leaped in, and started the engine. The thug was only ten yards down the road. For good measure, I drove straight at him, not really caring whether he lived or died. Someone threatening your life with a knife will do that to you.

He stopped, standing solid in my path.

I accelerated.

At the last second, he dived into the gutter. I think I clipped his foot.

Gas pedal flat to the floor, I hastened down the street, giving a great impersonation of a fleeing man. A smarter man *would* have fled.

A mile down the road, I turned right, slowing right down, so the engine purred rather than roared. I then weaved my way to a position in a side street around five hundred yards to the west of the Best's house. I flicked off the lights and drove two hundred yards to the junction, getting as close to the shadow man as I could without attracting attention.

I locked the car and proceeded carefully on foot. I made slow progress, clinging desperately to every bit of darkness, frequently climbing fences and crossing front gardens rather than exposing myself on the street.

Eventually, I found myself in a lush garden, lurking a dozen yards behind the shadow man's position. He was still there, and he was good. Even at that close distance, it took a great deal of concentration to make him out.

I settled down. The waiting game had begun.

The greatest danger with surveillance is remaining focused… and staying alert.

I hadn't slept for longer than I could recall. At least forty hours. My eyelids seemed reluctant to follow orders. I would have sworn they had fishing weights attached to them. A couple of times, the weight became too heavy. Each time I shook myself awake, the thought of Jack Greatrex and Amanda Best languishing in inhospitable hands did the trick.

The first rays of the early morning sun touched on the leaves of the kapok tree as the shadow man made his move. Of course, what is a shadow man without a shadow?

I ducked down low. To come this far and have him see me was unacceptable.

As the light cast its glow down the street and the shadow man moved from behind the tree, his features became clearer. He was tall, slender, and looked extremely fit. His dark skin had aided his concealment. He now moved purposefully, with long strides and a quick step.

In comparison, I felt like a worn-out slug. Still, I waited until he'd traveled further down the road before I followed. He took a left turn at the intersection where I'd left the Prado.

Great minds.

I paused for thirty seconds before following. Just before turning the corner, I glanced back towards the Best's house. The police pickup remained out the front, but another, similar police vehicle was drawing to the curb. Everybody's shift was ending.

I craned my head around the corner. The shadow man had reached a red Mitsubishi SUV. He stopped, put his hand into his pocket and pulled out what I assumed to be a key. The car lights flashed, and the man jumped in. Before he drove off, he put a cell phone to his ear, perhaps reporting in. But to who?

I yanked my head back and slipped behind an overhanging bush.

Ten seconds later, he roared past me, turning left toward the town center. I sprinted up the road, climbed into the Prado and followed. This would not be easy.

Pursuing a subject discreetly at night is hard. Pursuing a subject discreetly in daylight is harder. Following someone over any distance with a single pursuit car while remaining undetected is almost impossible. I hoped this would be a short journey.

Turns out I couldn't have been more wrong.

The light early morning traffic on the streets of Georgetown made it more difficult to conceal myself. I couldn't hang back too far for fear of missing the Mitsubishi making a turn. For obvious reasons, sitting too close was out of the question. My hopes of a short journey ended when the SUV passed through the heart of the town and sped toward the southern outskirts.

Several miles and many turns later, the red SUV was around half a mile in front of me as we powered along the Linden-Lethem Road. Having been in the country only a few hours, I had no idea where we were, never mind where we were going. The Google map app on my phone helped me get my bearings, but my destination was in the hands of the vehicle ahead.

Fifty miles further down the same road, another issue arose. Gas. The Prado began the trip with less than half a tank. At some point, I'd have to find a gas station to refuel. As the surrounding population grew sparser, I figured that should be sooner rather than later. My eyelids grew heavier with every mile. The longer the journey, the more likely I'd doze off and end up in a ditch.

The bottom line remained; it would be pointless to turn back. The shadow man was my one shot at locating Greatrex. The Beretta and spare rounds sat on the passenger seat next to me, a comforting sight.

At times I drew closer to the Mitsubishi, at other times I pulled back. I didn't think he'd marked me as a tail but wasn't certain.

Several hours into the trip, I caught a break. The red SUV pulled into a gas station. I braked hard, pulled off the road, and waited. As soon as he pulled out, I drove in. A few minutes later, with fuel in the tank plus some sandwiches and a pile of energy drinks on the seat next to the Beretta, I accelerated briskly down the road. The SUV fled out of sight. I needed to catch him before he turned off.

Another two hours of driver's fatigue and questions began bouncing around my brain like neutrons. Was I driving away from Greatrex and Amanda Best or toward them? No idea.

Should I keep going or turn back and try to press the police for more information? No idea. What would I do when the journey came to an end? What was my plan? No plan, no idea.

In the end, I forced myself to stop thinking about anything but the road ahead… and staying awake. There's only so many times you can reach the same overwhelming conclusion that you have no idea what's going on.

After a while, the surrounding bush seemed to feature more substantial trees, the undergrowth thicker. A towering mountain range appeared in the distance. Beside the road, a river emerged, running in a parallel direction. The map told me it was the Essequibo. We passed a sign that indicated the Kurupukari Crossing lay ahead. That worried me.

Two minutes later, I knew I was in deep trouble. The Kurupukari crossing wasn't a bridge. It was an ancient car ferry. Waiting in the front row to board was the shadow man in his red SUV. Fortunately, there were a few cars between his vehicle and mine. The chances of him not spotting my vehicle were non-existent. The likelihood of him recognizing the Prado seemed strong. I didn't know whether he knew my face, but I wouldn't risk the chance.

Too late to turn around without creating an incident, I waited in line. When the ferry reached our side, I motored on. As soon as I stopped, I searched the glove compartment, pulling out whatever papers I could find. I held them in front of my face, attempting to look like I was reading.

Nicholas Sharp, more Maxwell Smart than James Bond.

On the far bank, the red SUV sped off. I hesitated before following at a slower pace, wondering whether I'd gotten away with the ruse, or if the shadow man was humoring me.

It might go either way.

The road began to rise, the scrub grew thicker and taller, slowly turning into rainforest. My phone indicated that we were in or near the Iwokrama Nature Reserve.

A simple pursuit through an unfamiliar town had ended up a spectacular drive through one of the world's most pristine environments. Even in my beyond exhausted state, I appreciated the view.

But not for long. Once again, my eyes grew heavy. I must have dozed because I woke up with two of the Prado's wheels sliding into a ditch. The perfect recipe for a rollover. I flicked the steering wheel to the right and accelerated. The car momentarily lurched forward before settling back toward the ditch. As I sensed the front right wheel begin to rise off the road, I repeated the process with my foot flat on the gas pedal. The vehicle shuddered violently before launching forward again. This time, the left front wheel slithered up the gutter toward the gravel surface. The rear followed but swerved wildly as I over corrected. I turned into the skid and the Prado returned to some semblance of control.

It had been close. If the pursuit didn't end soon, it would end badly.

Twenty minutes later, I rounded a corner. A rare straight stretch of road appeared. It should have revealed the red Mitsubishi around three quarters of a mile ahead.

It didn't.

I refused to believe I'd come this far, pursuing my prey for nearly eight hours, only to lose him in the final stages. I pressed hard on the brakes. As I did, a cloud of dust surrounded the Prado.

Perhaps there was one slim chance.

I drove slowly forward, scrutinizing the forest on each side of the road. There was no space to even ride a motorbike through, never mind a large SUV. I'd traveled two-thirds of the way along the straight before something caught my eye.

More dust.

The cloud rose from the ground beyond a clump of bushes to my left. A previously unnoticed flattened section of undergrowth now became obvious. A closer look revealed another narrower track on the dirt beyond it. I gazed ahead up the hill into the thick vegetation. Now that I was looking, the trail of dust became more apparent.

This is where the shadow man exited the road. For a brief second, I thanked the heavens I hadn't stolen a town car. I heaved the Prado's wheel leftward, instigated the four-wheel drive and pressed on into the bush.

Another twenty minutes of winding track, semi-submerged boulders and sheer drops, and I reached the end of the world, or at least civilization as we know it. A wall of rainforest blocked the road. Perplexed, I got out of the car. Initially camouflaged by vegetation, I noticed a chain swinging between two trees, padlocks on each end. Hanging from it, a small sign commanded:

No Entry Under Any Circumstances

Beyond the sign lay a track even less inviting than the one I'd just driven. There were no choices to be made here. It was time to go hiking.

I retrieved the gun and ammunition from the Prado, filled my pockets, locked the vehicle, and began the upward trek along the path. For whatever reason, and I assumed it to be nefarious, someone had chosen to camp out in one of the most remote areas of South America that I could imagine.

61

Each bend revealed nothing but another one. Each hill the same. I walked uphill for over an hour, my feet constantly slipping on the thin layer of gravel across the track, reflecting favorably on the time when I was merely exhausted. Each bend and hill required caution. I didn't want to stroll uninvited, straight into an inhospitable environment.

Eventually, by looking up at the rainforest canopy, I detected some sort of break ahead. Probably a campsite clearing.

I rounded the final bend just as the sun began to set. The twilight announced the failure of my assumption.

There was no campsite.

Set into the side of the hill, in the middle of a three-acre cleared grass area, stood a two-story stone and cinderblock mansion. A wide veranda straddled the building's girth while two outbuildings were positioned to the right. The red Mitsubishi SUV sat in front of one of them.

Surprising. Impressive. Impossible.

Who the hell owned this place?

Chapter 12

Careful not to break cover from the rainforest, I started circling the perimeter of the clearing. Ten minutes in, I realized it was a waste of time. The forest floor was so thick it would have taken me over an hour to perform the task. I didn't have an hour.

I settled back into the bush and watched. I figured around twenty minutes of light remained. I'd scope out what I could and then let the darkness be my cover.

At first, I saw nobody. It took less than a minute to realize my error. The veranda that surrounded the house provided ample shadow across the lower walls. Perched in the darkened doorway on the right-hand side of the building, a figure emerged. I only pinged him when he stepped out to scrutinize the cleared grassed area. In the half-light, the strap over his shoulder supporting some sort of automatic weapon became obvious. Probably an AK-47. Three minutes later, I spotted a similar outline coming around the other end of the structure. He was also armed. There was no sign of the shadow man.

I allowed myself to believe the long and arduous drive may have been worth it after all. Armed guards are only posted if there is something to guard. These two weren't there to discourage burglars. I figured they were guarding someone or something that wasn't meant to leave the house.

Greatrex? Amanda Best?

The glimmer of hope gave me energy. Of course, even if Greatrex was imprisoned on the property, I still needed to devise a strategy to get him out. At least two guards with automatic weapons, probably more, versus one man with a single pistol. The odds weren't stacked my way.

Assuming Greatrex and Amanda were in the house, how would we escape if I got them out? Would an eight-hour car chase being pursued by heavily armed and pissed professionals succeed? Probably not.

No plan. Little chance of success. Potentially a deadly outcome.

It was going to be one of those times.

I waited, hidden in the forest as darkness fell. As the light faded, the sounds of the rainforest built to a crescendo, an awesome symphony of nature's prowess. I shuddered to think what creatures may be lurking behind me or slithering under my feet. A pack of human predators was enough to contemplate.

Two lights flicked on in the dwelling's bottom story, another upstairs. Because of my limited view, I had no handle on activity elsewhere in the building or surrounds. Fortunately, the guards stuck pretty much to their positions. That would be helpful.

Twenty minutes after the darkness set in, I made my move. Weaving in and out of the trees, I headed up the clearing. I'd take the man on that side first, provided he didn't see me coming.

The cacophony of forest sounds masking the rustling of

twigs breaking underfoot, I edged forward. Twenty yards before I drew level with the corner of the house, I pushed five yards into the undergrowth. Although it would take longer and possibly be noisier, I'd be hidden from the guard's sight. Once level with him, I'd re-approach the periphery of the cleared area.

Standing fifteen yards away, the guard now seemed unassailable. His eyes scanned from the forest to the front door guard's view. Each scan took about a minute. He was focused, spending no time lighting cigarettes or browsing his cell phone. Another indication that he was a professional.

That would mean at best I'd have around fifteen seconds to slip silently across the clearing before he saw me. Even then, he'd probably catch me in his peripheral vision.

I grudgingly accepted that my plan was unachievable.

Plan B. I moved further up parallel to the house until I perched ten yards up from the guard. What I had in mind was risky but needed to be done. As the sentry commenced his downward scan of the clearing, I bolted for the building.

That was the moment the floodlights flicked on. Instantly the garden flooded in a mosaic of light and shadow.

Now pressing flat against the cinderblock wall, I froze. There was just enough darkness to conceal me if I stood perfectly still. I hoped.

With the new light, every moment I waited increased my chances of detection, so when the lookout began his next sweep, I scampered down the edge of the house toward him.

A yard short of my target, everything went to shit. He must have heard a footstep, so he swiveled around simultaneously raising his gun. I dived right to avoid his aim while launching a fist at his jaw. It connected hard. The man grunted and took a step sideways. If he yelled out, it was all over.

He swung the automatic around as he moved. I ducked under the barrel. This battle had to be fought at close quarters, and in silence. Then my attack faltered. A searing pain radiated through my head as his forehead pounded the bridge of my nose. I felt the blood wash down my face as I started to sway backward. Aware another rearward step would be the end of me if he brought his weapon to bear, I lunged awkwardly forward, wrapping my arms around his torso. It was an amateur move, but the only one I had. I prayed he didn't have an accessible knife.

The guard struggled to break free of my grip. My senses still reeling, I held on for dear life. We wrestled like that for at least five seconds, close and personal. Aware that eventually he'd break away, I decided to go first. I thrust my chest forward, pushing him against the wall. In one swift motion, I relinquished my hold and plunged my hand into my pocket. The sentry was already bouncing back at me. I yanked out the Beretta, flicked it around in my palm and brought the handle crashing down on the man's right temple.

He folded to the ground. It was messy, but it had worked.

Now I had two guns. One for me, one for Greatrex. If he was here and if I could free him.

Creeping along the front of the building, I stopped at the first window. Block out blinds obstructed any view. The worst-case scenario: going into a potentially hostile environment without any intel. Were the outside guards the only obstacle, or were there more armed men inside?

Who the hell knew?

Next on my shopping list. Guard number two. The guy by the front door.

I could only assume he hadn't heard the previous scuffle. Either that or he'd gone for help. Clinging to the shadows, I hugged the wall as I edged across the facade of the building.

There would be no reconnaissance here. Just attack.

Once again, I pressed myself flat, back to the shadows, steeling myself to move forward. A single deep breath and then...

Suddenly, a face appeared around the corner. The guard. I was surprised. Fortunately, he was more surprised. That fraction of a second difference allowed me to drive my balled fist hard into his cheek. He lashed out with his free arm as he recoiled. I sidestepped the swing and hoisted my knee full force into his groin. Without waiting to see the results, I repeated my previous move, raised the Beretta, and smashed into the side of his skull.

He crumpled. First in wins.

The ball was now in my court. I scanned the clearing, the outbuildings, and the house for any sign my intrusion had been discovered.

Nothing.

I propped the second guard's rifle beside the door. After heaving the other automatic over my shoulder, I gripped the Beretta tightly with my left hand. The two different types of weapon would allow solid coverage in any kill zone.

The front door handle twisted slowly beneath my right palm. I edged it ajar before grabbing the grip of the automatic, my finger resting on the trigger.

One, two, three... I slammed the door open with my heel and stepped into the room.

Chapter 13

It happened with lightning speed.

First instant: scan the area for any armed combatants.

Next second: confirm no other hostiles immediately visible.

Three seconds in: identify any likely places of hostile concealment.

Four seconds in: Check for innocents; potential collateral damage.

A simple and brief process, my main aim being to live through it.

The room was large and sparsely furnished. A chunky wooden bench ran down its center. On the right, midway down, stood a staircase, presumably leading to the upper level. I kept it in my peripheral vision.

More to the point, so far, nobody had shot me.

A dark slate floor led to a lounge area at the far end of the space. A glass coffee table sat between two semi-comfortable looking armchairs. Jack Greatrex sat in the chair on the left. A tall, slender woman with long black hair perched opposite him.

"In God's name, what the hell?" The big fella stood up, his bulky frame dominating the space.

"Nicholas. How did you find us?"

I stepped back out the door, grabbed the other AK47, and threw it across the room to Greatrex.

"Are there others?" I asked. Straight to business. Still scanning the room.

"At least six hostiles in total." Greatrex checked his weapon as he spoke.

"I've taken out two, albeit temporarily. Where are the other four?"

"They've been working in shifts, one pair outside, another pair at the rear of the house and two men off duty, I assume upstairs," he replied.

I looked toward the woman.

"Amanda?"

She nodded.

"All right, Let's go," I said. "This is far from over."

"I'm afraid you're wrong about that, Mr. Sharp."

Greatrex's face crinkled in alarm the same instant I registered the voice behind me.

I pivoted fast, swinging the AK around. I'd made it less than halfway before a freight train stuck the side of my head, sending me spinning to the stone floor.

It had ended with the same lightning speed.

Then a different voice.

"Raise that weapon one more inch Mr. Greatrex, and you're dead."

In my dazed state, lying flat on the ground, I made out two men standing on the internal staircase. They each had their guns trained on Jack Greatrex's chest.

"Now, place the gun on the floor."

I swung my head back towards my own assailant. He was

69

a tall, fit-looking white man. He bore several days' growth and extremely cold dark eyes. He'd returned his weapon to a firing position. Naturally, the muzzle was directed at me. Another figure, equally formidable, stepped out from the doorway behind him.

Two plus two. The other four men.

I guessed I'd never get a job with International Rescue.

Twenty minutes later, Greatrex, Amanda Best and I each sat bound and bolt upright on separate wooden chairs.

"We did try to make this venture a little more civilized," announced my attacker. "At least until we were due to receive further instructions."

'*Further instructions*'. So that buck didn't stop with him.

"But I'm afraid your intrusion, Mr. Sharp, has changed the nature of our relationship."

All six men now occupied strategic positions around the room. Two of them stared at me, their anger barely concealed behind their professionally passive faces.

No sign of the shadow man.

"For what it's worth, my name is Muldoon. I'm in charge of this squad," the man continued. We're under instruction to bring you here, hold you incommunicado and await further orders. Do you understand Mr. Sharp?

I understood that I'd chased the shadow man up here for hours on end just to do these bastards' job for them. I also understood that it seemed likely we wouldn't be leaving here at all.

"I get it."

"We should have further information in the morning. In the meantime, you will remain restrained. For toilet and food breaks, you'll be released one at a time. There'll be no conversation between you. Two of my people will stay in this room to ensure that."

No psychology degree needed to see this guy's exaggerated need for power.

Muldoon turned and ascended the staircase. His immediate offsider and the two men I'd previously dealt with left with him. The pair from the stairs moved apart to the room's corners.

It would be a long night.

Chapter 14

It should have been a long, uncomfortable night. For Greatrex and Amanda Best, I suspect it was. Within thirty minutes of eating the cold pies provided, and after dealing with the necessities of life, I slept like a child.

I woke like an old man.

The sun's rays filtered through the edges of the blinds, sending shards of light across the room. My neck felt as though someone had clamped it in a vice.

"He lives."

Greatrex's voice penetrated my consciousness.

I looked around. Save for Amanda, Greatrex and myself, the place was empty.

"Where's the guard of honor?" I asked.

"They were called upstairs at sunrise. I've been listening to them stomp about through the floorboards. They haven't abandoned us."

"Pity," I replied.

"I've got a bad feeling about these people, Nicholas. Something isn't quite right."

"You mean, apart from the fact they're holding us captive in some remote rainforest retreat in some far-off country?"

Despite my sarcasm, I had more regard for Jack Greatrex's

character assessment than almost any person on earth.

"Yup," he began. "They act like professionals, just doing their job, following orders, etc. but I think there's more to the story. An undertone of some sort."

"Do you have any idea where they're from?"

"I don't reckon they're zealots, nor terrorists."

"Mercenaries?"

"Could be," replied the big fella.

A blisteringly loud mechanical roar swept over us, drowning out our conversation. It rose to a crescendo, seemingly above our heads, before settling and eventually dwindling away.

"A chopper," I observed.

"Rescue party?"

"Don't count on it."

We waited, listening for gun shots or explosions that might signal conflict. We heard nothing.

"No cavalry today," I announced.

There was noise coming from upstairs. Doors being slammed. The scuffling of feet. Then raised voices. I couldn't make out what was being said, but it sounded emotionally charged.

Three minutes later, Muldoon came stomping down the stairs. Two of his men followed. One marched over to me, the other to Amanda Best. They began to untie us. They left Greatrex to last. Probably because of his size. The man had a threatening demeanor when he was unsettled or frustrated. Currently, he was both.

"Upstairs, now," ordered Muldoon, seemingly unhappy with what he had to do.

We climbed the steps, our uncertainty palpable.

73

Halfway up the staircase, a landing split the remaining steps into two strands. One left, one right. Our guards pushed us to the left. That is, they pushed Amanda and me in that direction. Even though they had the guns, I don't think either of them fancied pushing Greatrex anywhere.

The area upstairs appeared the polar opposite of the space downstairs. Polished wooden floorboards were covered by an array of high-quality Persian style rugs. Impressive looking antique furniture had been elegantly placed around the room, including a large eight-seater dining table. The look was completed by a Chesterfield sofa and chairs facing the enormous windows that overlooked the rainforest. Overcrowded bookshelves lined the two end walls.

"Mrs. Best, Mr. Sharp, Mr. Greatrex, please accept my profound apologies for the manner in which you've been brought here. It appears my men have been overzealous in their approach and exceeded their remit. I do apologize."

We turned away from the window. The figure who spoke was tall, over six foot in height, had gray salt and pepper toned hair, a little too long to be called well-kept, and a full beard that matched. His deep velvet voice resonated across the room as he spoke. He was dressed in jeans and a slightly crinkled open-neck shirt.

As the man stepped forward, hand outstretched, two thoughts stuck me. First, Marlon Brando had arrived on set. Second, I'd seen his face somewhere before. Maybe it was our host, perhaps the rainforest or even the arrival of the helo, but I was definitely having an 'Apocalypse Now' moment.

"My name is Deagan Jones."

"Crimson Wave," said Amanda Best

"For better or for worse, yes," replied Jones.

A plethora of screen images flashed across my mind. Foaming waves crashing over ships' bows in the cold Antarctic. Crews casting out lines to tangle the propellers of illegal Japanese whalers. Fleets of small boats protecting pods of dolphins from traditional hunters. Irrevocably linked to each image was the man who stood before us. More often than not, in each image, he perched at the ship's helm, barking instructions. I even recalled a 'Sixty Minutes' interview with Captain Deagan Jones. Hero to many, outlaw to many others.

"You better have a fucking good reason for keeping us here against our will," I said, declining his hand.

"Your anger is noted and totally justified, Mr. Sharp. Please, all of you, take a seat and I'll do my best to explain."

I looked at Greatrex, so far silent, then Amanda Best. Despite not knowing her, we were in this situation together.

"Very well," she said. "But only because my husband thinks so highly of you, Mr. Jones."

Greatrex shrugged his shoulders. We sat, Amanda and I on the sofa, Greatrex on one chair and Captain Deagan Jones on the other.

"Before I begin, Mrs. Best. I'm so sorry to be the bearer of tragic news. I'm afraid your husband's remains were washed up in the mangroves just north of Georgetown. The authorities say that it was a diving accident."

Amanda Best's sharp intake of breath, accompanied by the shudder that seemed to radiate through her body, spoke to her grief. She bowed her head. Out of respect, no one spoke as the next few minutes dragged sluggishly by.

Eventually Amanda raised her head, her dark hair draped over her face, intermingling with the flow of tears.

She inhaled again before speaking, her voice low and purposeful.

"Teddy did not die in an accident." She looked at Greatrex. "Jack, you and I know he was too careful to allow that to happen." The grieving widow then glanced at me, before arcing her gaze round to Captain Jones. "I have no doubt, gentlemen, and neither should you. My husband was murdered."

To his credit, Jones didn't respond immediately. He sat, weighing up her words.

"Mrs. Best. Permit me to offer my condolences. You should know that I knew Teddy quite well. He took part in several Crimson Wave campaigns and was highly respected amongst our people."

Amanda stared straight through him.

"You should also be aware," Jones continued, "that I was in touch with Teddy the day before he disappeared. He provided me with some startling and worrisome intelligence."

"The detonating system," said Greatrex.

"You're aware of that then, Mr. Greatrex. I had wondered," replied Jones.

The big fella nodded.

"Based on the facts at hand, Mrs. Best, I concur with your conclusion. I believe your husband was killed to stop any further investigation into his discovery. Your thoughts Mr. Greatrex?

"No doubt."

"Mr. Sharp?" Jones looked directly at me.

"I'm the one who's late to the party here," I began. "I didn't know Teddy very well. I only met him occasionally through Jack." I turned to Amanda Best. "I'm sorry for your loss, Amanda." I then squared up to Jones. "Captain Jones, you still owe us one hell of an explanation as to why you've broken a string of laws that could see you imprisoned for life by kidnapping Jack, Amanda, and now me. My patience for a decent response has run out."

Nicholas Sharp, man of compassion.

Jones stood and nodded to Muldoon, who had been skulking in a corner. Still armed.

"Muldoon. Can you please ask Soloman to join us?"

A minute later, a tall, lithe dark-skinned figure entered. The shadow man.

"This is Soloman Triak. He's been my right-hand man for more years than I can count. He needs to be part of this conversation."

Jones stared out the window at the imposing view.

"Spectacular, isn't it?" he asked, probably not expecting an answer. "The Iwokrama Rainforest. Do you know how many species of wildlife and fauna live here?" Again rhetorical. "Countless, most likely. Over fourteen hundred square miles of pristine habitat. Many of the species here are endangered, some that exist here have already been branded extinct. The Iwokrama truly is a lost world."

Jones paused. Despite his passion, I was still impatient for answers.

He continued. "Forgive me everyone. I see you're restless for information, rather than a wildlife lecture. Please bear with me."

I remained silent.

"I've dedicated my whole life, my very existence, to protecting the planet we've been blessed to inherit. Let me tell you, it's been a fight and a crusade. Have I broken laws at times? Absolutely. When the action is warranted, have I ordered human lives to be endangered? Yes, but not intentionally. When I see a whale mother and calf being chased down by ruthless hunters in the name of false scientific research, I've never wavered. Intervention, action… whatever you choose to call it. When ships collide, there can be collateral damage. All my people stand firm with me on this, or at least they did. But I'll come back to that."

Jones hesitated, seeming to weigh up how far to take this.

"I'm personally a wanted man in several countries and jurisdictions. In other locations, I'm a hero. Sometimes I'm both in the same place. Either way, across the globe, there is work that needs to be done. My organization, The Crimson Wave, has been successful in saving so much habitat and wildlife. We respect nature, and we respect the rule of law… mostly. What we don't respect are laws created by environmental vandals. As it turns out, the media seems to thrive on that contradiction. Conflict brings good news stories, and at Crimson Wave, we are happy to oblige."

Amanda spoke. "Teddy believed in you and your people. But what he told me doesn't correlate with our involuntary presence here."

Jones turned to her.

"You are completely correct. Once again, I'm sorry. The truth is that when your husband disappeared, I became concerned. Not only for what he may have discovered, but also for his own safety. When we learned that Pedro, his informant, had been murdered, we were under no illusions. Anyone involved in this situation could be in danger. Crimson Wave is a large organization, and we need effective coordination to respond quickly to evolving situations. Accordingly, I spoke with some key people on our international board. They not only concurred, but insisted we employ some security experts for everyone's wellbeing."

"Who exactly is everyone?" I asked.

"Our first concern was you, Mrs. Best. Then, when Mr. Greatrex appeared and began asking a lot of questions, he set himself up as a potential target. Accordingly, Mr. Muldoon's team were contracted and dispatched to offer you sanctuary up here while we sorted things out."

I could sense Greatrex's frustration rising. The popping veins in his arms the tell.

"Mine wasn't an invitation. It was a kidnapping," he announced, his voice on edge.

"Likewise," interjected Amanda. "I was instructed to pack a small bag and come immediately. No option to decline."

Jones looked at them both. His shoulders sagged.

"While Mr. Muldoon's men were being activated to provide you some respite, I flew out of the country to seek help from experts in the field. Representatives of the board communicated our needs to Muldoon's organization. I fear it was a miscommunication that resulted in your forced exile. It should never have happened that way. When Soloman called me to explain the situation, I made plans to return immediately. I also requested he go back to Georgetown and keep an eye on your house himself, Mrs. Best, just in case any other interested parties materialized."

"Meaning me," I responded.

"Yes, Mr. Sharp." Soloman Triak spoke for the first time. "You performed excellently by the way. May I ask, did you manage to get inside the Best residence?"

I nodded.

"Exceptional skill, I had no idea. In fact, I didn't know you were in the area until I spotted you in my rear vision mirror as I left Georgetown."

"That early?" I responded.

"Don't be disheartened, Mr. Sharp," said Jones. "Before he came to work for me, Soloman was an undercover detective for the Guyana Police Department. Those skills were part of the reason I employed him."

"So why didn't you lose me on the drive here?" I asked.

"I considered it. To be honest, I wasn't planning on returning to Iwokrama last night. But as I drove, I contacted some old colleagues at the department. They informed me of your meeting with Station Sergeant Persaud. I did some research online and through my old connections. It seemed you were a stand-up guy with certain skills, and I don't mean your musical abilities. Given my concerns regarding the events here, I figured you may be a useful ally."

"You didn't consider that stopping your car and giving me a heads-up would have helped?" I asked.

"I did, but I figured you'd be more productive working on your own. And I was almost right."

Almost.

I took a breath. A lot of information needed to be processed and assessed.

"Two questions," I said, scanning between Deagan Jones and Soloman Triak. "First, what is the name of the contract firm that Muldoon and his thugs work for?"

Jones nodded at Muldoon. The latter seemed unimpressed by my position description.

"We are part of an organization called Compass Black," Muldoon responded.

If blood could run cold, mine would have. Many years

earlier, I'd dealt with some members of Compass Black in London. They were ruthless, immoral, free-range mercenaries. I saw no need to bring that familiarity to light here. The London situation hadn't ended well for team Compass Black… at all. I glanced at Greatrex. I'd have bet everything I owned he was thinking the same thing.

This new information tainted my expectation of the response to my next question.

"Second, are you saying that we are free to leave here at any time?"

"You most certainly are," replied Deagan Jones. "In fact, if that is your wish, we'll supply you with the transport at your earliest convenience."

Amanda slumped back in her chair. Relief. I didn't echo her reaction, although I was surprised at Jones' words.

I stood up. "Well, now is as good a time as any."

"Sit down Mr. Sharp. You're not going anywhere," announced Muldoon.

As he spoke, the remaining five guards piled into the room. One in each corner and two, including Muldoon, covering the stairs. All their guns were raised.

Expectations met.

Chapter 15

"What the hell is going on here?" demanded Jones.

"I would suggest that you are no longer master of this vessel, Captain Jones." I replied.

Jones took a step towards the Compass Black leader. "Muldoon, tell your men to stand down. Immediately."

"Not another step, Jones. Not a single one," replied Muldoon.

The captain's skin color had morphed to a deep red, his anger evident.

"In God's name, I employed you. Your duty is to ensure my and my guests' security. I insist you follow my directions."

Muldoon stared at Jones as though he'd heard nothing the man said. His gun remained pointed at the furious environmentalist.

I glanced at Greatrex. His face showed no evidence of surprise. Then to Amanda Best. Her mouth was agape.

Eventually Muldoon responded.

"Captain Jones, my company was contracted by your organization. In that, you are correct. However, you are not the person who employed us, nor the one we are answerable to. As for our task at hand, our orders are a little more complex than you suggest."

Muldoon spoke courteously, but without the slightest tremor of empathy.

"I think what Muldoon is saying, Captain Jones, is that you are now as much a prisoner here as we are." I added.

Jones' brow furrowed; his eyes drawn close in confusion. A moment later, a brief look of acceptance crossed his face. But he said nothing more.

"All of you, downstairs," ordered Muldoon. His men stepped forward, guns still aimed at each of us.

"Where is Joshua, you sick bastard?" Jones took another step in Muldoon's direction. He was greeted by the handle of Muldoon's weapon smashing across his jaw. He dropped to his knees, his face awash with blood.

"I'll have him brought here," said Muldoon before nodding at the man beside him who disappeared toward the rear of the house.

"Joshua?" I asked.

Jones, still on his knees, gaped at me, as though I had spoken in a foreign tongue.

"My son."

He turned back to Muldoon.

"If you harm him, in any way, I shall kill you Muldoon."

"Dad."

The voice came from a rear corridor. A second later, a young boy, around fourteen years of age, was shoved into the room. Behind him, an impatient-looking guard with an AK-47 prodded the boy's back.

Quite naturally, the lad appeared flustered. With his unkempt blond hair, intelligent blue eyes, and strutting jaw, he was the spitting image of his father.

"Josh, are you hurt?" asked the Captain.

Joshua shook his head. "No, but you are. What's going on?"

"Enough," said Muldoon. "Downstairs now, all of you."

The Compass Black men shoved, pushed, and cajoled us down the wooden staircase. Muldoon followed.

"Sit at the dining table, but with your hands clearly in sight. Four of my operatives will remain here with you."

A pointed finger at each of the designated men tasked the order. Jones and the remaining Compass Black operators disappeared back up the stairs.

We sat, our hands resting on the tabletop.

"At least they haven't tied us up," I observed.

"That may change overnight," said Greatrex. "Also, they don't seem too worried about us talking."

"Acknowledged, but that may not be a positive sign." I didn't want to say more and upset the boy.

There were a lot of dots that needed connecting. Now was the time.

"Captain Jones. I think you have a better idea of the situation than you've revealed. Would you care to share?"

Jones scrutinized me, likely assessing what he knew and how much he would disclose. After a few moments, he shrugged his shoulders in acceptance.

"This could take a while."

"Apparently we're not going anywhere," I replied.

Jones used a sleeve to wipe the blood from his face.

"Crimson Wave began as a small group. As I indicated earlier, our methods have always been direct and frequently confrontational. Our approach achieved results, and a great deal of media attention. Don't misunderstand me, with that scrutiny came an overwhelming growth in membership and sponsorship. Like-minded individuals and businesses donated money and time. Our pool of resources grew. After a few years, we'd become a formidable force in the environmental movement. Some said, the cutting edge of progress. While others held meetings, we advocated direct action, and we demonstrated to the world what that meant."

Amanda interjected. "That's why Teddy joined. He'd always been impatient for change and Crimson Wave seemed to offer a clear path forward."

Jones nodded.

"A decade ago, we realized we had to restructure. Everything just got too big. We had campaigns running all over the globe, protesting the illegal whalers in the Antarctic Ocean, fighting unlawful overfishing in the Mediterranean and Baltic Seas, protecting pilot whales and dolphins in the Faroe Islands, seals in Canada, and monitoring and opposing offshore oil drilling near vulnerable habitats. There is more, but you get the picture."

We all nodded.

"Our new structure involved a number of key countries establishing their own Crimson Wave entities, with all activities being monitored and overseen by Crimson Wave International. As founder and probably the most recognizable face of CW, I was appointed chairman of the International Board. The arrangement served us well for several years until…"

Jones' eyes appeared to glaze over; he'd gone somewhere else. We waited. Young Joshua reached his hand across the table, placing it over his father's. The boy had empathy.

"Sorry, regret can be somewhat of a stalker," said Jones. "As I began, operations moved along soundly for a long time. Our new corporate structure seemed to attract even more sponsorship and much more money. To be honest, I should have paid more attention to where the money was coming from, but the benefits were undeniable. My only concern was that no sponsor should be able to limit our actions or influence our decisions."

"So, what changed?" asked Greatrex.

"Over time, more jurisdictions took legal action not only against Crimson Wave as a group, but many targeted me personally, as CW's figurehead. It didn't particularly worry me except that I needed to be careful where I traveled. The authorities caught me in the wrong place twice. I spent a short period in an Italian jail before our lawyers got me out. The second occasion I was arrested, I just shot through on bail. Can't find me, can't catch me type of thing. Then tragedy struck. Joshua's mother, who I loved dearly but didn't live with, became seriously ill. Her death shocked us all, but it also meant my son had to be my priority."

Josh squeezed his dad's hand. The silent understanding between father and son.

"From that moment on, I started spending more time in Iwokrama."

"You bought this place?" asked Amanda.

"No, my dear," replied Jones. "No one buys land in the Iwokrama Rainforest. This building has been here for years and was largely unused since the British agreed to Guyana's independence. I'd performed several favors for the council in charge of the reserve, helping them with environmental matters. They offered me sanctuary here, and I accepted. This is our base, but Josh and I travel extensively and carefully when we can. He's home schooled. Between Soloman and I, we've done a decent enough job with the boy's education."

Joshua smiled. Triak nodded his head.

"Even with the regular contact, my influence on the organization began to wane. I should have seen it coming, but I didn't. My colleagues on the board suggested that perhaps I should step down as chairman, take a more advisory role, for the good of our cause. They argued that it would be more difficult to maintain substantial sponsorship with a fugitive as the head of the group. Effective campaigning for the planet was my main concern. I put my ego, and believe me, I have a healthy one, aside and stepped down... fool."

I leaned forward. "What happened next?"

"It began well enough, but then the signs of what I'd regard as moral disintegration took hold. Certain members of the board proposed we adopt more conciliative strategies within our campaigns. They suggested we work with other groups, even local authorities, to achieve greater cultural change. I argued against it, saying we'd tried that before, and it only resulted in frustration. Coastguards, police, and other official bodies had mostly feigned interest in our hard gathered information, before they initiated minimal action, that was often too late, and frequently ineffective. I stated other organizations existed for that approach. Not Crimson Wave."

"What was their response?" asked Greatrex.

"The board outvoted me."

"So, you came back here?" Amanda inquired.

"Reluctantly, yes. I needed to regroup, and, of course, look after Josh. I used the time to do some research, dive deep into the backgrounds of not only of some of our sponsors but also some of our newer board members. Some of Crimson Wave's most generous supporters branded themselves as good corporate citizens. They advocated climate change as

87

the major issue of our era and put their money where their mouths were."

"But?" interrupted Greatrex.

"But what I discovered under the surface displeased me."

"What did you find?" I asked.

"It was unbelievable. Deep down, behind a myriad of shell companies, bogus charities, and confusing corporate entities around the globe, I uncovered links to traditional energies - oil, gas, even nuclear. These were not 'our' people."

"And these sponsors eventually brought their influence to bear?" suggested Greatrex.

"Exactly. It was done slowly, with great skill and subtlety. They gradually loaded Crimson Wave's international board with individuals who secretly endorsed a traditional energy agenda. In effect, they nobbled the most productive and radical environmental protection group in the world. I'd call it brilliant if they weren't so damn evil." Jones held his fists clenched tight.

"So, what did you decide to do?" I asked.

"I considered leaving, but that seemed cowardly. I thought about attending a board meeting and confronting them, but that would have been pointless. I'd been biding my time, procrastinating, when I received the email from Teddy Best the other night."

"That spurred you to act," said Greatrex.

"It did. Teddy's information implied a direct and major threat to the environment off the northern coast of South America. If the oil line between Georgetown and the Reardon 3 platform was ruptured, the result would be catastrophic. I spoke to an underwater explosives expert, a former Navy SEAL, who is a close friend. He confirmed my fears. I no longer had a choice. I requested an emergency meeting of the board and flew to Stockholm."

"And?" prompted Amanda.

"I laid out the case. There was agreement, or at least it appeared that way. I suggested we get one of our expert teams to Guyana immediately. The deployment was approved. The new chairman, Rahmat Beras, said he would attend to it personally. As I met with the board, further information came through. The disappearance of Teddy Best was confirmed, as was the murder of his informant Pedro."

"What was the board and the chairman's reaction to that?" I inquired.

"They expressed alarm, requesting we consult closely with the Guyanese authorities and stipulating personal protection for me and my family. I indicated I'd be fine with Soloman and whatever local men I could muster up. They insisted on a professional security crew being sent in. I was told that if we were to initiate proactive measures, that would be non-negotiable. Reluctantly, I agreed."

"Then you returned here this morning," added Greatrex.

"Yes, to discover not only had the security team arrived, but instead of requesting you join me here until it was safe, they forced the matter. I was ropable."

"And now we find ourselves incarcerated together," said Soloman.

"Captain Jones, one question," I began. "Didn't it occur to you that the new security personnel made it here unusually quickly? Unless they were locals, which they're not, it should have taken them at least twenty-four hours for them to assemble here?"

"Damn."

"I suggest your board had the Compass Black team on standby, waiting for you to pull a trigger to enable them to act," I suggested.

"And that's exactly what I did."

"Yes sir, you did. But don't forget, I have the advantage here of knowing how this group acts, and what little, if anything, they stand for... apart from a substantial paycheck."

Silence.

I continued. "We're left with one option."

"What's that? asked Jones.

"Get the fuck out of here."

Chapter 16

The next couple of hours dragged on. Our guards hadn't put a stop to our conversation, but planning an escape within their earshot was counterproductive. Greatrex and I looked at each other, words unspoken. We'd been through enough together to understand this would be an improvised scenario. Not ideal.

This would be about opportunity. To take on four extremely focused armed guards, currently out of our physical reach, guaranteed a fast track to instant death.

Sometime close to two in the afternoon, opportunity walked through the door, or at least a glimmer of hope presented itself. Muldoon descended the stairs.

"On your feet, we're moving you," he ordered.

Jones swung around. He looked tired, defeated, and every bit of his fifty something years.

"Where are you taking us?" An intense fury simmered under his words. That was good. Anger may serve him and us well.

"That's for me to know," replied Muldoon. "We have our instructions. Get up."

A guard opened the lower front door, the one that I'd entered by a lifetime ago, before the others herded us out.

"Can we grab our things from our rooms?" Asked Soloman Triak, referring to Jones, Joshua, and himself.

"No need," came the curt response.

Not a good sign.

We turned left and marched up the slope beside the house. The afternoon sun glared down. Within a dozen paces sweat oozed from every pore. As we rounded the corner of the building, things became clearer. On a large flat pad cut into the hillside stood two almost identical choppers. One sky blue, one black. They were obviously the main transport in and out of the retreat.

The guards pushed us along. I expected the front man to lead us to one of the helicopters. They'd probably need both to get everybody out. To my surprise, he kept walking straight ahead. I glanced over at Jones and then to Triak. They would know what lay beyond the helipad. Their creased brows and taut mouths indicated high-level concern. It didn't take much to put two and two together.

"What about the boy?" asked Triak.

"We have our instructions," repeated Muldoon.

Triak's expression morphed briefly into grief before his eyes darkened with rage. He clearly cared for the child he had helped raise.

If I'd thought I'd have a chance, I'd have leaped across the space between us and taken Muldoon out then and there. Callous bastard. I glanced at Greatrex. I knew the signs, balled fists, veins swelling out of his neck. The big fella despised a lot of things that were wrong with the world, but he abhorred people who harmed kids more than anything. Right then, I didn't give much for Muldoon's chances of surviving the afternoon. Jack Greatrex would pay any price required to save that kid.

Enough of the emotion. It was time to get strategic. Four guards accompanied us, one in front, one at the rear, and a sentry on either side. Their weapons were raised and ready. Muldoon stood a little away, well out of my reach. His weapon tilted downward, although I held no doubt he'd be able to raise and fire it within a second.

Soloman Triak's eyes were darting left and right. He was a professional and would surely be looking for every opportunity. The trouble being the men in charge were also trained professionals and so far had presented no chink in their armor. Jones, who had first appeared grief stricken, now appeared to let his anger consume him. He seemed ready to act if there was a way through.

We all knew there wasn't.

We needed a distraction. The Compass Black crew wouldn't fall for one of us feigning injury. They'd probably just shoot the complainant then and there.

Any moment, desperation would overtake sense, and Greatrex or I would do something. But we didn't.

It was Soloman Triak who took decisive action. Soloman Triak beat us to the punch.

Without warning, Triak sprung himself sideways towards the sentry on his left. He grabbed the guy's weapon and swung it toward the rear guard. He pulled the trigger, showering the man with bullets. Because the gun's sling remained around the first guard's shoulder, his potential moves were limited. Heaving hard, Triak then pointed the barrel upward and smashed it against the surprised man's forehead.

It took Greatrex and me a millisecond to react. Ignoring the guard two yards away, I bolted sideways and launched myself toward Muldoon. The leader raised his AK-47, aiming at my chest. I barrel rolled to the right, hitting the hard ground with a shuddering jolt. I stretched my arms towards his legs in desperation. Muldoon read my move and stepped back… but a second too slow.

I swept my hands under him, and he hit the earth beside me. The clatter of automatic fire filled my ears. I had to trust that the others were doing what they could. As Muldoon landed, I lurched forward, slamming my shoulder into his neck. He grunted before a deep wheeze betrayed his lack of oxygen.

Now it was all about the gun. Whoever controlled it would win this skirmish, whoever didn't, would die. At that moment, neither of us was in control. The Compass Black man recovered quickly. As I reached for the weapon's trigger guard, he chopped both arms upward, sending a sharp, debilitating pain through my wrists. Still gasping for air, he rolled toward me, pulling the weapon backward in an attempt to place the barrel against my chest.

I extended my arm and punched him in the face with my right fist. Simultaneously, my left hand grabbed the automatic's muzzle, desperately trying to point it upward to the sky. Muldoon got off a few rounds, but they went wide. I pounded his face again. For a split second, his grip on the gun weakened. I wrenched it forward. Suddenly it was free. I held it close, as though my life depended on it, and rolled away. Once I passed the second turn, I sprang to my feet, pointing the gun behind me. Muldoon had risen to one knee, about to pounce. When he saw the weapon aimed at his torso, he froze.

"Please Muldoon, give me a reason," I said.

He didn't move a muscle.

The pause gave me a chance to assess our status. Greatrex had confronted the sentry I had avoided to reach Muldoon. They now scuffled in the dirt. My money was on the big fella. Triak still struggled with his man for control of the guard's weapon. His surprise attack had caught the guy unaware, but he was a large man and more than a match for Triak. That left the lead guard. He stood motionless, his weapon pointing at Deagan Jones, who had launched himself at Joshua, sheltering him from the gunfire. He lay on top of the boy, looking up at the gun. Amanda Best hunched down next to them.

"Shoot Jones," yelled Muldoon.

The guard began to squeeze his trigger. At the same moment, Soloman Triak landed a fatal blow to the side of his man's head and turned toward Jones' executioner.

"No," he yelled, his voice strained with emotion. He dived at the lead guard, who sprang into action, swinging his weapon from Jones to Triak. The burst of gunfire caught Soloman Triak's chest mid-dive. The assault was not survivable.

Jones took the opportunity to lunge forward, bear hugging the shooter to the ground. He reached for a nearby rock, grabbed it, and pounded the man into unconsciousness.

Hearing Muldoon's order to shoot was all the excuse I needed. I squeezed the trigger on my weapon.

'Click.' The damn gun jammed.

"Now it gets interesting Sharp." Muldoon's leer bore total malice.

At that instant, more gunfire erupted from the direction of the house. The two remaining guards had obviously heard the sound of shots and reacted. With Triak dead we were outnumbered and out flanked.

Muldoon lunged toward me. I was trained to fight with

strength and logic, not anger, but I was pissed. I wheeled the weapon around and smashed it across the Compass Black man's face. He went down.

Jones stood, his features crumpled at the sight of his old friend lying mortally wounded beside him. But he put the welfare of his son before his own grief.

"The helicopter," he yelled. "I can fly us out."

The helipad lay midway between our position and the approaching guards. We had some functioning weapons, so we had a chance.

"Let's go," I roared.

Greatrex had finished off his man and grabbed his gun. I ripped the automatic off the dead rear guard and bolted down the hill. Deagan Jones helped a sobbing Joshua to his feet. He hadn't armed himself.

We fired a smattering of rounds as we ran. Greatrex and I ahead of Jones, his son and Amanda. Our gunfire slowed the advance of the men coming up the hill, but it didn't stop them. Halfway to the helipad, I heard shots fired behind us. Probably Muldoon with the remaining guard's weapon.

This was going to be too damn close.

"The blue helo, head toward the blue one." yelled Jones. He'd now placed himself behind Josh and Amanda, attempting to protect them from the rear attack.

The men down the hill were gaining ground. Automatic rounds hammered the earth at our feet. We were within their range, but too distant for accuracy. Greatrex and I continued to fire blindly, trying to slow them down.

As we reached the helipad, the surrounding earth spewed dirt into the air. Bullets came from all directions.

I made it to the blue chopper first. I wrestled open the

hinged pilot's door before standing back and firing several bursts down the slope. Deagan Jones jumped in, slipping straight into the cockpit. I ushered Joshua into the aircraft and seated him in the middle of the back row. On the far side, the helicopter Greatrex yanked open the sliding door, and pushed Amanda into the front passenger seat before letting off another burst and climbing on board.

Jones had the rotors turning within seconds. As his hand reached down to pull on the collective and send the bird skyward, the safety glass next to me fragmented into a series of spiderweb lines.

They were almost upon us.

The aircraft rose quickly and cleanly under Deagan Jones' hands. The metallic sound of bullets striking steel echoed through the cabin as the assault on our helo continued. Soon we ascended beyond the rainforest canopy, I allowed myself a hint of hope. Apart from the heroic Soloman Triak, we'd made it.

I looked down. My relief had been premature.

Below, on the helipad, the rotors on the black helicopter had begun to turn.

Chapter 17

We'd all placed headphones with mics on our heads.

"They're coming after us," I announced.

Jones focused on the task at hand. He finessed the controls like an artist.

"Can we outrun them?" asked Greatrex.

"Maybe yes, maybe no," Jones responded.

"You seem to know what you're doing," I observed.

"Too many years as a Navy flyer. It was a long time ago, but I kept up to date. I've used this bird numerous times in recon and photographic sojourns for Crimson Wave."

In the back seat, Joshua remained silent, almost frozen in the moment. A couple of tears rolled down his cheeks.

"Soloman…" he murmured.

"I'm sorry, son," replied Jones. "Our hearts will be heavy with the loss of our good friend. He died saving us all, and I'm not about to let his effort be wasted."

As he spoke, Jones pushed the aircraft's nose down slightly. It picked up speed as we dived downward. Mid-descent, he pulled back again on the collective. The helo surged its way skyward.

"Just testing our weight," said Jones. "We're pretty much at capacity for this bird."

"Can we outmaneuver them?" I asked.

"The good news is this is a Messerschmitt-Bölkow-Blohm Bo 105. It may be getting on in years, but the MBB Bo 105 is one of the most agile helicopters ever built."

"I suppose that is good news," said Greatrex skeptically, as he craned his head for a view of the ascending aircraft below us.

"However, the bad news is that the helo following us is almost identical. It's going to come down to pilot skill and weight. I'm pretty confident I can match most flyers, but we're running on close to maximum weight for this baby. A lot will depend on the load of the craft pursuing us. Can you get a look?"

Jones grabbed a set of binoculars from under a shelf beside his seat and passed them back to me.

I scanned the sky before finding a distant black dot. "They're below us and seem to be getting closer," I said.

Jones didn't respond. My guess was he didn't want to alarm the boy.

Three minutes later, I declared, "I've got them. It looks like Muldoon flying and one of his men is in the rear seat."

"He may be a dickhead, but he's not stupid," said Jones. "He's given himself an advantage from the get-go. What's their current position?"

"They're just about level with us and around four hundred yards behind," I replied.

"Tell me when they're level."

A minute later: "Now."

"Well, here we go." Jones thrust the nose of the helo down, as before, but far more extreme. We dove straight down toward the rainforest, faster than I could have imagined possible. I

99

couldn't see how we could pull up from this.

"What's his current position?" yelled Jones.

"He's mirrored your move. Same distance behind. No... I think he's gaining slightly."

"We're dropping quicker because of our weight. He's gaining because he has less weight, so increased airspeed. Much of a muchness. It'll be a different story going up," said Jones.

The chopper's dual engines were screaming. Even with the headphones on, we had to shout to be heard.

Jones briefly looked at me in his mirror.

"You seem a little on edge, Mr. Sharp."

I checked out Greatrex. His expression was similar to what I imagined mine to be.

"Jack and I shared a bad helo experience in Iraq a few years ago. We were shot down; it didn't go well for many on board."

Jones nodded.

"Apologies then. You're not going to enjoy the next few minutes."

As he spoke, I involuntarily closed my eyes. The rainforest canopy seemed inches away. Suddenly, there was a sharp change of mechanical tone. The screeching transformed into a laboring grind. Instantly we were surging upward, the skids almost touching the treetops as we followed the hill upward. This man was a magician.

"Sitrep?" asked Jones.

I looked out the window.

"They just emulated your move." Two magicians.

"They're going to gain as we ascend. If I was Muldoon, I'd try to pick up a little height and push us down into the trees."

Almost on cue, the black chopper pointed its nose upward

as they closed the gap. Now barely fifty feet back, they started pushing down toward us.

"Hold on to something," announced Jones. Instantly, our aircraft tilted sideways at close to a ninety-degree angle. The black helo's skids were about two feet from our rotors. The aircraft behind us responded, jumping upward, while Jones maneuvered us in a backward curve partially down the mountain before heading off towards the north, away from Muldoon.

"He'll catch us again," said Jones. "But we'll put as much distance as we can between us while the opportunity is there."

We sped down the valley, gradually gaining height.

Throughout this, Amanda Best sat stoically in the front seat, her only movement reaching a hand over to young Josh.

"Sitrep?"

"I can't see them. Jack?"

Greatrex twisted in his seat. "Nope."

Jones pushed the craft toward the southern side of the valley. "We'll cross the first mountain range at the end of the basin. I'll stay low. They won't be able to come at us from underneath."

A few minutes later, we'd closed in on the valley wall. Jones eased the machine up and over the crest. The other craft was nowhere in sight.

We passed over the ridge into clear skies, climbing higher with every second. Abruptly, the sound of automatic fire overrode the roar of our engine. The black helo appeared from the other side of the ridge, approaching us on a collision course.

"He's shadowed us up the far side of the range. Now you need to really hold on. So far, it's just been a joyride."

Jones pulled back on the collective, shooting us virtually

straight upward, like a rocket. Could helicopters do this?

The rounds went wide as we rose. The black chopper swept around and then matched our ascent, inching towards us. Skids to skids. I didn't see how this could possibly end well.

The climb felt as if it was taking forever, with both choppers' engines maxing out. Inch by inch, the black chopper's skids clawed their way closer to ours. Jones didn't react, he just pressed on.

With the aircrafts inches away from each other, and the prospect of running out of flyable airspace a distinct possibility, Jones did the unthinkable. As the skids touched, he brought the helo backward on itself. Again, we arched rearward, but this time totally inverted as we formed a great loop across the sky. The black chopper peeled left.

I should have felt relief at the avoidance of a collision, but flying upside down in a roll, plummeting back to earth didn't seem to offer much sanctuary from the terror we were escaping.

Jones held the craft firm. As we came out of the roll a hundred yards above the forest, he once again ran parallel to the treetops. If I were religious, I would have crossed myself.

"Sitrep?"

Greatrex sat closest to the oncoming black helo. "A thousand yards away coming straight at us, port side."

Relentless.

Jones inhaled. The chopper's engine had now returned to its normal quiet roar.

"Lady and gentlemen, we could keep this up all day, or at least until we run out of fuel, but Mr. Muldoon is clearly an extremely capable pilot. Better than I would have expected. I suppose there'll be some strong aviation history in his resumé.

Either way, I hate to tell you that at some point, due to his weight advantage, he will outmaneuver us, and that will be that. I'm open to suggestions."

Jones glanced at his son in the mirror, judging his son's reaction to his harsh pronouncement. Joshua held firm.

No one reacted. No one offered any ideas. Every second that drifted past, the black helo drew closer.

"I have one idea," I announced.

"Shoot," replied Jones.

"I believe that's exactly what Nicholas was about to suggest," said the big fella.

I continued. "At the moment, our opponent is matching us move for move or attempting to splatter us with wild gun fire. Hit and miss. I'm suggesting something more tactical."

"Go on," said Jones.

"If I wanted to bring that chopper down with a bullet, would I be better taking out the engine or the pilot?" I asked.

Jones considered his response. The black helo edged closer.

"If you take out the engine, unless you hit a fuel line and it explodes, he still has a chance for a forced landing. A good pilot can land with autorotation under the most trying of circumstances. Take out the pilot. They're done."

"Would a round from an AK-47 penetrate the front screen of the black helo?"

"I think you know the answer to that already."

I glanced down at the spider's web of fractured glass beside me.

"However," continued Jones, "if you could target exactly the same spot twice, there's a chance. But you'd have to be a hell of a marksman to do that to a moving chopper *from* a moving chopper."

My mother taught me to embrace challenges.

Chapter 18

"If I could, I'd drop off Amanda and my son before attempting something like this, but apart from the lack of a place to land, anytime spent on the ground would leave us vulnerable to attack," said Jones.

I nodded.

"So how do you want to play this?" he continued.

The black helo was swooping in. At fifty yards out, he changed direction, running parallel to us. A gun barrel appeared from the side window.

"Shit, he's reading from our playbook," said Jones, immediately pointing our nose down and diving under the other chopper. A burst of gunfire erupted from the other aircraft, passing over our heads.

"Jack, Let's swap seats. I'll need the sliding door."

"Roger."

We took off our headphones. I exchanged places with Joshua and then with Greatrex. I didn't like leaving the boy on an exposed outside edge of the aircraft, but there was no choice. I checked my AK's magazine.

Four rounds. Not much.

Greatrex unclipped his, holding up two fingers.

"Keep the damn thing close, just in case," I instructed,

pointing at his weapon. "Deagan, can you bring us up underneath the black helo but in front, hovering parallel to my exposed flank?"

"Can do, but I can't hold that position long with him closing in on me. How far out do you want me to come up?"

"Five hundred yards," I replied.

I saw his eyebrows raise, but he remained silent.

Jones guided our chopper on a perpendicular angle to the black helo. On cue, he turned it on a dime, coming in below the other aircraft.

"Prepare for some more fire."

No sooner had he spoken than a burst of gunfire rained down upon us. Jones was ready, swinging the aircraft right. A metallic staccato sounded from behind as some of the rounds hit our tail, but Jones kept our bird upright and on course.

"I hope you're a better shot than him," he said.

"Me too," I replied.

Greatrex grinned… slightly.

Before we knew it, Jones opened the throttle, shooting past beneath the black helo, coming up five hundred yards ahead of it and dead level. He swung our craft around and hovered as the other bird powered toward us.

"Hold my belt," I yelled to Greatrex. A second later, I felt a forceful tug behind me.

I heaved the sliding door open. The aircraft's cabin filled with the mechanical roar of our rotors. I flicked the AK's selector switch to semi-automatic. With only four rounds in the magazine, it would be single shots only. Sitting sideways, I slid across my seat and out the doorway, coming to rest with my feet braced on the chopper's skids. With half my body hanging out of the aircraft, I was battered by the airstream from the rotors. Not a great environment for accurate shooting. I grasped the rifle tightly, raised it, and took aim. The wind and the turbulence buffeted us around. One minute the black helo sat centered in my sights, the next it disappeared. I estimated my target to be approximately four hundred yards out and closing.

I drew a deep breath, exhaled, and fired… just as our helo dipped sideways. My shot went high. Sparks flew off one of the rotor blades on the other craft.

"Can't hold for much longer," said Jones.

I adjusted my aim. Three hundred yards out, I leaned against the frame of the doorway, waited a few seconds until our helo flew steady and then three, two, one…. I squeezed the trigger again.

The familiar spider web spread across the black helo's windscreen, its center in front of the pilot, Muldoon. But they kept coming. Way too fast, way too close.

"I'm going to have to break," yelled Jones, "and we won't be able to surprise him like this again."

"Wait," I roared back. One hundred and fifty yards. Our chopper bucked relentlessly in the thin air, so did my target. The first shot was the relatively easy one. Now I had to match it.

"Take the damn shot, man, or we're going to have a mid-air."

"Steady her up," I shouted. Probably a pointless instruction.

One hundred yards. If one aircraft didn't move or change course in the next five seconds, we'd both be going down the hard way.

"Hold it," I bellowed, before focusing on the job at hand.

Slight dip, wind gushing against my weapon, pushing it downward.

Pause.

Inhale.

Slow breath out.

Focus on the center of the spider web. Nothing else matters.

Squeeze.

Fire.

The instant the gunshot resonated through the cabin, Jones broke to the right and down, once more arcing backwards, away from the target. The black helo surged forward, its bulk invading the airspace we'd just vacated.

Unimpeded.

I'd missed again.

I swiveled my head to get a better look out of the aircraft, the wind and noise all consuming.

"Sitrep?"

"He's flying straight," I yelled, feeling the frustration in my voice.

"No, wait."

The black bird faltered, raising its nose upward for a fraction of a second before settling back on its path. Then a minute dip. This time, there was no correction. The bird nosedived, then heaved over on itself, before spinning around in a repetitive spiral, closer and closer to the ground.

The ten long seconds seemed like forever. Still, there was no correction, nor did I expect one.

Finally, the flight of the black helo ended, as it succumbed to an enormous fireball erupting from the forest canopy. A deafening explosion accompanied the flames.

Goodbye Muldoon, you prick.

Chapter 19

LOS ANGELES - THREE WEEKS LATER

The colorful stylings of Venice beach beckoned me as I looked down from my apartment. I planned a long stroll as soon as I'd knocked off the remains of a cold enchilada waiting in my fridge. It had been a long morning in the recording studio.

My cell chirped to life. Greatrex.

"You watching the news?" Straight to the point.

"No."

"Turn it on."

I picked up the remote and flicked on a news channel.

We are receiving reports that there has been some kind of oil spill in the Guyana-Suriname Basin off the coast of Guyana on the northern coast of South America. We have more from our South American Bureau correspondent Rodrigues Charles, who is on the scene.

I turned up the sound.

Thanks Tom. Unfortunately, the news of an oil spill is accurate. It's believed that the oil line leading from the coast to the Reardon 3 Exploration Platform has been severely breached. Initial reports indicate the spill to be massive. The pipeline appears to have ruptured in several places. There are rumors that the only way

ECHO BLUE

this could happen is through some sort of sabotage. Authorities are yet to make a statement, but we understand clean-up teams have been dispatched. Here in Georgetown, Guyana, there is a great deal of concern that the crude oil may flow into one or more of the country's main rivers. The Essequibo and Demerara Rivers are particularly vulnerable.

We are going to cross to a representative from Reardon Energies in just a moment...

"Holy Shit," I exclaimed.

"Exactly," replied Greatrex. "Have you heard from Deagan Jones since we returned?"

"One call to check we'd made it safely home. He told me that he and Josh were heading off the grid for a while, trying to sort out a way forward. I wouldn't be surprised to hear from him now," I added.

"This reeks worse than a sewer," said the big fella. "Everything in my gut says something is mighty wrong here."

"Everything in *my* gut agrees with you. But in all honesty, are we in a position to do anything?"

"I guess this isn't really in our wheelhouse," replied Greatrex, "but I still don't like it."

"I…"

Right on cue, my cell vibrated with another call.

"Jack, I'll call you back. Jones is on the other line,"

I hung up.

"Deagan."

"Nicholas, I'm glad you picked up."

"Have you seen the news?"

"Sure, I've seen it, and I'm worried as hell. But there's something worse."

Jones paused, I waited.

"Nicholas, they've got Josh."

Chapter 20

COUNTY WICKLOW, IRELAND

DEAGAN JONES

Deagan Jones strode up the narrow path towards the small stone cottage that he and Josh were holed up in. The place belonged to Jones' extended family. As an Irish American, returning to his ancestral roots in County Wicklow seemed like a sound idea, as did slipping quietly out of sight for a while. Drystone walls flanked either side of the track. Beyond them, an endless panorama of green undulating hills rolled off into the distance. A layer of fine Irish drizzle reminded the environmentalist they weren't in the tropics now.

Jones drew his collar tight. It may have been decidedly colder here than in the Iwokrama Rainforest, but then he couldn't imagine a better place to slip off the grid. Acutely aware that he and Josh, in addition to Nicholas Sharp, Amanda Best and Jack Greatrex, had been lucky to escape Guyana with their lives, Jones knew he had a great deal of thinking to do. Foremost in his mind was a rising concern for his son's safety.

He'd told no one where they were going.

Jones continued to be tortured by the fact he'd let the Crimson Wave situation deteriorate this far. He should have seen the signs, or at least some of them. Was it ego that blinded him or a dumb underlying belief that the cause he believed in was so just that nobody within the organization would consider betraying it? How wrong could you be?

Using his cell phone and internet connection for limited periods, while making efforts to mask where his signal emanated, Jones had made discreet inquiries. His name still carried enough clout and enough loyalty that the right people could be cajoled into passing on any information they had. The trouble, of course, was picking the right people.

All too aware of the danger of asking questions of those whose alliances may lie elsewhere, Jones carefully began to gather more intelligence. The depth of the intrusion by covert traditional energy advocates into Crimson Wave appeared staggering. Piece by piece, the intelligence he gathered started pointing toward the Middle East. That probably shouldn't have surprised him.

Jones also made some inquiries as to who on Crimson Wave's international board may have had any past dealings with Compass Black. Judging from the attack in and above the rainforest, not to mention Nicholas Sharp's previous encounter with the group, they appeared unscrupulous and merciless. He'd never forgive that they had attempted to murder his young son.

By association, whoever had hired Compass Black shared their same moral vacuum. Jones' research had led to two names. Both were current Crimson Tide board members. Both had a well-disguised relationship with several movers and shakers within the oil industry. Jones had found out that both men had some sort of prior association with Compass Black. One instance involved a wife that had been abducted for ransom, the other a security issue in Japan.

Jones was confident that only one of the individuals on his roster was implicated in the treachery that almost claimed his and Josh's lives. His reasoning was simple. The second name on the list was his own.

The thought of his son's brush with death subconsciously caused Jones to increase his pace. He didn't like spending any time away from Joshua given the current circumstances, but supplies had to be obtained from the local village.

The act of walking helped Jones think. But try as he might, he hadn't yet formulated a plan to deal with the current situation. Eventually, he would. He'd have to.

As he pushed open the cottage's heavy wooden door, Jones was relieved to see the lad at his laptop playing some game or another.

"Offline, I hope Josh."

"Sure Dad, just like you said."

Josh looked up at Jones as he spoke. That alone made him different from most teenagers. The boy brushed his long blond fringe back across his forehead. The warmth behind his son's eyes told of how much they needed each other at the moment.

"Did you get the cheese slices? I'm hanging out for a grilled cheese sandwich."

Jones' remorse was instantaneous. He'd been too busy thinking of other things. His shoulders, sagging in defeat, must have given him away.

"Dad, you promised."

Josh stood up. He was nearly as tall as his father now.

"It's all right Dad, I'll go and buy some. You haven't let me out of the house once. I need to get some air."

Jones knew the boy was growing restless. Josh understood their necessity for secrecy and solitude, at least in his head, but he still retained the impatience of a child.

Jones hesitated.

"I'll go back," he said.

"No, Dad, I've gotta get out of here. It'll be fine. I'll only be gone half an hour."

Like any caring father, Jones felt himself weaken. This wasn't a time for unneeded risks, but he couldn't keep Josh cooped up forever.

"All right mate, but straight there and straight back, no talking to anyone. Okay?"

Josh was halfway to the door before his father had finished speaking.

Deagan Jones sensed his stomach churn, but he couldn't retract his decision.

"I'll come with you," he said.

"No Dad, I need some solo time and a walk."

His father's son.

Decision made.

Probably the worst decision Deagan Jones had ever made in his life.

Thirty minutes passed without Josh returning. Jones was mindful of the clock, but not overly concerned. Teenage dawdle.

At forty minutes, he felt his internal tension rise.

After forty-five minutes, Jones stepped out the door and began retracing his earlier steps down the path to the village. No external thoughts intruded. He just wanted to find his son. Walking slowly, eyes peeling from side to side, he noted nothing out of the ordinary. Twenty minutes later, he shoved open the door of the small mini mart. A glance around the room and a quick check down each aisle told him Josh wasn't there. He approached the counter.

"Hello there, second trip for the day, I see. What did you forget?" asked the cheerful shopkeeper.

"Sorry, I'm just wondering. Have you seen my son? Teenager, fourteen, longish blond hair. He popped down to buy some…"

"Cheese slices," interrupted the shopkeeper. "Yes, he left here with them about, oh I don't know, maybe forty-five minutes ago, perhaps closer to an hour."

Jones felt a chill radiate through his body.

"Thank you." He turned and bolted out the door.

As tempting as it was to run back to the cottage, Jones knew he'd be better served by a slow, careful perusal of the track. Step by step, he worked his way along the path. He moved left and right, peering over the drywalls on each side, hoping for a glimpse of… anything.

Suddenly, there it was. On the side of the pathway, behind the wall, semi-covered by long grass, a packet of cheese slices lay unopened.

"Josh," he whispered quietly to no one at all.

After taking several deep breaths, Jones ran the remaining length of the route. He burst through the front door, not even registering its weight.

"Josh, Josh…" Nothing.

Jones reached for his cell before realizing he had no idea who he would call. The local authorities, not a chance. What good could a county Irish copper do against the forces they were up against? Law enforcement agencies in the states? FBI, CIA. Who would listen to him? Someone at his own organization? But who could he really trust at Crimson Wave?

As he stared down at his phone, searching his thoughts for some clarity, a news grab popped up on the screen.

"Massive Oil Spill off Guyana, South America."

Jones quickly scrolled through. Then he made up his mind and pressed dial.

"Nicholas, I'm glad you picked up."

Chapter 21

The cab taking us from George Bush International Airport into the heart of Houston scurried through the busy traffic. Our destination was a large office building inside the Interstate 610 loop.

"Why here?" asked Greatrex.

"Jones didn't get too specific," I replied. "When he requested help, of course I said we'd do what we could. Then he insisted we meet him in Houston in twenty-four hours."

"But if his boy disappeared in Ireland, why did he want to rendezvous here?"

"That was my initial reaction too," I replied. "Jones insisted that tramping around the villages of Wicklow would get us nowhere. He believes Joshua is long gone."

"But alive?"

"Yeah, clearly he's a bit emotional about that. Who wouldn't be? But his intuition was that they took the boy to silence him, so keeping Josh breathing is in their interest."

"Makes sense," said the big fella. "Does Jones figure Josh's disappearance relates to the oil spill in Guyana?"

I turned my head to face Greatrex. "There's the thing. He

118

was coy about that, and reluctant to say more over the phone."

"And to ask the obvious - why us?"

"Why is it ever us?" I replied.

The cab pulled to a halt in front of an enormous building. The skyscraper's silver and glass façade towered upward. Set diagonally on a city block, it appeared to have views snaking through the gaps in the neighboring structures. An imposing circular enclosed portico protruded onto the street.

We strode through the huge automatic doors, still unsure of our specific destination within the building. A figure materialized to our right, his gait purposeful.

Deagan Jones looked exhausted. His face revealed more craggy lines than it had three weeks earlier. The dark bags under his eyes spoke of his lack of sleep. I wasn't sure if a person could age ten years in such a short period of time, but the proof seemed to be standing in front of us.

"Deagan," I stretched out my hand.

"Nicholas, Jack, thank you for coming. I had no right to ask."

"I don't know what we can do, but if someone took your boy, we'll do everything in our power. We're both so sorry you're in this situation."

Greatrex tilted his head forward in agreement.

Jones nodded.

"Before we go into our meeting, we must talk. Follow me."

The environmentalist led us into a large café that consumed a fair proportion of the ground floor. The tables were spread out with partitions topped with large plants dividing the areas. The Texans obviously like their conversations private.

We sat in an area well away from everyone else. Jones ordered coffee for three. After they'd been served, he began

119

to speak.

"I've given you gentlemen an overview of how Josh's disappearance went down, but I believe there's little to gain from going over the minute details."

"Why so?" asked Greatrex.

Jones scanned the room before answering. Either paranoid or rightly cautious. I'd vote for the latter.

"These people are playing a significantly bigger game. A child's kidnapping is nothing compared to the level of destruction they seek."

"How can you be sure, Deagan? I know this sounds a little condescending, but given the circumstances, do you have a clear perspective of what's going down?" I asked.

Jones reached into his pocket and withdrew his cell. He tapped on the screen a couple of times before passing it over. I held it where both Greatrex and I could read it. The message read:

'Jones, you're out of it now. Stay out. If you do what we say, you'll see your boy again. If you don't...'

"I guess that's why you're staying away from the authorities," said Greatrex.

Jones nodded.

"No caller ID, I presume?" Stupid question, but all bases had to be covered.

"None," Jones responded.

"There were many people you could have asked for help, Deagan. Professional investigators, international kidnapping crisis negotiators and the like. I don't know how much expertise we can offer," I asked.

Jones seemed to ponder the point.

"I understand that," he began, "but I've been doing some research. It appears that when you dig in the right places, a bit of interesting information about you two comes to light."

I had a fair idea where this was going.

"So, it seems the pair of you have helped quite a few people through some serious situations, including some quite powerful people."

Jones paused. Neither Greatrex nor I reacted.

"Combining that closely guarded information with what I observed of you both back in the Iwokrama Rainforest and the fact I no longer have any idea who I can trust, well... here we are."

"Fair enough," replied the big fella. "By the way, you were no slouch flying that bird over the treetops yourself."

"Okay, let's move on," I said. "I'm assuming you believe the threats on your life, the Guyana debacle, Josh's kidnapping and possibly the oil spill off Georgetown are all related."

"Interwoven and totally integrated, without a doubt," Jones responded.

"Can you explain why?" I probed further.

"Yes, at least partially," Jones replied. "The one thing you left off your greatest hits list is the disintegration and disruption of Crimson Wave. In my mind, that's where it all begins.

We must have looked doubtful.

"I see your uncertainty, but bear with me. As I've already explained, things were going pear-shaped within the organization prior to this last week of misadventures. But it was Teddy's discovery of that detonator cord that escalated events. The environment shifted abruptly from disagreement to danger. My research led me to search for names within CW that had any ongoing relationship with traditional energies, i.e., oil and gas, and also some sort of previous association with Compass Black."

"Fair enough," responded Greatrex.

"Two names within the organization met the criteria."

"So, there you have it, two main suspects," I said.

"Yes and no," replied Jones. "To be honest, I've not been totally straight with you both. It's time to fix that. I matched both criteria."

If there is such a thing as deep silence, that's what we were experiencing now.

"You have our attention," I said.

Jones nodded.

"First, the Compass Black issue. Years ago, I was part of a demonstration that blockaded Japanese whalers in Kushiro. It was the very early stages of Crimson Wave. We were passionate and angry, but not particularly well organized. The people we opposed had various reasons for not calling the traditional authorities to put a stop to our actions. Instead, they brought in outsiders. A bad bunch, ruthless in their approach."

The environmentalist faltered, a watery mist appearing in his eyes.

Jones continued. "This group operated without limitation. It got ugly. My best friend at the time, Billy Ora, another dedicated activist, was killed. Knifed through the heart in the shadow of a whaling ship on the docks. The blockade had been broken, as was our sprit, at least temporarily. We returned to the States to regroup and find out who we'd been dealing with."

"Compass Black," observed Greatrex.

"Yup, I never forgot that name. It has instilled fear and anger in me for years. Discovering Muldoon and his men being from the same organization horrified me, but I didn't speak up. What difference would it have made?"

"Fair point," I responded. "That explains the Compass Black connection, but what about your links to the oil companies?"

"In war and politics, things can get heated and downright ugly. I've been at war, an environmental war, most of my life. After we lost Billy, I realized that just like the USA and Russia, as well as confrontation, we needed to establish diplomatic back channels."

"Back channels. You and who?"

Deagan Jones stood up and waved an arm. Come with me, gentlemen. It's time for our meeting.

Chapter 22

Jones led us through the impressively grand lobby to a bank of elevators. We entered one and Jones pressed the button for the seventy-fifth floor. The express service didn't stop for the first sixty floors, reaching our target quickly.

We stepped out into a luxurious landing area with all the bells and whistles, comfortable couches, exotic pot plants and thick pile carpet. On three sides of the lobby were large, frosted glass walls. Engraved along the biggest wall were the words:

Reardon Energies

Suddenly, all is revealed. I wondered who Jones' contact was within the company.

The environmentalist led us to a main reception desk, behind which sat an impeccably dressed young man and middle-aged woman. Greatrex and I hung back while Jones did his business. A moment later, two automatic sliding doors to the right of the desk opened.

The young man beckoned us through. We followed him down a wide, wood-paneled passageway. At the end of the passageway stood another elevator. Surprisingly, two burly security guards were stationed on either side of the elevator doors. They both stood in the classic pose, hands clasped in front of them, feet eighteen inches apart, looking solid and fit in their dark suits. Each man had an earpiece and a bulge in his jacket, indicating a concealed weapon.

Our guide nodded, and the man on the right pressed a hidden button. The elevator doors opened. We entered.

I felt the elevator rise briefly before settling.

The small foyer we stepped into made the previous one look like Macy's basement. The carpet was so thick you could lose a shoe in it. Four comfortable-looking Chesterfield upholstered chairs sat around a coffee table near the left wood-paneled wall. Lavishly framed oil paintings, each with its own light, hung elegantly on the walls. Each showcased a panorama of ocean waves swelling about an offshore oil platform.

A lone woman sat behind a large desk with a sole computer screen and keyboard perched on it. There we no filing cabinets or other extraneous office paraphernalia within sight. This was most definitely the executive suite.

As I gazed around the space, I noted two more security guards flanking the elevator. Unobtrusive. They could have been twin brothers to the ones below.

Deagan Jones ambled up to the lady behind the desk.

"Please go straight in, Mr. Jones. He's expecting you."

Another automatic sliding door parted a pair of wood panels. Jones led the way through. The young man remained.

Executive utopia. The space we entered could have housed two reasonably sized apartments. It was certainly bigger than the President's Oval Office.

I knew because I'd been there.

It was a corner suite, of course, but each of the enormous walls consisted of oversized glass panes. Not an external wall in sight. Behind the windows, an unimpeded view stretched across the city of Houston toward Galveston Bay.

Spectacular.

Two more Chesterfield couches sat parallel to a large coffee table in front of one window. At the apex of the corner of the windows, an oversized teak executive desk filled the foreground. Behind it, a broad-shouldered male, probably mid-fifties, totally bald head, dressed in an expensive looking dark blue suit, stood up.

Our host stepped around his workspace and straight up to Jones.

"Deagan, good to see you. I'm so sorry about your son."

Jones shook his hand and nodded.

Turning his attention to us, the man reached over, hand open.

"Mr. Sharp and Mr. Greatrex I presume."

We shook.

"I'm pleased to meet you. My name is Jim Reardon. Thanks for dropping by."

Jim Reardon, president of Reardon Energies, one of the largest gas and oil producers on the globe. When Deagan Jones establishes a 'back channel' nobody could accuse him of lacking style.

"Gentlemen, sit down, please," Reardon waved us over to the couches by the window. As we sat, I glanced up at the sliding door we'd just passed through. No security guards were on the inside.

Deagan Jones began, "I see the surprise on your faces, Nicholas, Jack. I guess it does seem a bit unusual, a highly aggressive environmental activist sharing a direct dialogue with the president and CEO of one of the largest suppliers of traditional energy."

"The thought had occurred to me," I responded.

"Well, there's a bit of history involved," added Reardon, "and believe it or not, a tad of common interest."

I assumed my eyebrows were raised as high as Greatrex's.

"From where I stand," said Jones, "anything that gets the job done and protects and conserves our environment is a valid methodology. As you know, I don't particularly care if we act within or outside the law, neither do I care if we act within or outside normal conventions."

"Always thinking beyond the norm," observed Greatrex.

"Exactly," Jones responded. "When Crimson Wave mounts an action, our aim is, or at least it was, twofold: we need to put a stop to any environmentally damaging activity and it's equally vital we bring public opinion along with us. Revolution is willed by the people. Now don't get me wrong. I loathe everything Reardon Energies and other environmental abusers represent, and I would shut them down in an instant. However, like most warriors, I'm a realist. While my group, and others similar, are slowly turning public opinion - and make no mistake, we *are* turning public opinion - we must also be effective today. Sometimes immediacy involves negotiation, through back channels."

Jim Reardon settled into his seat and smiled. "To concur with Deagan, I would gladly rip his organization apart for all the grief his people have caused my company. But at the end of the day, I'm also a practical man. I see the direction the world's supply of energy is heading in, so Reardon Energies sometimes needs to be strategic in our long-term approach."

"So, one of you just invited the other over for dinner and said, 'let's chat'," I offered.

"Yes and no," Jones replied. "I'd read an article, an interview with Jim, where he stated longevity requires an element of open-mindedness. I would have thought nothing of it, bar for the fact that his company had instigated a significant name change. They moved from Reardon Gas and Oil to Reardon Energies. All the associated spin suggested the transformation was simple minor corporate rebranding. But it got me thinking, so I made an approach."

"And you opened the door, Mr. Reardon?" I asked.

"Just an inch," Reardon replied, "and please call me Jim. I agreed to meet with Deagan, although covertly. I couldn't have my shareholders believing I'd gotten into bed with the enemy."

"We met," continued Jones. "There was a situation in Australia. Reardon Energies was exploring the possibilities of some exploration off the country's North-East coast. The area they were considering sat too damn close to the Great Barrier Reef. It was legal, but morally questionable. Anyway, I put my case to Jim, laid out all the facts, unemotionally, scientifically. When our meeting concluded, I didn't expect too much."

"And?" asked Greatrex.

"You could have blown me over with a light Artic breeze. A couple of months later, Reardon Energies announced it was canceling the Australian exploration, saying it was economically unviable," added Jones.

"And a relationship was born," I said.

"Basically yes," replied Reardon. "The surprising thing to both of us, however, was the fact we got on pretty well. Two stubborn and determined peas, but in very different pods."

"That was over fifteen years ago," added Jones. "Our meetings have always been on the quiet. Almost no one else has been aware of them. Alternate locations, out of public view."

"Yet here we are, sitting in the Reardon Energies CEO's office for all to see," said Greatrex.

Jim Reardon leaned forward on the couch. "Yes, unfortunately so. Given the recent attack on our Reardon 3 platform in Guyana, and other threats made to the organization, covert meetings are no longer a luxury I'm able to afford. I'm sure you would have noticed the extra security precautions on the way in?"

"The guards," I said.

"Indeed, my board insisted. They are highly trained professionals, but I can assure the three of you, they are not from the group you call Compass Black."

We took a moment to absorb what we heard, while Jones and Reardon anticipated our reaction.

Eventually, I broke the silence.

"All right folks," I said. "We have a situation here. Let's talk business."

Chapter 23

"Let's work backwards," I began. "The attacks on the Reardon 3 platform. What can you tell us about them?"

"The pipelines were blown in three places. The forensic team informed me that it was Trinitrotoluene, TNT. The attacks were professional and effective. Of course, we monitor the pressure on all our lines. As soon as we detected the decrease in pressure, our people shut the lines down. That information was released to the media."

Deep lines etched across Jim Reardon's brow as he spoke.

"What we didn't disclose was data regarding the delay in our shutdown process. To cut a long technical explanation short, our network didn't react as speedily as it should. Someone had gotten in somewhere and done some high-level reprogramming of our default settings. Our team fixed it eventually, but a great deal more oil was released than should have been."

"So, these people are thorough and skilled. I assume finding a way into your well-protected network would be no easy task," said Greatrex.

"We have more redundancies and firewalls built into that system than you could possibly imagine," replied Reardon.

"Yet they got through," said the big fella.

"They got through, yes. We're still trying to work out how."

"Okay," I said. "How about the threats you mentioned?"

"Well, it's hard to tell the forest from the trees," replied Reardon. "The company, board members, and I all receive death threats regularly. It's part of doing business in a conflicted world. But the frequency and strength of the warnings has escalated dramatically. Given that one assault has already happened, our company is, at this moment, extremely security minded."

"What about threats to other platforms?" I asked.

"Yes, our people are wading through them now. Our team is thorough and experienced, but this is a whole new level."

"Obviously, the authorities in Guyana acted swiftly, to protect the environment," said Greatrex.

"Extremely quickly, Thank God. We've also been offered help from the EPA and other relevant agencies in the States."

"All right then," I began, "let's lay this out. How are you two connecting the blown pipelines to Teddy and Pedro's deaths, Compass Black, and the penetration of Crimson Wave?"

"This is where the picture becomes too big for Jim's team, local authorities and other bodies investigating the disaster," began Deagan Jones. "I believe tracking down the person or people behind the takeover of Crimson Wave will lead us to our saboteurs, Joshua's kidnappers and, of course, those who saw fit to include murder in their method of operation. They will be one and the same."

"That's a big call," I said.

Jim Reardon interrupted. "Yes, it is a big call, but I happen to agree with Deagan."

"How so?" asked Greatrex.

"Ours is a large industry," replied Reardon, "there are times we work together, usually when the sector is under threat, but as competitors we can be cutthroat, bordering on immoral."

"Bordering?" Jones interjected.

"Point taken Deagan. Most established energy companies have been known to operate well over the moral line in the sand… at times," confessed Reardon. "Either way, a community like ours hosts more than its share of gossip, rumors, and verbal combat. The fact is, I've heard some things that lead me to believe Deagan's conspiracy theory may be correct."

"What things?" I asked.

Jim Reardon paused for a moment, sitting back on the couch. Possibly considering how far to take this. Eventually, decision made, he began.

"Although the traditional energy industry attempts to present a united front to the world, we are divided along several fault lines. Despite what they say in public, the Saudi and American interests have little trust in each other. Since Russian troops invaded Ukraine, no one trusts or relies on Russian oil and gas. Canada mostly side with the States, and everyone regards China as an unpredictable force. Add to that, we all hate the environmentalists because they threaten our very existence."

"Only because you threaten the planet…" began Jones.

"I understand where you stand, Deagan, and you know I'm not without empathy…"

"Gentlemen, back to the rumors please," I insisted.

Jones relaxed his posture, going off the boil. The oil man continued.

"Last week, an individual from my security team came to me. He'd heard from someone in Indonesia that one of the loudest voices in the environmental movement had been compromised. He didn't know if his source meant a group or a person."

Reardon smiled at his counterpart.

"That marries up with Deagan's theory regarding the infiltration of Crimson Wave," I pondered.

"That is exactly my point, Mr. Sharp, Nicholas," said Reardon.

"All right, let's take a walk down hypothesis lane," I suggested. "If you wanted to discredit an environmental organization, how would you go about it?"

Reardon considered my question, but only briefly.

"To be honest, our people have run this case scenario many times, sort of like a war game."

Jones' face crinkled in consternation.

"Don't be overly concerned, Deagan. We, at least Reardon Energies, never acted on any of those war plans. It turned out the most effective scenario was also the most brutal. Simply launch a violent assault on an offshore drilling facility. In other words, attack ourselves. Such an attack, or more to the point, the environmental damage caused by it, would cause outrage throughout the world. We would then begin backgrounding the media, through third parties, that a particular activist group had been responsible. Blame the environmentalists for destroying the environment. Cost effectively, the plan stacked up. Our short-term losses would be more than made up for by our long-term gains. Being able to open new areas of exploration unhindered by those radical lefties would be a free road to a cash cow."

Deagan Jones seemed about to blow up. His face turned beetroot red, and his veins seemed on the verge of popping.

Reardon raised a hand of peace.

"Deagan, as I said, we'd never do it. I regarded the environmental cost as unacceptable."

An inhospitable silence permeated the room.

"I've been rude to you all. I apologize. Would anyone like some coffee?" Reardon was clearly trying to tone down the tension.

Reardon buzzed an order though to his personal assistant.

"There is one thing I've got to ask you, Mr. Reardon, Jim," I said. "*You* may have had the moral gumption not to enact that plan, but many of your competitors would have figured out the same scenario. It is possible that one of them saw it through?"

"That's why we're here," replied the CEO, no lack of severity in his tone.

At that moment, the personal assistant entered with a tray of coffee and Danishes. She placed it on the table in front of the sofa. She seemed to hesitate, not wanting to interrupt her boss's meeting.

Reardon sensed her discomfort.

What is it, Rebecca?

"It could be nothing Sir, but given the presence of everyone in this room, I thought you should check the news headlines," she replied before turning and leaving.

On cue, we all reached for our cells. A headline popped up.

Environmental Warriors Crimson Wave Implicated in Reardon 3 Oil Attack. Has Deagan Jones Gone Too Far?

My question had been answered.

Chapter 24

The silence was stony, if not rock-solid cold.

I glanced toward the door. The two security men from the foyer had now positioned themselves inside Reardon's office. Clearly Rebecca the PA wasn't taking any chances. I wouldn't be surprised if the guards we saw by the lower lift doors had been repositioned close by.

"I fear your world has just been turned on its head once more, Deagan," said Reardon.

Jones appeared deflated, his shoulders hunched forward, his forehead resting in his hands. Eventually, he looked up.

"It's bad, but at this point, all I really care about is getting Josh back safely. Since losing Soloman, you three are the only people I can trust. Will you help me?"

A desperate plea from a desperate man.

"Without a doubt, Deagan," Reardon replied. "I'm speaking here for both of you as well, Nick, Jack. Are you in agreement?"

I looked across the coffee table to Greatrex. An imperceptible nod.

"We'll help. At least we'll do what we can," I replied. "But you have scores of people much better qualified to follow this through. Why us?"

"Trust," Jones responded, "and perhaps a little belief."

"From my side, I'd say unconventional ingenuity and dogged stubbornness," added Reardon.

"But, with respect, you don't know us, Reardon," replied Greatrex.

Reardon smiled. "True, but I should confess, before you arrived, I did some digging. In this environment, a couple of strangers couldn't be allowed to walk in here unchecked. It turns out I have friends in some quite influential places who have relationships with some of your friends. Does the name General Colin Devlin-Waters mean anything to you both?"

That explained it. The general was our former commander in the US Marines. Our relationship had been rekindled in a situation in Iraq some time ago. We'd frequently worked together since then. General Colin Devlin-Waters acquired information like others acquired socks, his list of connections endless.

"Point taken," I said.

"Now, we need to do some planning, and I believe not all the available intel is on the table yet," announced Greatrex.

I nodded. "Deagan, you mentioned that there were a *couple* of names that matched your search criteria. Who was the other one?"

Jones sighed. "Yes, it's about time we discussed that. The way I see things, this man is our only lead back to Joshua, or anything else. But understand, to achieve what he's done has required cunning, ruthlessness and brains. We must tread carefully lest he be warned."

"Agreed," I replied. "But who is he?"

"His name is Rahmat Beras," began Jones. "His wealth is at least in the tens of billions. Ostensibly, according to his published profiles, Beras made most of his money out of healthcare. It's a massive cash cow, and he owns funds across the USA and Europe. He has reinvested a lot of his fortune in stocks and real estate. Rahmat Beras' riches earn him more per day than most people earn in a lifetime."

"What's his connection to oil and traditional energies?" asked Reardon. "I've never heard of him within my industry."

"This is where the subtext becomes more complicated," said Jones. "Over the last five years Beras has been investing in green and alternative energies. He owns several offshore wind farms and has made substantial investments in solar energy."

"Doesn't that make him a good guy?" asked Greatrex.

"Well, at least according to my playbook, it should," replied Jones. "And those are the credentials that got him a spot on the board at Crimson Wave. That, and some significant donations to several of our projects. But the research I've done lately indicates some anomalies that are difficult to explain. His wind farms aren't producing as much energy as the industry anticipated. There were rumors of turbine sabotage. A few local fishermen reported small explosions and an unusual number of turbines out of action at a Beras-owned farm off the Massachusetts coast. Plus, the solar companies that he's invested in are generating lackluster results."

"Maybe energy production just isn't in his tool kit. The competencies and knowledge required are a long way from healthcare and the stock market. He wouldn't be the first tycoon to overreach," I suggested.

"That had been my first reaction," said Jones, "but the more I thought about it, the less logical it sounded. Even if he didn't have the skills, he had the money to buy the best people who did. More to the point, he's known as a hands-off investor. Unlike some, he doesn't interfere with decisions made by the expertise he hires. And there's something else."

We waited while Jones collected his thoughts.

"In our CW board meetings, Rahmat Beras speaks fervently about the imperative to liberate the environment from mismanagement. He also speaks of accord, partnering with others in the industry and government to accomplish that accord."

"Why is that a problem?" asked Greatrex.

"It may be a great ideal," replied Jones, "but it's also the argument he's used to blunt our teeth at Crimson Wave. Consensus is his justification for taking a less radical and confrontational approach. And it's how he's edged me out of the picture."

Jim Reardon looked directly at Jones.

"Respectfully, Deagan, are you sure this isn't just bad blood from you?"

The two men sat eye to eye for several seconds before Jones answered.

"Not for one second do I blame you for suggesting that, Jim. I pondered it myself."

Jones sat on the edge of his seat, his eyes now traveling in an arc between the three of us.

"Until I found this."

Jones reached into his pocket, pulling out some neatly folder papers. He laid them flat on the coffee table.

"These are printouts of contracts for security arrangements regarding Beras' Massachusetts operation. You'll see they cover several facilities."

We studied the documents. The contract was between Adventure Energies and NorthStar Security Services. Nothing appeared out of the ordinary, except the amount paid for the services seemed quite high.

"I'm not getting it Deagan," said Reardon. "Apart from an extremely generous fee-for-service, this all seems pretty standard."

Neither Greatrex nor I contradicted him.

Jones pointed to the bottom of the final page.

"Have a look at the signature."

Richard Muldoon

"The name ring a bell?" asked Jones.

Reardon opened his palms indicating he had nothing.

"There are plenty of Muldoon's in the world, Deagan. It's not an uncommon surname. We don't even know if Richard was the first name of the Compass Black leader at Iwokrama," I said.

Jones reached back into his pocket and produced another printout. It appeared to be from a website.

NorthStar Security Services
Meet the people keeping you and your facilities secure.
Our Squad Leaders:

Underneath the heading, clear as day, was a head and shoulder shot of Richard Muldoon. The very same Richard Muldoon who had recently met his death in a helicopter crash in Guyana.

"Shit," said Greatrex.

"There's more," added Jones. "It took me a long time and

a great deal of playing join the corporate dots, but buried deep in a maze of shelf companies it became apparent that NorthStar Security Services are owned by the same entity that own the much harder to find Compass Black."

"NorthStar is the legitimate front for Compass Black," I said.

"Precisely," replied Jones.

"Where did you come across all this information, Deagan, particularly the contract??" asked Reardon.

"Part of the role of being an effective activist is the ability to perform deep research, not always legal. Let's just say that Beras' Adventure Energies doesn't exactly have fireproof firewalls."

A lot of new data was coming at us. It needed to be processed and put into perspective.

"All right," I began, "you've linked Rahmat Beras to Compass Black. That's significant. How does he tie in with the traditional energy industry? Despite his seeming lack of success, all his effort within the industry seem to be toward renewables. What do you have Deagan?"

Jones sighed.

"That connection is still somewhat tenuous, although my gut tells me I'm right."

"Go on," I replied.

"Beras works out of Indonesia, that's where he was born. However, he has offices all over the world and spends a significant amount of time traveling between them. He doesn't come from a rich family. His father was a doctor. They weren't on the breadline, but certainly didn't have the required cash to set the young Beras on the investment path he needed to achieve the success he's had."

"So, you think his seed money came from somewhere else?" asked Greatrex.

"Correct Jack."

"Here's the thing," continued Jones. "Beras was successful enough in his studies to gain a place at the Harvard Business School in Massachusetts. Turns out his best mate there was one Ahmed Faez."

"Let me guess," interjected Greatrex. "Young Ahmed was from the Saudi based Faez family, who own amongst a lot of other things, Faez International, one of Saudi Arabia's largest oil producers."

"Got it in one," replied Jones.

"I know Kalid Amir Faez, the patriarch of the Faez family. He is shrewd and quite ruthless in the way he does business, but he is also well respected. The link is very tenuous, Deagan," said Reardon.

"Yes, but less so as you look into it," the environmentalist replied. "It turns out young Rahmat and Ahmed were great mates. They were both ambitious, smart, liked girls and liked money. Of course, Ahmed had a heap of the latter, at least his family did. Rahmat spent most holidays with Ahmed in Saudi Arabia. He became close to the family. They were impressed by his brains and ambition. He, undoubtedly, was awed by their wealth."

"A match made in heaven," said Greatrex.

"Apparently so," Jones responded. "After their time at Harvard, Ahmed went into the family business. Rahmat stayed in the States and began buying up smaller health funds and turning them into bigger, more profitable health funds. Everyone presumed his money came from his familial ties in Indonesia."

"Followed the family tradition into medicine like his dad," said the big fella.

"Why didn't you place Beras with this link to Saudi oil earlier, Deagan? Surely when Crimson Wave were scoping him out as a major donor and then later, as a board member, the connection would have surfaced," I asked.

"The association never emerged for a good reason. When they finished at Harvard and Ahmed Faez returned to the Middle East, he and Beras broke all contact. Apart from being two kids at college together, nothing since then links them."

"Maybe they had a falling out," suggested Reardon.

"Or perhaps the Faez family had a long-term strategy," replied Jones.

We drifted into a thoughtful silence as we processed Deagan Jones' proffered scenario.

After a minute or so of spinning thoughts, I spoke.

"This information regarding Rahmat Beras is all we have to go on. We have nothing else, and to be honest, somewhere in my gut alarm bells are ringing."

Greatrex nodded. Reardon tilted his head to one side, maybe not yet totally convinced. I continued.

"If we take the front foot and assume Beras' involvement, the first thing we need to figure out is where he would instruct his people, the Compass Black team, to hold Joshua captive. Assuming that it's their intention to return the lad to his father, and Deagan I'm sorry to say this, but that is quite a large assumption, it would have to be a secure but unreachable location."

Greatrex chimed in. "The necessity to keep Deagan at bay by holding the boy suggests Beras has plans. If we find Josh, we may also find what Beras is up to."

"Good point," said Jim Reardon, slowly coming onboard.

"All right, there are two ways I see to proceed," I began. "Our priority is to track Rahmat Beras. We must find out where he's been and where he's planning to go. Second, we should look at all known links and locations for NorthStar Security Services. I'm certain we'll uncover little or nothing on Compass Black, but NorthStar may provide some clues."

"How do you propose to do that?" asked Reardon.

"Jack and I will return to LA. Jack has access to some very sophisticated equipment. He can search places on the dark web that no one even suspects exist. Having a military communications background comes in handy sometimes."

Greatrex nodded.

"In addition to that, I'll make some calls. There are people who know people who may be helpful," I concluded.

"Why waste time?" asked Reardon.

"We'll need that information..." began Greatrex.

"No, I don't mean that," responded Reardon. "Of course you need that information, but the flight back to LA takes over three hours, meaning you'll lose most of a day with travel time. We have an incredibly sophisticated communications system here. We don't lack for funds. Jack, I can guarantee that you will be impressed, and I am confident that you will find everything you require."

I glanced at Greatrex and again received the standard imperceptible nod.

"Makes sense," I responded.

"I want to be part of this, I need to be part of this," Deagan Jones spoke with an underlying intensity.

Jim Reardon stepped in. "Deagan, I know you do, course

you do. I'd feel the same in that situation. I imagine everyone in this room would feel that way. But you can't be involved. Not now."

"I insist…"

"No Deagan, Jim is right," I began. "If Rahmat Beras is behind all of this, he'll be keeping eyes on you. He's probably also responsible for tipping off the press by suggesting you and Crimson Wave are implicated in the Reardon 3 attack. The result being, he's cleverly arranged for the world's press to be keeping an eye on you too. If Beras gets any indication of your presence close to where Josh is being held, you'll jeopardize your son's life."

Jones shrank in his chair.

"Of course, you're right. Again, this jerk outsmarted and outplayed me."

"But Deagan, there's one thing Beras hasn't counted on," said Reardon.

"What's that?"

"Us," I replied.

Chapter 25

Two hours later, the four of us were back in Jim Reardon's office.

In the preceding one hundred and twenty minutes, Reardon had been overseeing his company's inquiries into the Reardon 3 attack while Jones spoke to the press congregated in front of the building. They'd been extremely surprised when radical environmentalist Deagan Jones had actually walked out of the enemy's lair to deny all involvement in the incident.

During the same period, Greatrex had been downstairs in Reardon Energies' communication center, closeted away in a dark room chasing positional data. I'd been speaking to the General and several others, attempting to gain intel on Rahmat Beras, Faez International and the infamous Compass Black.

"I'm afraid our company can't make a public declaration denying your participation in the sabotage of our oil line yet, Deagan. My board is insisting that the investigation by authorities be completed before such a statement is issued. I have stated to them that it's my belief that the assault had nothing to do with you or Crimson Wave and I'm pretty certain they believe me. The fact that you spoke to the press outside this building will also help, but sadly, you'll still have the world's media on your back for quite a while. I'm sorry I couldn't do more."

"That's as much as I could expect Jim, thanks for your efforts," Jones responded. He turned to Greatrex and I, both now sitting opposite him. "Nicholas, Jack, what have you got?"

Greatrex began.

"Flight manifests are a useful tool. I've managed to track Rahmat Beras' movements over the last two days. After the Crimson Wave board meeting in Stockholm, at which you were present, Deagan, Beras returned to his London office where he spent twenty-four hours. He stayed at Claridge's."

"Of course he did," said Jones.

"He then flew to New York on his private jet."

"That doesn't give us much," Reardon remarked.

"Normally it wouldn't," responded Greatrex, "except for one thing. When was the last time you flew from London to New York via Barcelona, Spain?"

"That's quite a detour," said Jones.

"It sure is. Especially when he was in Barcelona for less than two hours," replied Greatrex.

Jones turned to me. "Nicholas?"

"I spoke at length to the general and a couple of his contacts within the security sphere. As expected, there is very little information available on Compass Black. They operate way off the radar. Word of mouth through previously established relationships is the only way they gain new business. Few people know who Compass Black's operatives are, and many of those only found out just before they died."

"What about NorthStar?" asked Reardon.

"That's a different kettle of fish," I replied. "Those I spoke to were aware of NorthStar, but unaware that they could be a legitimate front for Compass Black. However, there's still not much public information about the group, apart from what they've published themselves. One contact suggested they may use confidentiality clauses in their contracts. It's not an unusual practice within the industry."

"Protect the client, protect the organization," observed Greatrex.

"The general did a little digging of his own," I continued. "He discovered that there had been rumors that NorthStar ran its own training camp, but nobody knows where." I swung around to Greatrex. "If you owned a training facility for covert security operatives, what would be your criteria for a location?"

The big fella thought for a moment, giving his goatee beard the usual rub as the cogs turned.

"It would need to be remote, difficult to access, dry so that weather wasn't an impact on schedules, and preferably in mountainous terrain. More physically challenging and greater seclusion."

"Okay, so ten minutes ago, I received a return call from one of the general's contacts. He'd been talking to a few more of his own connections within the business. The owner of a European contractor told him that he'd heard rumors of an instructional base for black op security in… Spain."

"Bingo," said Jones.

"So, given Beras' unscheduled stop over in Barcelona, the rumor of a facility in Spain and Jack's selection criteria for a camp location, what do you come up with?" I cast my eyes across the table.

"The Catalan Coastal Mountain Range. Remote, challenging, and accessible from Barcelona," replied the big fella.

"That's a long shot," said Reardon, "based solely on a series of assumptions. Besides, it would be like looking for a needle in a haystack."

"What else do we have?" I asked.

Silence.

"Exactly. We can sit around and wait for more shit to go down, or we can get active."

"We should move," said Greatrex.

"All right, that's it." I said. "We go looking for that needle and hope to God we find it."

I couldn't look at Deagan as I spoke my next words.

"A child's life depends on it."

Chapter 26

CATALONIA - SPAIN

"This is the third village, Nicholas. We've asked around, staked out the local stores and eateries and got nothing. What are our chances?" asked the big fella.

"More of a chance than staying home and twiddling our thumbs. I reckon that's our only yardstick."

We'd been in Spain for almost fourteen hours. The trip from Houston had been quick. While Jack and I were mucking around with airline schedules and connections, Jim Reardon had simply said, 'Why don't you take my Gulfstream?' Of course. Why didn't we think of that? Less than ten hours after leaving the George Bush Intercontinental, we'd landed at El Prat Airport in Barcelona.

Immediately hiring a nondescript but reasonably powerful VW T-CROSS, we set off toward the *Serralada Litoral Catalana,* the Catalan Coastal Range. When we reached the type of terrain Greatrex had in mind, we began searching for the proverbial needle in the haystack. It was never going to be an easy task. We found some comfort in the fact Jim Reardon's security team had been able to supply us with a small portable armory, at least enough weaponry to perform the job on hand.

The perfunctory customs check when we arrived at El Prat came nowhere close to finding the arsenal hidden away in the bowels of Reardon's Gulfstream G800. A perk of affluence.

Our strategy was to search village by village, putting our floundering Spanish to the test by chatting with locals and hanging out in town squares. We also maintained a weather eye for any signs of outsiders. Fortunately, the area was sparsely populated, and the towns were mostly small. That made an impossible task vaguely doable... with a truckload of luck.

So far, Lady Luck was conspicuous by her absence.

"Let's give this place another hour and then move on. According to the map, there's a town called Vilada less than forty minutes from here. We'll really be hitting mountainous terrain. There could be a chance," I suggested.

Greatrex shrugged his shoulders. "I guess we've got no other plan. Forward ho."

A while later, we found ourselves weaving up a steep mountain road. Darkness had fallen, making the drive precarious. The route frequently changed between sharp drops falling off into the blackness on our right, and cliff faces embracing the mountain on our left before interchanging to the complete opposite.

Even at night, you could feel the age of the town we arrived at. Although set high in the hills, the ancient buildings of Vilada stood as a monument to time as they perched surrounded by the high peaks of the mountains, an even greater nod to the passing years. We inched through the heart of the village, eventually pulling up fifty yards down the road from a venue that was clearly the local hotspot. Set at street level, the *Buen Tiempo Restaurante y Bar* formed part *of an old structure towering four floors.* Spotlights lit the walls accenting the simple but captivating stone façade. Diners and revelers filled the tables and chairs arranged on the footpath, the atmosphere vibrant.

The music and chatter wafted down the street and through our open windows. With the car engine turned off, we embraced the warm night air.

"Let's sit here a while," I suggested. "I'm wondering if going in asking questions straight away is putting people's backs up and shutting them down. We can just observe for a bit."

"Point taken," responded Greatrex.

We let the time steal past. Drowsiness wasn't a problem since we'd slept on the plane. However, our lack of progress was.

"I've been thinking," said Greatrex.

"Great wonders will never cease," I replied.

Nicholas Sharp, man of infinite wit.

"Ha. Consider Rahmat Beras' flight. Why did he detour to Barcelona, and why such a quick stop off? He wouldn't have had time to make it up here, so was he just meeting someone in Barcelona, or is there more to it?"

"Consider the timing," I replied. "It wasn't too long after Joshua Jones disappeared that Beras left London. Although, by my reckoning, there would have been enough time for a chopper flight between County Wicklow and London."

"He didn't come to visit anyone. He was dropping someone off."

"Exactly. I'd say he dropped off some of his people and young Josh."

"The timing works," agreed the big fella.

"And the location."

A thought to spur us on.

"You know I could use a drink and some food," said Greatrex. "There's a couple of tables emptied up. How about we go in but ask no questions?"

"Better than leaving our post," I replied.

Greatrex heaved the door open before I'd finished speaking.

We wandered up the street, enjoying the balmy air. As we reached the sidewalk outside the bar, a maître d' appeared through the doorway.

"*Mesa para dos*," I said, holding up two fingers to aid my struggling Spanish. 'Table for two.'

"*Si, de esta la manera*," he responded, leading us inside.

Indoors, the temperature soared. The chatter of customers added to the cacophony of the music as their voices bounced off the thick stone walls. The maître d' led us to a table at the rear. Greatrex sat with his back to the crowd. I sat against the wall, watching.

"*Dos cervezas*," said Greatrex. Our Spanish seemed to be holding up. The advantage of living in LA.

Three minutes later, a smiling young waitress placed two large, cold beers on the table in front of us.

"*Te gustaria comida?*" she asked before repeating in English, "Would you like food?"

"Is it that obvious?" I queried; our cover blown.

"Si, senor, we get quite a few Americans and English here."

Greatrex raised an eyebrow.

"A lot of tourists I expect," I replied.

"Si, but we also have a few of your fellow countrymen that work in the area from time to time."

"Ah, local industry?"

"Yes and no. They say they are engineers and designers

helping with civil construction. But I think maybe not."

"Why so?" asked Greatrex.

"Well senor, I am probably wrong, but they spend a lot of money, and they seem awfully fit for engineers." The waitress patted her shoulders as she spoke, then pulled her hands away. "How you say...broad shouldered."

Aware we sat on the brink of being perceived as too nosy, I risked one more question.

"Have any been in tonight or last night?"

Her eyebrows furrowed, confused, ready to back down.

"*Lo siento*, I talk too much," she replied.

"No," I said. "The apology is mine. It would have been nice to chat with some fellow Americans. No problem."

The young woman appeared to relax.

Greatrex held the menu open. "Could we have two *Mandonguilles amb sípia i pèsols* please?

The waitress nodded and walked away.

"Impressive," I said, "So what have you ordered?"

"White beans with grilled pork sausages, and I got you out of a jam."

"I guess I was getting a little ahead of myself. Desperate times."

Greatrex nodded.

The beers barely hit the sides. We requested more as our food arrived.

"This is good, very good," began the big fella. "You know I reckon it even compares to..."

"Hold that thought," I interrupted. "Two men, one large, one very large, just walked in. Dark clothes, like workwear. One guy, the smaller one, has a beard. I can't make out the other guy's face, but even at this distance, I can see a slight bulge under each of their jackets."

Greatrex reacted by not reacting. "What is your gut telling you, Nicholas?"

"Maybe."

"Well, 'maybe' is the best we've had since we arrived in Spain."

The two men strode up to the bar and ordered beers.

"They're keeping to themselves, not mingling," I observed. The larger figure stood leaning against the counter, back to us, his face looking out towards the street.

"How do you want to play this?" asked Greatrex.

"I don't know if there's anything to play yet," I replied. "This could be our furtive imagination amidst a frustrating search."

"It could."

At that moment, another patron strolled up to the bar. He accidentally knocked the larger bloke's arm, spilling some of his beer. The patron's body language seemed apologetic. The big bloke swung around, tense, but then as the patron produced the peace offering of a fresh beer, he relaxed.

I didn't relax.

"It's not," I said.

"It's not what?" asked the big fella.

"It's not a waste of our time or our imagination."

"Why so?"

"Don't look around," I instructed.

I reached across, grabbed Greatrex's serviette and slid it under the table, dropping it to the floor.

"Pick that up. Scan to your right along the bar, where the big guy in blue is grabbing a new beer."

Greatrex did as instructed.

"Shit," he replied, now sitting upright once more.

"Shit indeed, you make him?"

"The big guy from Muldoon's team. One of the goons that watched over us downstairs at Jones' Iwokrama retreat."

"It makes sense," I began. "If you're going to kidnap someone, take along somebody who can clearly identify the victim. No mistakes that way."

"Yup, it adds up."

"Well," I said, "despite the odds, it looks like we just found the needle."

Greatrex looked directly at me before indicating over his shoulder.

"And at the end of every needle, there's a prick."

Chapter 27

Greatrex kept his back to the room. I kept my eyes down.

"We need a plan, and we need it quickly," I said.

"Chances are we'll find the NorthStar/Compass Black base in a remote location somewhere in the surrounding hills. That said, tailing these guys at night without being detected is an impossible task. We'd probably be the only two cars on the road. Headlights on and they'd spot us, headlights off and we'll be taking a flying lesson into one of those valleys," Greatrex pointed out.

"Couldn't have put it better myself. It's a shame Reardon's team didn't provide a tracking device."

"Mmm," said the big fella, "maybe we just use what we've got."

"A cell phone?" I suggested.

"We can do better than that."

"What do you have in mind?"

"The beauty of simplicity."

"Great." I still had no idea.

"An Air Tag. I've got one in my case in the back of our car."

"You do have your moments."

"Thanks... I think. If we wangle the tag into their possession, I can track their movements on my cell. We can hang back and then arrive on location at our leisure," said Greatrex.

"Short of strolling up and asking one of them if they'd mind taking an Air Tag with them, I'm thinking the only way is to place it into their vehicle," I concluded.

"Do you have a plan for that?" asked Greatrex. "Considering we have no idea which car is theirs."

"Of course I do," I replied. "I just don't know if it'll work."

"I feel like you've said that before. So…"

"So, follow my lead. Although we can't make a move until they do."

We sat there in the corner of the bar for another hour, the only exit too close to the two Compass Black men for us to utilize. The beers ran out quickly, so we stuck to water.

"They're paying their tab," I said. "When they go, we go."

"Roger that."

A minute later, they were moving. Fifteen seconds after that, we pushed our way through the crowded room.

When we reached the street, the men were in sight. They strode off to the southern end of a row of parked cars before crossing the road. It was only when they crossed the road that I picked up their slight sway.

"I guess everyone needs a night off," said Greatrex.

All the vehicles along the road were positioned at a forty-five-degree angle to the curb. As the men moved southward, shadows enveloped them.

The big fella immediately peeled right and headed across the road to our car to retrieve his tag.

A minute later I met him on the far side of the street. He clenched the Air Tag in his fist.

"Jack, give me the tag, then hang back, but stay on the sidewalk. I'll follow parallel, but behind the cars. When they find their vehicle and open their doors, pull out your pistol and smash a car window with the butt, then yell something and run like hell."

"Distraction?"

"Exactly."

"How are you going to get the tag into their car?"

"I'll improvise."

Our pincer movement continued up the road for another two hundred yards. All the parking spaces were full, yet thankfully, no one else appeared. The men stopped at a dark late-model SUV. The bigger man, our guy from Iwokrama clicked the keys and the parking lights flashed. A few seconds later, both front doors opened, and the SUVs internal light flickered on.

It was now or never.

A second later, an almighty crash of glass echoed down the street. The sound was followed by a desperate voice screaming out 'Hey, you'. Another crash followed. The theater of deception.

Both men instinctively stepped back and gazed in the direction of the sound. By this point, I'd reached the back of their vehicle.

"What the hell was that?" said the shorter man.

I stretched up and clicked the latch on the rear door of the SUV.

"No idea, but it's none of our business." Our guy.

I eased the liftgate open slightly. The light didn't matter because it was already on. Slipping my hand through the gap, I groped around the floor. There was a rubber grip mat over the carpet. Not surprising. I slid the Air Tag under it.

"Let's get the fuck out of here," said the big guy.

They climbed into the SUV, immediately reversing out.

In a second, I had to hit the deck and roll under the car next to me. The SUV's front tire missed my foot by an inch.

A minute later Greatrex stood facing the empty space, as I dusted myself off.

"All good?"

"All good," I replied. "Let's get the car. We need to lag behind them, but I don't want to be too far out of touch, either."

The road surface transformed from asphalt to gravel fifteen minutes into the pursuit. Again, the valleys and hillsides seemed steep and threatening, perhaps even more so than earlier. It was hard to tell in the dark. I focused on driving while Greatrex remained glued to his cell.

We'd given the Compass Black men a ten-minute head start.

"Still got a signal?" I asked.

"Yup, but in these mountains, it could be unreliable. It was a good call to stay reasonably close."

"Does the map give you any indication of where we may be going?"

"Hard to say. There are not too many villages or signs of human habitation around here. At the moment we seem headed to a place called *Castell de l'Areny*, but that could change with one turn."

Impatient, I gripped the wheel. If young Joshua Jones was being held at the end of this road, I wanted to get there and extract him as quickly as possible. People's plans alter at the drop of a hat. I didn't want to arrive too late. On the other hand, giving our presence away would be foolish.

"They've changed direction. Now heading northwest," announced Greatrex.

159

"Possible destination?"

"Could be *Sant Roma de la Clusa*, could be Santa Monica Pier."

Funny guy that Greatrex.

The darkness hung like an oppressive blanket as the dust dissipated either side of our headlight beams. No lights indicating any form of civilization cut through the blackness. An hour had passed since we set off.

"We'd never have tracked these guys without the Air Tag," I said.

"Not a chance. Hold on, they've turned again. East. Well, it's official, there's no road marked where they're going, yet they haven't slowed down."

As we followed the arrows on Greatrex's phone, the road began to disintegrate.

"Now I know what a pilot feels like doing an instrument-based landing." As I spoke, a large rock thumped up against our undercarriage.

"Slow down, Nicholas."

"I reckon I can keep the speed up, but it'll be a rough ride."

"No, slow down," the big fella insisted. "They're slowing down... shit...no...."

"What?"

"The signal's gone. We've lost them."

Instruments down.

Chapter 28

Our choices were limited to none.

"How far ahead of us were they when they went dark?" I asked.

"Around ten minutes."

"Then there's only one thing we can do: drive on for five minutes, stash the car and proceed on foot."

"If they're still miles away from their destination, we'll never catch up or probably even find them," said Greatrex.

"But if we stay with the car, we could suddenly find ourselves driving straight into their compound. I doubt that would end well for us… or Josh."

"Point taken. Foot it is."

Five minutes later, we pulled to a halt. Greatrex grabbed a flashlight out of the glove compartment. As we stepped out of the car, he flashed it up and down the road. More of a track, really. When he shone the beam to our right, it revealed nothing, because nothing was there. Just air suspended over a drop that seemed to extend down to hell itself. The same beam aimed to the left revealed a sheer cliff face rising from the road.

"Nowhere to hide the car here," said the big fella.

"Give me the light and I'll check ahead, see if there's any

turn off. Maybe use the flashlight on your phone to check the way we just came. I didn't see anything, but you never know. I'll meet you back here in fifteen minutes."

"Got it," said Greatrex.

Fifteen minutes later, we stood in front of the T-CROSS.

"Nothing," said Greatrex.

"There's a small left turn about three hundred yards ahead. It seems to lead nowhere, but I reckon there's enough cover to hide the car," I said.

"Let's go, we're losing time we haven't got."

"Indeed."

A few minutes later, the car was hidden. I remained confident it wouldn't be seen by a passing vehicle at night, but daylight could tell a different story. Still, we had no alternative.

We marched up the track, using the flashlight as sparingly as possible. Greatrex regularly glanced at his cell, willing the signal to return. It didn't.

Half an hour into the foray, our spirits began to wane.

"This could go on forever, with no result," observed the big fella.

"Do you want to turn back?"

"Hell no."

I smiled. What had Reardon said? 'Dogged stubbornness'.

Twenty minutes later.

"Nicholas, have you thought about how to approach this, if we find them?"

"*When* we find them. I've thought of little else. We're armed, that's a good start."

"Two automatic pistols, a fair amount of ammunition, a pair of binoculars and a few flash-bangs doesn't maketh an army."

"True," I replied. "Just once, I'd love to walk into one of these situations suitably equipped."

"Kind of makes you miss the Marines, doesn't it? We were always well resourced."

"Not enough to go back," I replied.

"No," agreed the big fella, "not enough for that."

"I figure we wait until dawn. If we can't scope out the lie of the land plus do a body count of hostiles, we'll be walking to our graves."

"Running."

"Yeah, running. I'm just hoping we make position before sunrise, or the job gets a whole lot harder," I said.

"Roger that."

The rough gravel gave way to uneven rock, stones that slipped under our feet and the regular ruts across the road. In the darkness, each obstacle seemed designed to trip us or roll our ankles. We trekked on.

Suddenly...

"Wait, what's that?" I asked, raising my hand.

"I can't hear any... ha... got it... an engine."

"It's coming up the road behind us. We better make ourselves scarce," I instructed.

We both looked around. A cliff wall of stone and rock stood to our right. On our left was a sheer drop.

"You know what we've got to do," I said.

The roar of the vehicle's engine grew louder.

"Jack, jump!"

Greatrex threw himself over the edge.

The glare of headlights flooded the rock wall ten yards away.

I leaped into the darkness.

And kept going… down.

Too many seconds later I hit the ground with a thud that seemed to connect my stomach with my backbone. I lay there motionless.

Once I regained my breath, I scraped around the dirt with my hands. Almost instantly my right hand touched nothing but thin air. Some sort of ledge had blocked me from plunging to the valley floor, but I had no idea how far I'd actually fallen.

I tried to move my legs. Slow to react and hurting like all hell, everything appeared to be working. I rolled into the cliff face and rose to my knees. So far, so good.

I listened for the passing vehicle. I listened for Greatrex. I heard nothing.

"Jack?" I yelled.

Nothing.

"Jack?"

The same.

I assumed the vehicle had passed, but I'd been too busy to notice. I didn't want to think about Jack Greatrex.

I stood up and stretched my arms. More pain, but that was all. Nothing broken. Nothing I couldn't live with. I craned my neck upward. The gray shadow of the rock face towered high into the darkness. It must have been twenty-five feet.

I could wait for a rescue that would never come, or I could climb to a near certain death.

I raised a hand searching for the first crevice, before hoisting myself up.

Rock by rock, crevice by crevice and inch by inch I tortured my body upward. I don't know how long the climb took, but I do know I didn't have another minute's worth of strength

CHAPTER 28

when my right hand reached the gravelly surface of the track.

I took a deep breath and began to sweep my left hand upward when suddenly I found myself flying through the air.

Shit.

No.

What the hell? I was catapulting up not down.

"Come on Indiana Jones, we've got work to do."

Greatrex.

"You all right?"

"I'm here. aren't I?" I responded as my knees thudded onto the road surface.

"Sure are. I just made it myself. What a dumbass thing to do."

I sat back on the ground with a thump that radiated pain through every limb.

"Dumbass, sure. But still better than the certain death of meeting the people in that car."

"I'm okay too. Thanks for asking."

Typical Greatrex.

"Well, apart from my new appreciation of the Catalonian mountainside, there's at least some good news to emerge from this." I announced.

"What's that?"

"We're still in the hunt. There is no innocent explanation for a vehicle traveling on this road at this hour."

"Fair point."

We continued the slog, Greatrex shuffling along slightly ahead of me on the track. I reached into my pocket to check the time on my cell. My fingers grasped the mangled mess of my former phone, killed by the fall. First casualty. Fifty

165

percent of our communication capability down.

"Shit," I said shortly afterward.

"What?"

"I can see you, or at least your silhouette."

"The sun's coming up."

We shuffled faster.

It turned out we were closer than we thought. As we reached a crest in the track, two small lights danced on a distant hill. We stopped and watched. Provided we didn't use any flashlights ourselves, we'd be out of sight, at least for now. The sun was gaining strength as a shadowy pre-dawn light began to reveal its mysteries.

"If we hurry, we should be able to make it to that ridge there," I said, pointing to a crest roughly level with our own position. "That should give us an overlook to the lights."

"In fifteen minutes, we'll be on view to the whole world."

We half marched, half ran across the ridge, the rising sun threatening like a spotlight. The uneven ground caused a few falls and stumbles, not to mention cursing.

Seconds after we'd hunkered down, the whole valley lit up. It was as though someone had clicked a light switch. We were up high and the view from our hide revealed miles of mountains trailing off into the distance.

Windswept stands of bushes with craggy trunks interspersed with rocky outcrops cluttered the steep slopes. As the morning sun released its final secrets, two deep valleys strewed with sheer escarpments appeared. It was a wonder we'd both survived our falls the night before. The trees below were denser and lusher. There was even a smattering of green pasture. Goat country.

But it wasn't the overpowering power of nature's beauty that we'd come here to see.

I reached into my jacket pocket, my hands wrapping around the small field binoculars Reardon's team had loaned us. I looked down at a ridge similar to our own, but lower.

"Okay, it looks like a compound with…." I paused. "I make it six huts. Makeshift, military style."

"Fences?" asked Greatrex.

"Nothing insurmountable, just normal post and wire boundary fencing. I don't think this is a location anyone planned to lay siege."

"Hostiles?"

"Well, there's the thing. We're going to have to wait this out, count heads, and then do our own math. Logic dictates that if big man and his mate could wangle a night off, then there must be enough remaining guards here to cover their duties. If they are holding a prisoner, i.e., Joshua Jones, they'd have to have enough personnel to cover at least three shifts, eight hours a shift. Minimum two guards a shift, probably three, possibly more. That makes a minimum total of…"

"Six bodies, nine if the shifts are in threes," said Greatrex.

"And however many more we haven't considered," I added.

"Questionable odds," suggested the big fella.

"Wouldn't have it any other way."

Despite our cocksure attitude, and some history of success battling probability, we both knew the chances of retrieving Joshua Jones from these men's hands and making it out alive was, at best, minimal.

"So now we wait, observe and count," said the big fella.

"And plan," I said.

"It better be a damn fine plan."

"I'm working on it."

By mid-afternoon, I had a reasonable idea of how this may play out. We'd identified the building Josh was held in. Frequent movement in and out, one man at a time, sometimes with a tray of food in hand, told the story.

We'd physically counted eight men but figured there'd be more. To the left of the compound sat the SUV that big man and friend had driven the night before, a jeep, possibly the car that passed us by on the track and two old Toyota troop carriers. All up, the vehicles could carry at least twenty-eight people. We both fervently hoped they hadn't.

"Okay, so what have you got, wise one?" asked Greatrex.

"Try this on for size," I responded. "We go in at dusk, disarm three of the vehicles, keep the SUV for our escape."

"Check."

"Working below the tree line, we scout down the sides of the compound and initiate a surprise rear attack on whatever guards we're able to take out. Silently, of course."

"Check."

"When we've done all we can, use our flash-bangs to create a diversion, then make a beeline for the hut that we figure Josh to be in."

"Check."

"Can you stop saying check, please?"

"Ch…" The big fella smiled. "If we're going to go down, at least we'll go down fighting."

"That we will," I replied. "But I'm worried about the boy. If we go down, he goes down too."

For a moment, the conversation faltered.

"Nicholas, do you think they'll release Josh to his dad when this is over?"

"Considering they seemed happy enough to take him out at Iwokrama, I'd say not for a second. I think they're only keeping him alive for now to have a hold over Jones."

"So, no choice," stated Greatrex firmly.

"You know, this semi-arid countryside reminds me a little of Bolivia."

"What brought that up?" asked Greatrex.

"Let's just hope we do better than Butch and Sundance."

Chapter 29

"There's something wrong," I announced, offering the binoculars to Greatrex.

"I'm seeing more guns."

"Exactly. This morning there were spasmodic patrols, mostly single guards, sometimes armed with an automatic. As the day progressed, there have been more patrols, always two guards, always armed," I said.

Greatrex looked through the lens as he spoke. "Personnel are stationed at perimeters in groups of two with a guard on each corner of the target building. The hostiles posted on the fence line all have weapons and binoculars."

"There's more," I replied. "Have a look at what's hanging off their belts."

"Shit," said Greatrex. "NVGs, they've all got night vision systems."

"They know we're coming. My guess is they found the tag."

"That changes everything," Greatrex responded.

"Sure does. There goes the surprise party."

Our chances of success had evaporated, and we had no alternative plan.

Then Greatrex's cell buzzed in his pocket.

"At least we're getting a signal now," he said, holding up the screen with one hand, sheltering the bright glow with the other. "Number blocked."

"Answer it," I suggested.

He clicked it onto speaker. "Yeah."

"Mr. Greatrex, my name is Muldoon."

I looked at Greatrex. This wasn't possible. We saw Muldoon die in a ball of fire in Guyana.

"I assume Mr. Sharp is with you. Now, just to clarify, my name is James Muldoon. I believe you met and murdered my brother, Richard."

Head spinning moment.

"What do you want?" asked Greatrex.

"It's simple, really. Of course, we've been running a jammer all day, so you couldn't call for help. It's turned off for this interaction and will reactivate immediately after. We know you're here, both of you. The Air Tag in the back of my men's vehicle was a commendable improvisation. Sadly for you, we perform an electronic sweep of all incoming vehicles. That's when you would have lost your tracking capability."

Greatrex glanced at me, his face a picture of consternation. This man's language appeared concise and professional. Our reactions in the next few seconds would be crucial.

An idea occurred to me, although it reeked of desperation. I raised a hand and drew a forefinger across my throat. Greatrex nodded.

"Sharp is dead," he announced into the phone.

"I don't believe you."

"You've got no choice. It's a fact."

Silence.

"How did he die? Before you answer, remember I have a child's life in my hands."

The fish tugged at the line but resisted biting.

"Sharp was with me until shortly after we lost your signal. When the second vehicle appeared, we both dove off the track, on the cliff side. I made it, he didn't. Essentially, you've already murdered him."

Pause.

"Prove it."

"How the hell do I prove that? I can take you back to the location, but even then, you won't find his body without a long search."

Another pause.

Finally.

"All right, we'll leave that issue for the moment. Now, here are my instructions. You are to come to our front gate. I'll have men, heavily armed men, waiting to escort you into the compound. You must be unarmed. If you so much as blink the wrong way, Joshua Jones will be shot immediately. Do you understand?"

"I hear you."

"With regard to Sharp, there is a remote chance you may be telling the truth, but only remote. Accordingly, if your dead friend should suddenly partake in a resurrection, both you and the child will be killed. Am I clear?"

"Yes."

"Do you agree to our terms?"

"Do I have a choice?"

"Of course you do. You can flee and save your own skin. But if you don't appear here within the hour, the boy will die. The choice is yours."

Some choice.

"I'll be there," replied Greatrex.

The cell went dead. Greatrex checked for a signal, showing me the screen. There was none.

"That's changed things up," I said.

"Do you think he bought the 'Sharp's dead' bit?"

"Unlikely, but I reckon we've sewn enough doubt for him to proceed cautiously with his plan to bring you in," I responded.

We sat there on the hill, silently as we considered the new situation.

"Jack, if you walk through those gates, you're a dead man."

Greatrex nodded. "But if I don't, Joshua will be killed. What sort of choice is that?

For some people, it would be a choice. But for a man like Jack Greatrex, who cared deeply about honor, but even more than that, found the abuse of children horrific, there was no option.

"The way I see it," I replied, "I've got less than an hour to get Joshua out of that place. If it goes wrong, we all die."

"If you make a noise, we all die," added the big fella.

No guns, no flash bangs. Probably no chance.

We slowly descended from our position to the lower ridge where the Compass Black compound stood. The twilight probably worked to our advantage. The daylight was fading, but the NVGs wouldn't be effective yet. We made good progress, even though we'd had to dash from cover to cover or stay below hill lines for the entire journey.

The focus on the approach acted as a diversion from our lack of a plan. Sometimes distraction eases the mind to think creatively about other issues. This time, it didn't.

Until it did.

We both lay belly down in long grass twenty yards from

the perimeter fence when I turned to Greatrex.

"I've been thinking. Muldoon was full of threats. Every single one ended with taking the life of young Joshua, but I'm not convinced that's his intention."

"Go on," said the big fella.

"I don't believe he has the authority to murder Joshua if alternative solutions were available. In this case, there are lots of alternatives. I think Rahmat Beras would have Muldoon for breakfast if he needlessly jeopardized his long-term plans, whatever the hell they are."

"So, what's he after?"

"Us. This has become personal. We killed Muldoon's brother. I reckon he's using a professional situation as an opportune time to settle a blood vendetta."

"There's an element of logic in that," replied the big fella. "But is it a big enough element to risk the boy's life?"

"That's the million-dollar question. I only know one way to find the answer."

"We proceed as originally planned," said Greatrex.

"Yes, we do. Simultaneous entry, front and rear, after the initial silent assault, it's all noise, smoke and mirrors. But there's a variation."

"I've got a sinking feeling in my stomach," said Greatrex.

"You probably should," I replied. "Your entrance needs to be public. You are the diversion."

"What if Muldoon shoots me on the spot?"

"You'll be dead."

Pause for effect.

"But I don't think he will," I continued. "He'll want to question you about my death, test the story, gauge your ability to lie."

174

"I can lie."

"I know you can. You were quite convincing on the phone. By killing me, you may have just saved us all."

"I'll remember that for the future." Greatrex grinned sheepishly.

"So, the problem I'm seeing is that you can't be armed when you pass through those gates. That makes you pretty much a toothless tiger facing all those trigger-happy operatives."

"It had occurred to me," Greatrex replied. "So, how do I access a weapon?"

"You don't, at least not immediately. If I can get myself into a position within the compound where I'm able to take out the guards closest to you and then distract the others, you can make a grab for their guns. You've done it before," I said.

"Nicholas, you're taking the term 'exposed' to a new level. But I don't see we have any other choice."

"We don't."

Greatrex grunted.

"While you head back up to the track to make your grand and public entrance, I'll work my way around the back. Before you go, give me your pistol."

"You just want to see me naked."

Greatrex handed over his weapon.

"Let's give ourselves fifteen minutes. That will take us right up to James Muldoon's deadline. My cue will be hearing them react to your appearance," I stated.

"You'll have to move quickly," said the big fella.

"You'll have to walk slow... real slow."

Fifteen minutes later, I lay gut down in the long grass three feet away from the compound's rear fence line. In full daylight, I would have been an easy mark. In this fading light, not so much. I needed to be close enough to hear anything that happened inside.

Two hostiles were visible in the semi-darkness at each corner of the perimeter. They all held automatic rifles. My guess was Kalashnikovs, but I couldn't be certain. As I approached, I noted they patrolled along the fence at spasmodic intervals. Smart, no routine to predict. All eyes were peering outward, searching for any alien approach, searching for me.

It would all be about the timing. If a patrol from either end walked the perimeter now, they would likely make me at such a close distance. I needed them distracted.

Where the hell was Jack?

Suddenly, I caught movement in my right-hand peripheral vision. The guard in the north-eastern corner had begun advancing along the fence line. I reckoned I had about ninety seconds.

Still nothing from the front gate.

Sixty seconds.

Zip.

Thirty seconds, I'd have to make a move, but in these circumstances, it could only end one way... badly.

Then.

"Hey, somebody's coming down the road... it's him... the big guy," someone yelled.

"All stations stay on full alert, front and rear. Don't be distracted."

I recognized Muldoon's voice crackling on a transmitter.

Despite training and regardless of orders, human beings have natural instincts, embedded reactions. The two men approaching my position stopped and looked up, just for a few seconds.

What momentarily ago had been a threat was now an advantage. I had no distance to travel. Leaping to my feet, I lunged over the fence at the guard closest to me. I chopped across his throat and used all my power to launch a fist into his chin. He hit the ground hard. I caught a passing glint of metal as he fell to the ground.

The second man turned, raising his weapon. I struck out with my right foot. At best, the blow would slow him down. He grunted, and the automatic's barrel lifted. He hadn't fired... yet. As he raised his arms, I noticed a knife in his belt. I reached down, grabbing the knife from the first guard's belt. Guard number two now aimed his gun directly at me, although, through no choice of his own, he stood too close. I dived underneath his weapon and came up at him. Like the first guard, I chopped across his throat, but this time, I held eight inches of steel in my hand. I felt the wetness of his blood splattering my face as he lost his grip on life.

Two down. Too many still to come.

I swung around, searching for the guards in the southern corner of the perimeter. They were looking outward, down the hill. I grabbed a second knife from guard number two's belt before taking the opportunity to step back into the shadow of the closest building. A moment later, one of the corner guards looked up along the fence line. He seemed to note the absence of his colleagues and motioned his partner to follow him.

By this point, darkness had fully fallen. The second lot of guards wouldn't notice the first, slumped on the ground, until they virtually tripped over them. I was counting on that.

Two minutes later.

"Hey, what the fuck?"

They'd found the bodies.

Both men raised their weapons, scanning in an arc from inside the compound where they presumed the intruder to be, to the outer area. Concealed, I waited until the rifles pointed in another direction. It would have been a simple kill to take both out with two quick rounds from my pistol. But that was not my intention.

Both guards scanned the hill below.

"NVGs," said one of them, his voice urgent. "It's dark enough now."

Both men temporarily lowered their barrels to don the night vision goggles.

Again, opportunity arises. After placing both blades in my right hand, I leaped forward. I figured they'd hear me, and they did. Both men swung around, raising their guns as they did. I elevated my left hand and aimed my flashlight at their eyes. They had no choice but to hesitate while they ripped their glasses off.

I didn't hesitate.

I ditched the flashlight and transferred a knife to my left hand. A single step forward with both hands raised, I plunged the blades into their throats. The only sound was a haunting gurgling.

Despite my previous training and experience, up to this point, I knew I'd been lucky.

Then luck ran out.

"Hey." The voice out of the blackness startled me. A guard I hadn't seen, presumably from the building behind me.

"Turn around slowly, hands in the air."

If I did as he asked, I'd only see the business end of his weapon and the collapse of the operation. Sometimes survival is about commitment. I pivoted, flicked both blades through the air and dived right. No time to assess, no time to aim.

"Fuck."

Even in the darkness, I saw the hostile reach for his shoulder. I pounced, but he reacted quickly, his free elbow smashing against my chin as I landed on him. He hit the dirt, but the force of his blow brushed me aside. Waves of pain pulsed through my jaw. Fighting against it, I pushed myself up and smashed my fist hard down on his face. We wrestled; our bodies too near for him to use his gun. I sensed his arm pressing against my chest, reaching for his knife.

I reached for mine. The fact it remained stuck in his shoulder helped. He cried out as I purposefully dragged it through his flesh and muscle as clumsily as I could. We lay facing each other, as close as lovers, sharing breaths. At that proximity, I couldn't get his throat with my blade, so I raised it above his shoulder before thrusting it full force into the side of his neck.

I held the blade in place. Several seconds ticked by before his breathing ceased.

Lovers no more.

Aware Greatrex couldn't stall for long, I hurried on.

With the shadows providing cover, I edged my way around the building's perimeter, working toward the front. No more hostiles intercepted me. The compound lights allowed me a clear view down the driveway from the corner of the building.

Greatrex walked slowly up the drive. Two men on either side had automatic weapons aimed at him. Each man left a clearance of four feet between their guns and the big fella.

Professionals who didn't want to be surprised. They looked to be heading towards a structure just up the hill, to my right. If they made it inside, my job became impossible.

The pressure cooker of time bore down.

A quick scan of the area. Apart from the four guards escorting Greatrex, two more stood beside the door to the building. Two additional guards remained down by the gate. I knew there'd be others concealed in the dark, but I couldn't do anything until they appeared.

Because I didn't know what James Muldoon looked like, I couldn't identify him. No one seemed to be giving orders. If I could, I'd have taken him out first. Shoot the beast's head. The building with the two guards out front appeared to be the compound's epicenter. If Muldoon wasn't out here, he'd probably be in there. Most likely, Joshua Jones would be in the hut as well. Muldoon wouldn't want him too far away.

A visual on eight hostiles. Six within range, the men at the gate too distant. It was a certainty other armed hostiles would appear out of the darkness when the shooting started. I had two pistols. There was no chance of me taking them all out… not without help.

Greatrex's entourage stood ten yards from the hut's door by the time I finalized my strategy. If I remained hidden under the cover of the building, the going would be slow. The result would be a prolonged firefight I couldn't finish. So, Wyatt Earp style, I stepped out from the building's shelter and fired, a pistol in each hand.

Right hand, first shot, the guard on Greatrex's left. Left hand, second shot, the man on the right. The two hostiles lagging behind Greatrex began stepping out to get a clear shot. That would take half a second. I spun toward the guards on the door, simultaneous shots, one hand for each guard.

Assessment.

Four men down. The two hostiles behind Greatrex stepped out and fired. I ran the width of the building, rounds splintering the wood in front and behind me. I dropped down to one knee and took out the right-hand man. That left a single man still firing, his gun on automatic. He wasn't caring about the real estate. I dived low.

Six Compass Black men came out of the shadows on the right of the driveway as I looked up. Their fire virtually shattered the structure behind me. Without doubt, I was seconds away from a pulverizing death.

Suddenly, the torrent of bullets eased. I glanced up. The remaining man that had stepped out from behind Greatrex was down. The men lining the drive began to buckle under a barrage of automatic fire. They either died or ran.

But it wasn't my fire.

Greatrex.

Still lying on the ground, I turned my attention to the hostiles on the right. Before firing, I reached into my belt and grabbed two flash-bangs. I launched one down the left-hand side of the drive and another toward the hut.

Smoke and mirrors.

In rapid succession, I fired down the drive, picking off the men Greatrex had missed. Behind the big fella, two men from the gate stormed up the drive.

"Jack, at your six," I yelled, doubtful he'd hear me above the gunfire.

As the first round kicked up the dirt at his feet, Greatrex swung around, taking out his would-be assailant with a brief splatter of automatic fire. The second man ducked behind a

181

water tank. I dropped the pistol out of my left hand. Raising my right hand and using the left for support, I waited. Three seconds later, a head appeared out of the shadow beside the tank. A millisecond after that, he was dead.

Suddenly, everything went quiet. The lull before the storm or the end of a battle? The remaining Compass Black men would be regrouping. But we didn't know how many remained. Greatrex made a beeline for the far corner of the main hut. I got up and bolted across the yard to the closest corner.

Nobody shot me.

I wondered about Muldoon. Was he dead? Had he hit the deck with the boy inside the building when the bullets started flying? I sensed a chance of success here, despite the odds.

Greatrex and I now stood on either side of the door. I held up three fingers. We'd go on my count.

One…two…three….

I kicked the door open, getting down on one knee so Greatrex could aim over me with the automatic. We were ready to shoot, but there was nothing to shoot at.

"Shit and damn," I muttered.

Greatrex pivoted behind me to cover our backs, but nobody was there.

"What the…" he began.

Then we heard it.

The recognizable mechanical roar of an aero engine. A chopper. We raced back into the yard.

Its landing lights on, the familiar silhouette of a helicopter was approaching the same ridge that Greatrex and I had previously occupied. It was too dim to discern any human shapes, but I could make out a torch waving around halfway up the hill.

"Quick, the SUV. Let's get the headlights focused on the top of that ridge."

The big fella bolted down the drive. The keys must have been in the vehicle, because a second mechanical roar joined the first. The car fishtailed on the gravel surface as Greatrex floored the gas pedal. On reaching the yard at the top of the drive, he swung the SUV around, perching on the highest point available. A small hillock on the eastern side. The vehicle's high beam illuminated a spot one hundred yards below the ridgeline.

I ran to the nearest fallen hostile and wrenched a Kalashnikov from his frozen grip. I then sprinted toward the SUV. Carefully resting my elbow on the hood as it supported the barrel of the weapon, I lowered myself into position, aiming for the center of the area lit by the car's lights. The fugitives would have to pass through the illuminated zone to get to the chopper. I wasn't watching my back, figuring that if there'd been any more Compass Black operatives left in the compound, they'd have shot us by now.

We waited.

I considered attempting to take out the helicopter, but the distance was too great to guarantee an effective impact on metal.

We kept waiting. Seven minutes later, they came into view. From this vantage point, it was hard to be certain, but three figures, dressed in black barely two inches apart, scaled the hill.

I took aim at the lead man, hoping it was James Muldoon.

"Nicholas, time's running out. They'll be back in darkness

183

in a couple of seconds."

"Got it," I replied.

I checked the weapon was set to semi-automatic. I needed to be surgical about this. As I lined up the first head, my shot was clear.

I took the familiar deep breath.

Slowly exhale, like I'd done a hundred times before.

The trigger felt cold as I began to squeeze.

Then I saw it. The flash of blond hair between the shoulders of the first and second men. All up, there were four of them. Three Compass Black men cowering around Joshua Jones. Not to protect him, but to use him as cover.

Muldoon knew I wouldn't risk hitting the kid.

I stood up.

"Can't do it Jack." The words struggled to come out of my mouth.

Greatrex appeared perplexed, his face creased. Then a second later, he seemed to get it.

"The boy?"

"It's too close, and they know it. It's not worth taking the chance. I won't gamble a child's life on one chance in a million of making the shot."

Greatrex nodded.

I leaned against the side of the car, allowing myself to slide down onto the earth. Greatrex did the same.

"We've failed," I said.

"Yup."

Whatever energy that had kept the two of us going seemed to evaporate into the night air.

Nicholas Sharp, world-class marksman, just couldn't make the damn shot.

Chapter 30

"I'm sorry Deagan, we've let you down, and more to the point, we've let Joshua down," I said.

"No, Nicholas, you nearly succeeded, and at least now I know for certain that Josh is still alive. That brings great relief."

We sat in Jim Reardon's office, back in Houston. Once again, the four of us - Reardon, Deagan Jones, Greatrex and I - huddled around the coffee table.

"I've got to give you guys credit," began Reardon. "You found the needle slap bang in the middle of the haystack."

"Yes, but unfortunately we lost it again," Greatrex responded.

"So, what's next?" I asked. "Any news regarding Rahmat Beras' movements?"

"Well, I can tell you he's been hard at work discrediting me," replied Jones. "Crimson Wave has been linked to the Reardon 3 attack on a number of levels. Two of our American-based activists have been found with plans of the Reardon 3 rig on their computer. Another has been identified as being in Georgetown just before the pipeline was blown, and of course there's me. Apparently, my navy past, albeit a long time ago, sets me up as having the skill set to plan such an act of sabotage."

"Do you have those skills, Deagan?" I asked.

A sheepish grin appeared. "Well, yes, but I didn't learn them in the US Navy."

"Where did you learn them?" asked Greatrex.

An awkward silence.

"Planning to sabotage onshore pipelines in the Middle East if the Saudis and their friends didn't start working within international environmental guidelines."

Jim Reardon looked somewhat alarmed. "I don't remember any such attacks, Deagan, at least not in peacetime."

"That's because they never happened, Jim. The Saudis saw the light. The threat was enough," Jones responded.

"Deagan, think carefully. Can anyone bear witness to the fact you have those skills?" I asked.

"There lies the problem," replied Jones. "Several of us were trained up. I presume that includes the mystery person being interviewed on Sixty Minutes this Sunday evening. Apparently, he's a Crimson Wave whistle blower."

"This is all building up to something," I suggested.

Everyone nodded. I looked directly at Jones.

"I don't want to alarm you unnecessarily, Deagan, but I suspect there is a strong chance you'll be taken into custody by the authorities before the week is out."

"That's why I have made plans to disappear for a while," replied Jones. "I'll be out of reach of the American government, at least temporarily. I'm hoping that will appease Beras and buy Josh time."

"I'm not sure that anything will appease Beras," added Greatrex. "He seems to be on a roll, and we don't know where to."

There was a knock on the door. Rebecca the PA entered without waiting for an invitation. As before, the two security guards from the foyer took up position inside the office.

Reardon glanced up, reading the language of the room. "What's wrong Rebecca?"

"It hasn't made the media yet, sir, but there's been another attack."

"On us?"

"No, Mr. Reardon, not this time, thank God. It's a British oil and gas rig in the North Sea. Initial reports suggest the environmental damage is massive."

Reardon clicked on his phone, checking out the screen. "As Rebecca said, nothing in the media yet, but it will come soon."

Rebecca left, but the men stayed.

"This is a quickly changing landscape," said Reardon. "Whatever these people are after, it's no longer just an assault on Reardon Energies. It's an attack on the industry."

I leaned forward, about to speak, but then remembered the guys posted by the door. I looked to Reardon before glancing toward them with my eyes.

"Thanks gentlemen," he said, addressing the men. "I'll be fine."

"Yes sir," replied one as the other opened the door and they both left.

"Sorry, can't be too careful," I said.

"Considering you and Jack were the ones getting shot at, I fully understand," replied Reardon.

"I have a question, and it's for all of you," I announced. "Is it the industry that's under attack, or just a component of the industry?"

Reardon sat back in his chair. He wasn't a man who spoke

without thought.

"Are you suggesting that these attacks are focused solely on offshore rigs?"

"The thought had crossed my mind over the last few minutes," I responded.

"What would they have to gain?" asked Greatrex.

"It depends on who *they* are. Jim, does the Faez family have any interest in offshore production?" I asked.

Another pause.

"Not to my knowledge, and my grasp of the industry is quite vast," he replied.

"Is there a pattern within the pattern that we're not seeing here?" I asked. "I mean, even with the pressure from groups such as Crimson Wave and increasing demand from the public for green energies, oil production across the world is still immense. If somebody, one of the players, thought the industry might shrink, could they effectively corner the remaining market?"

"That's a big question, a huge question," replied Reardon. "I suppose if someone wanted to try that, now is the time."

"How so?" asked Greatrex.

Reardon continued. "Ever since the Russian invasion of Ukraine, there's been mammoth pressure on western lines of production to supply the world, or at least those that have come out against the invasion. And that's all of NATO and a whole lot more. That means less oil available for more countries, so prices creep up. OPEC regulates the price of much of the world's oil. They also have an enormous influence on supply. Most of their oil is produced onshore. If they could discredit offshore production, they'd…"

"Own the world," said Greatrex.

"Well… yes," replied Reardon. "Onshore drilling is more profitable too; the power the onshore oil producers would have would be immense."

Greatrex spoke. "And most of the onshore oil that supplies the world is found in…"

"The Middle East," responded Reardon. "But what you're suggesting is preposterous. Despite the popular image that the west holds of Middle Eastern terrorists, the movers and shakers behind OPEC are businessmen. Shrewd, ruthless at times, arrogant, but terrorists? No… no way."

Deagan Jones spoke. "Jim, it's been my observation that when governments and corporations go off the rails, and I mean right off the rails, it's not usually those at the top who start the fire. It's more likely those close to power who want more power. I'm talking about those dwelling on the fringe of where the big decisions are made. They paint events as they desire them to be perceived, manipulate reaction, then boom, suddenly they're the ones with influence. History reeks of the methodology. Hitler, Stalin. The list is endless."

"So, you're suggesting that while Kalid Amir Faez and his contemporaries may not be behind this, others, perhaps on the outer circle, could be responsible," I suggested.

"That's a scary thought," said Greatrex.

"Okay, so we're making progress here," I announced. "But how the hell do we infiltrate the inner workings of the Middle East Oil business to flush out a rat, or group of rats? I don't see how it could be done without a big-time CIA style operation."

Reardon turned to gaze out the window, again in thought. Everyone in the room read his body language and didn't interrupt the process. A couple of minutes later, he turned back, a half-smile on his face.

"Perhaps I can help with that."

Chapter 31

Fire and brimstone. Deagan Jones was in his element.

After our meeting in Jim Reardon's office, Jones let us know that he'd arranged a final press conference before making himself scarce. He felt he needed to defend himself, and Crimson Wave, against the latest slurs.

The conference took place outside Crimson Wave's small Houston office. He neglected to tell the press that he currently wasn't permitted inside the office. Despite their rejection, he'd defend his beloved organization to the end.

Greatrex and I stood back, behind the press throng.

"I stand before you today to declare I have nothing to hide. Every one of you, at least those that know my work, will understand that I've always fought to protect our planet and our future. Every action I've taken has been toward that end. I'll admit that sometimes the line of the law may have been stepped over, perhaps even ignored, but never would I sanction such environmental damage as we've seen off the coast of Guyana and in the North Sea. Whoever instigated these attacks, and it most certainly wasn't me, is an environmental vandal of the highest degree, an intolerable blot on humanity. The stench of evil behind these heinous crimes is as putrid as the worst villainy in our human history.

The people responsible must be caught and punished."

As Jones spoke, his booming voice resonated across the crowd. His gray mane swept back and forth across his forehead. Along with raised arms and clenched fists he embodied the theatrical experience. To all present, the man's passion was palatable.

"It's not hard to see how he captured the world's attention," said Greatrex.

"Thank God he's on the side of righteousness," I replied.

"Unfortunately, most people don't agree."

Right on cue.

"Captain Jones. How do you respond to the mounting evidence against Crimson Wave?"

"I'd ask you in return, sir, where did the evidence come from? I suggest you, the press, question the credibility of your sources."

Jones could take it as well as he could dish it out.

Another journalist.

"Surely you must concede that finding the plans of the Reardon 3 rig on a Crimson Wave member's personal computer is damning evidence?"

"What's damning is that no one has investigated how those plans got on that computer."

A doubtful murmur crept across the crowd. Jones wouldn't stand for it.

"I see and hear your doubt, but what I'm doing now is asking you to do your job and investigate. You'll need to dig deep, be real journalists, not the puppets of corporate sharks."

A voice from the back.

"And what are you doing, Captain Jones? What actions have you taken to uncover these subversive forces?"

A quietness fell across the rabble. Everyone wanted to hear Jones answer.

Deagan stared down at the podium. I figured he wasn't checking his notes, rather choosing his words. His life's work was at stake here, and although no one in the media knew it, so was the life of his son. Suddenly, I wondered if the press conference had been a huge strategic mistake.

Finally, Jones looked up.

"Have you ever been up close, I mean really close, to a breaching humpback whale? Have you felt the power as these giants disperse the water around them running for the breach and then launching into the air like a massive living skyrocket before crashing down onto their backs, their huge flippers arched against the water's surface as they disappear under a cascade of foam. Have you ever seen that? Have you ever felt that? I have, many times, in many locations across this incredible planet, and I can tell you it's a life-changing experience. I cannot believe that any human who has touched such majesty so closely, so personally, could ever do anything to endanger these great creature's habitat. That's why I'm able to stand before you in all honesty and say it wasn't me, nor my brothers and sisters in the environmental trenches who committed these gross acts.

"Ladies and gentlemen, there are waves within a wave. Currently there are differing views on how Crimson Wave conducts business. I've always been associated with direct action. You all know that. However, if the line has been crossed from within our organization, I will identify the culprits and bring them to justice. I emphasize the 'if' in that statement. If those responsible lie outside our group, I will lend the authorities every support in their investigations."

"So, you're saying Crimson Wave could be involved?"

Suddenly, the tone of the crowd changed. Jones furrowed brow suggested he recognized his own error.

The environmentalist then spoke loudly and firmly. The affirmative stance.

"No, not in the slightest. What I'm saying is Crimson Wave has always stood for the betterment and conservation of our natural resources and environment. If, like any corporation, political party or, dare I say, media organization, we find corruption or seditious action within our ranks, we will ferret out those responsible. But I can tell you emphatically that it is not our grass roots members who are deviating from our mission."

I glanced across at Greatrex. His face appeared as uncertain as I was sure mine looked. Had Jones just given the media and even the authorities the best hint possible that they needed to look at the bigger picture here, or had he unknowingly signed his own son's death warrant?

Deagan Jones continued.

"And ladies and gentlemen, I can tell you I have people working on it."

"That would be us," I whispered to Greatrex. "I suspect Jones has just made you and I huge targets, not only for Muldoon and Beras, but now also the press. We need to leave and take Jones with us. No matter his good intentions, he can't do this again."

But it wasn't to be.

At the back right-hand side of the throng, a man and a woman, both dressed in dark suits, stepped out of an equally dark car. They mounted the curb and began pushing through the crowd. There seemed to be a kerfuffle, people of the fourth estate complaining as they were gently yet professionally shoved aside. A minute later, the pair had reached the podium.

"Mr. Deagan Jones?" said the woman.

Jones looked down. The gathering ebbed into silence.

"Captain Deagan Jones, yes."

"I'm Senior Special Agent Spence, and this is Special Agent Fairweather."

The male nodded.

"We are from the Federal Bureau of Investigation and will be taking you into custody today."

Jones appeared stunned, his mouth agape. The press hung on every word.

"Do you have a warrant?" asked Jones.

"Yes, sir," replied Senior Special Agent Spence. She produced some paperwork from her coat and handed it up to Jones.

The environmentalist stepped down off the podium as he took the warrant. He read it carefully then looked up at the agents, before glancing toward Greatrex and me at the back of the crowd.

"May I finish my press conference, Agent Spence?"

"That would be Senior Special Agent Spence, and no, sir, we don't think that would be appropriate."

Jones seemed torn. He could step back onto the podium and make an even bigger issue out of this, or he could leave quietly with the agents. He chose the latter.

As the agents guided Deagan Jones back through the mob, the journalists frantically called out questions.

"What are the charges, Deagan?"

"Where are they taking you?"

"Will you take the fifth?"

"Is this the end of Crimson Wave?"

Wisely, Jones didn't respond.

As the crowd dispersed and reporters went to file what would be a huge story, Greatrex turned to me.

"That was an unusually public execution, wasn't it?"

"It certainly was," I responded. "And you know, I suspect there's a very well thought out rationale behind creating such a spectacle, but right now, for the life of me, I can't figure out what it is."

Chapter 32

Jim Reardon was as good as his word.

Greatrex and I sat in the rear of his Gulfstream G800, circling the sky above the King Khalid International Airport in Riyadh, Saudi Arabia. As the plane descended, the city of Riyadh appeared vast. Ancient stone buildings interspersed with the most modern office towers, many of their designs abstract and striking. A modern metropolis in a traditional environment, where, for at least the upper echelon, there was no shortage of money. Oil money.

Reardon's idea had been simple.

He'd explained: "There's a wedding next week, a huge affair. Kalid Amir Faez's daughter, Zafina, is being married. She is to wed Alem Abadi, the son of Ibrahim Mahomet Abadi, one of the most successful businessmen in Saudi Arabia."

"And Abadi's main source of income?" Greatrex had asked.

"Oil, naturally," Reardon had replied. "The fact is I, along with most CEOs of the world's oil and gas industries, have been invited. It's not that I am particularly close to either family, but the event provides an opportunity for a great display of wealth and, of course, power."

"And you're going?" I'd inquired.

"I've responded that I would attend, but with all that has

happened, I was having doubts. Given what we now suspect, I'll go. And Nicholas, Jack, you can be my security team. That will place you right in the heart of the world's oil movers and shakers. You guys seem to be pretty good at sniffing things out. Here's your chance."

We agreed.

Jim Reardon strolled down to the rear of the aircraft's cabin, sat in a seat opposite us and buckled up for the landing. He sipped a gin and tonic.

"My last tipple for a few days," he said, waving the crystal glass. "The Saudi laws are quite strict. Anyway, the latest itinerary for the festivities has been emailed though. It's going to be a busy time."

He passed each of us a printout.

"The actual wedding ceremony and reception are the day after tomorrow. It says here 'surprise guest international performer'. Do you have any idea who that is?" I asked.

"No, Kalid Faez likes his little secrets. If you're trying to guess, don't limit your imagination. Faez could afford the performance fee of any, and I mean any, artist in the world."

"There's a lot going on here," observed Greatrex. "Have you had a response to your request for a confidential meeting with Faez senior. Surely, if there are any rumblings from the outer ranks, he'll know about it."

"Good news on that, Jack. Kalid Faez's private secretary messaged me an hour ago. We've been given fifteen minutes with his boss this evening at 6 p.m. As my security, you two are authorized to attend."

"Gentleman, we'll be touching down shortly," came the pilot's voice over the intercom.

"I could get accustomed to this mode of transportation," I

said, turning to the big fella.

"We've certainly done a fair bit of traveling over the last few weeks, South America, back home, Spain, back home and now the Middle East. And all because I tried to help out an old friend," he replied.

I sat back in my more than comfortable chair and stared out the window at the approaching world below us.

"Isn't that the way it always seems to begin... just helping out a friend," I said.

"Would you change a thing?" asked the big fella.

"Perhaps we should have fewer friends."

Chuckle.

Touchdown.

The Ritz-Carlton, Riyadh, was a palace amongst a city of palaces. I reckoned the King of England would be happy to call this place home. It's long avenue of trees, leading up to a majestic fountain perched in front a boomerang shaped building several stories high, rivaled Buckingham Palace.

The black stretch limousine pulled up outside the impressive entrance. The dry, warm air was welcoming, not oppressive. It evoked memories of Iraq. A lot that I saw on our drive from the airport reminded me of Baghdad, but a bigger, more luxurious version.

"This place must be costing you a fortune," I mentioned to Jim Reardon as we climbed out of the limo.

"Not a single cent," he replied. "We are guests of Kalid Amir Faez. He refused any offer of payment for our expenses, he inferred it would be an insult. Multiply that by around two hundred Chief Executive Officers or company owners plus staff, there'll be quite a bill at the end of this party."

"Millions," said Greatrex.

"I doubt that's an exaggeration," agreed Reardon.

We stepped through the doorway, doors held open by two immaculately dressed doormen and into another world.

"Every time I think we've stayed in the most lavish place on earth, something comes along to beat it," said Greatrex.

"Perhaps we should have more friends after all," I replied.

Mild chuckle.

As the elevator powered upward, I pondered our accommodation. I expected Greatrex and me to be sharing a small room while Jim Reardon slept in style. Instead, as Reardon was led into the Royal Suite, the big fella and I were shown down the hall to another Royal Suite. More than one. Who would have thought? I guess there's a lot of royalty in Saudi Arabia.

As the porter let us in, I tipped him.

"*Shkran lak.*"

He smiled at my feeble attempt to speak the local language.

If heaven was a hotel room, it would be like the Royal Suite at the Ritz-Carlton, Riyadh. Luxurious, ornate, expansive. Choose any superlative and there'd be an area of this place to match it.

Greatrex ensconced himself in one of the puffy armchairs in the living area. I reached for the phone, ready to make my usual order for a bottle of Johnnie Walker Black, but then stopped. A dry country. Maybe not heaven after all.

Jack raided the bar fridge for soft drinks. A few minutes later, Cokes in our hands, we sat talking.

"I'm thinking we should refine some aims and objectives here," I said.

"Agreed. This is a complicated scenario. If we are to

have any success re-establishing a link to Joshua Jones' whereabouts, or finding out what else is going down here, we need a strategy," said the big fella.

"All right," I began. "One: Deagan Jones has established a connection from the attempted compromise of Crimson Wave to board member Rahmat Beras. Two: Beras is, or at least was, directly linked to the oil rich Faez family who are our hosts. So, we establish if Beras and the son, Ahmed Faez, are still connected and confirm Faez set Beras up financially early in his investment career."

As I spoke the words, I realized the difficulty of the task before us.

If that's the case, it's necessary to establish whether Beras is supported by Faez senior, or as Jim Reardon suspects, there is a breakaway group within the family, possibly a next-gen thing," I added.

"Then come the two big questions," said Greatrex. "What are they planning? There must be more, because what they've achieved so far won't drive the offshore industry to extinction."

"And the second question, the one that's really within our remit," I continued. "How can we use any of this knowledge to trace a connection from the Faez's to Beras, to his lackeys, Compass Black, and therefore the location of Joshua Jones?"

"When you say it out loud, that's quite a mountain to climb," said the big fella.

"And to be honest, I'm not certain we have the tools nor the window of opportunity."

We sat in a shared silence, considering our own words.

Then.

"I don't know Nicholas. This time, we may have bitten off

more than we can possibly chew."

"Next, you're going to ask me about a plan."

"We don't have one, do we?"

"Zip. But on the good side, we've worked in the dark before."

"So, for the next forty-eight hours, it's all about gathering intelligence?"

I turned to my old friend, feeling my lips pursing. "We need to gather it, make some sense of it, and then, for the sake of young Joshua Jones, figure out what the hell to do with it."

I needed a scotch.

Chapter 33

It felt like a gigantic movie set, waiting for Iron Man to power down from above. The Faez Center towered more than forty floors towards the cloudless blue sky.

It was nearly 6 p.m. Reardon, Greatrex and I were escorted through the doors and directly to an express elevator. Our personal escort, dressed in a smart claret red western-style uniform with gold braiding, pressed level forty-two. The elevator powered upward like a rocket. When the doors opened, a breathtaking view of the city presented itself. Ushered left, we followed the escort around the elevator bank to a suite of offices. A receptionist greeted us.

"Gentlemen, this way, please." No questions asked. She knew who we were.

As we'd arranged, Greatrex stopped when we arrived at the entrance to Kalid Amir Faez's suite. He'd suggested that by waiting outside, as a security detail was likely to do, he may glean additional information about the goings on in the building. He found it pointless for all three of us to attend the meeting.

The escort swung the doors open. Like Reardon's office, the view was spectacular, but this time the floor to ceiling window curved around the space, continuing the Tony Stark effect.

Behind a bespoke circular glass desk sat a striking figure. He wore a full length flowing white robe with a mandarin collar, a white ghutra over his head that revealed his face and thick once dark goatee beard dappled with gray. A black igal, a double loop of braided cord, kept his headdress in place.

The figure stood.

"*Salam Alaykum,* Jim. It's so good to see you."

"May peace be with you also, Kalid," Reardon responded.

The two men shook hands.

"May I present Nicholas Sharp? He is here as part of my security, but I must confess he has a greater role to play in my visit."

"I presumed that to be the case when I received your request, Jim. Mr. Sharp, *Salam Alaykum.*"

"And to you, sir." The Arab presented a firm handshake.

"Now, please sit down." Faez waved towards the chairs at the desk, indicating the visit was to be friendly, but still with some level of formality.

"May I get you anything?" offered the Saudi.

"No thank you Kalid, your generosity of spirit has already been substantial. The Ritz-Carlton is superb," said Reardon.

"I'm glad you find it satisfactory," Faez smiled.

"And warmest congratulations on the impending nuptials of your daughter, Zafina," added Reardon.

"Thank you, sir. It is going to be a great celebration. I'm pleased you could make the trip."

Reardon nodded.

"Time is pressing with much to do. Let us get down to business, gentlemen. You have requested this meeting. How may I be of service?"

"Kalid, you are aware of the attack on our rig, and the assault in the North Sea."

"Yes, they are most unfortunate events."

Reardon continued. "I'll be direct and to the point, and I'm afraid some of our questions may seem offensive. I can assure you that is not our intention."

"Message received and appreciated, Jim. Now please proceed."

Reardon paused; this would not be easy for him.

"We have a working theory that the attacks may be a strategy to eradicate the offshore oil industry."

"That is alarming, most alarming. With much of the world not accepting Russian energy supplies, I fear the pressure on our onshore production facilities would be excessive if that were the case," Faez responded.

"That is our view as well. We do believe there is a possibility that a group of oil producers, possibly based in the Middle East, may be behind the plan. Perhaps greed is the motivating factor at play," said Reardon.

Faez frowned. "I hope you are not suggesting I am part of this hypothetical scheme."

Tension suddenly filled the air.

"No Kalid, not for one second. If we believed that, we would not be talking with you now. It is your perspective we seek," chimed Reardon quickly.

The frown eased. "That is a relief for the warmth of our relationship."

"We do, however, have a name, and we understand it's a person who may be known to you," stated Reardon.

"Well, as you Americans say, spit it out."

"Rahmat Beras."

The Saudi oil magnate sat back in his chair and scratched his chin. His taut expression suggested concern. Both Reardon and I were aware that his response would tell us a great deal.

"Yes, I know Rahmat. He was a good friend to my son at Harvard. He's smart and resourceful. As I got to know him better, I became convinced of his inevitable success. His only hurdle was his family's modest wealth. To be honest, it was my own son, Ahmed, who suggested I provide the young man with seed money when they'd both finished their studies. I agreed and provided the funds. To me it wasn't much, but to youthful Rahmat, it was the world. I believe he has become extremely successful. He's repaid his financial debt to me many times over. My only regret is that he and Ahmed have lost contact over the years. I suppose they had some sort of falling out. It happens with the young. They can be so impetuous. Sadly, Rahmat's visits to Riyadh faltered. I haven't seen him in years, and Ahmed has not spoken of him."

"Thank you, Kalid. I know we had no right to ask such an intrusive question," said Reardon.

"It is fine. Are you able to explain why you suspect Rahmat is involved in such a despicable program?"

"That would be a lengthy story, my friend, more than we have time for. There are, however, some further aspects of the matter to discuss with you that may lead you to your own conclusions," said Reardon, tactful to the end.

"More questions?"

"I'm afraid so."

"Please, proceed."

Now, as arranged earlier, it was my turn.

"Mr. Faez, I certainly don't want to seem intrusive, but are you aware of any discontent from family members or high-level executives either within your own company, or your competitor's operations, who may have shown signs of disgruntlement? Perhaps they've been unsuccessful in suggesting new methods in the market?"

"Tactfully put Mr. Sharp. Your diplomatic skills defy your age."

I wished Greatrex had been in the room to hear that.

Faez continued. "You're asking me if there are there any rotten apples within my family who may be trying to usurp my own control of the business."

I nodded.

"I'm not happy with the question," Faez continued, "but I understand your need to ask it. I'm afraid I can offer no answer for you at this moment, but I promise to arrange another meeting for the three of us early tomorrow. I shall offer you a response, then."

Readon looked concerned.

"Don't worry Jim, I am not offended. I simply need time to respond. My man will see you out."

Chapter 34

"What do you reckon?" I asked.

"It got a bit hairy there for a moment, but I think we're all right," Reardon replied.

We'd returned to the hotel and sat in Jim Reardon's royal suite, almost a mirror image of our own, explaining what had transpired to Greatrex.

"Why didn't he want to continue the conversation then and there?" asked Greatrex. "It's a busy time for him. It would have been easier to sort it on the spot."

"Perhaps there are other factors at play," I suggested.

"What factors?" asked the big fella.

"I'm not sure, but I don't think we've offended him. Our suspicions were a lot to take in. He may just need to consider what we put to him," I replied.

"Either way," said Reardon. "We'll know tomorrow. If there's no meeting, the trail goes dead."

"That's it then. We wait," I stated the obvious.

That evening, the three of us ate together in the hotel's restaurant. The meal was exceptional. Afterward, Reardon made his apologies and left to network with some other oil supremos staying at the Ritz. Fortunately, the bill for dinner never materialized. It seemed we weren't off Kalid Amir Faez's Christmas card list just yet. Not that Sunni Muslims write Christmas card lists.

Back in the privacy of our suite, Greatrex and I studied the itinerary for the next two days. The big fella was correct. There was a lot happening. We needed to cherry-pick the events that could lead us to the most information.

"The wedding itself is the day after tomorrow," I began. "Normally I'd suggest it might be a case of 'loose lips sink ships', but as the event is alcohol free, no one is going to shoot off their mouth accidentally."

"True, but with that many movers and shakers present, we'll need to work the room; eavesdrop where we can, watch who gathers, maybe look for a clique of younger power brokers."

"Good idea," I replied. "What about tomorrow evening. Nothing is scheduled, at least nothing that involves the Faez family."

"Yeah, that seems a bit odd. We should follow it up. Possibly there is something exclusive planned that we don't know about."

"And that we're not meant to know about." I added.

Greatrex nodded.

"Any word about who the big guest star is yet?" I asked.

The big fella shook his head. "Nothing official, but while I was waiting for you outside Faez senior's office, the place was buzzing. I asked if they had any clue as to who it would be, but they played coy. The couple of younger staffers who worked on the top floor seemed pretty excited, though. I think it'll be a well-known name."

"We can't do much more tonight. I think I'll turn in," I said.

"Likewise," Greatrex responded. "You never know what

tomorrow might bring."

I'd almost dozed off in my bed of a thousand comforts when my cell chirped. The screen showed a message from Reardon.

"Meeting with Kalid Faez, 10 a.m. He's asked to meet in his office but indicated we may move on somewhere else. I've got no idea where. JR."

Well, at least now we knew tomorrow would bring something.

After a healthy breakfast that probably cost about a week's rent of your average house in LA, we headed back toward the Faez Center in the black limo. We didn't talk much, with such little intel, everything had been said.

At 10 a.m. on the dot, Reardon and I were shown into Kalid Amir Faez's office. Faez was dressed in identical clothing to the previous day. Again, he rose to greet us.

"Jim, Nicholas, thank you for returning. I'm sorry to delay the conclusion of our conversation. Please sit. And by the way, Nicholas, please ask your friend Jack Greatrex to join us."

I stepped over to the door. On cue, the assistant on the other side opened it and Greatrex walked in.

"Mr. Greatrex, *Salam Alaykum.*"

"And to you, sir." They shook hands, then we sat.

"I trust you rested well, however time is pressing, so we best get down to business."

The three of us nodded.

"The questions you so tactfully asked me yesterday, Nicholas. They were thoughtful, but they pertained to family. In our culture, family is a sacrosanct space. I would not dishonor my children by answering such personal, and perhaps in other circumstances offensive, inquiries about them without their knowledge."

Reardon chipped in, "As I mentioned, Kalid, no offence was intended."

"And none was taken, Jim. That's why I mentioned the proviso 'in other circumstances'. So, last night I spoke at length with Ahmed and my daughter Zafina. They have assured me that they have no awareness of any potential coup or takeover that would affect our operations. I also questioned Ahmed regarding his relationship with Rahmat Baras. He told me their friendship faded as they grew older. Their interests differed. I believe that's a natural progression in life."

Faez rubbed his hands together, as though washing them.

"So, as you can see," he continued, "I'm unable to offer any substantial information, but I wish you well in your investigations."

Faez rose from his chair. We followed suit.

"Now, before you leave, I have something much more immediately interesting to share. I'm going to take you to meet our special guest artist for the wedding. I think you'll be impressed. Please consider the introduction a good will gesture from me to you."

"Thank you, Kalid, that is very kind," Jim Reardon responded.

With Kalid Amir Faez accompanying us, we rode down in the elevator. As we entered the foyer, a tall man also in traditional Saudi attire stepped in behind us. Faez stopped.

"Where are my manners? This is Jabir, my bodyguard. I don't leave the building without him."

211

We shook hands. Jabir appeared polite and respectful, yet he still managed to convey a 'you touch my boss and you're dead men walking' look.

After the introductions, we proceeded through the hotel's front doors. Two stylish white Rolls-Royce Phantoms awaited. A uniformed chauffer stood beside the open passenger door of the first vehicle. Faez must have noted our reactions.

"Ahh… a small indulgence, I'm afraid. Jim, if you and Mr. Greatrex ride in the first car, the chauffeur will drive. Jabir will drive the second vehicle. Mr. Sharp, will you join me?"

Greatrex raised an eyebrow, but good manners meant following our host's instructions. Somewhere in my gut, I felt certain Faez had a reason for our prescribed travel arrangements.

Jabir opened the rear passenger door for his boss. I strolled round to the other side and let myself in, no longer amazed by the opulence.

Jabir gently eased away from the curb, following the first Roller.

"Please forgive me for being so explicit regarding the cars, Nicholas, but I have my reasons," said Faez.

I nodded.

He continued. "This conversation needs to be private. I've chosen to speak with you alone, as my research leads me to believe you are the driving force behind this investigation."

"Your research, sir?"

"Now let's not be coy. A person of my resources has great reach, as does Jim Reardon. I'm credibly informed that you've managed to insert yourself into a number of situations and aided some people who required a man of your special abilities."

"May I ask your sources, Mr. Faez?"

"You may, but I won't tell you. Suffice to say, we both have friends at a very famous address in Washington DC."

I asked nothing further.

"I'll need to be brief and to the point. This journey will take around twenty minutes. The expedition I'm about to suggest may be considerably longer."

"You have my attention, sir."

"Excellent. After our conversation yesterday, I did exactly as I told you, Jim and Mr. Greatrex, this morning. I spoke to my children, Ahmed and Zafina last night and questioned them regarding the matters you raised. Their responses were precisely what I relayed to you in my office. The trouble is, I don't believe a single word they said."

Surprised silence.

"I'm not a stupid man, Nicholas. For some time, I've sensed unrest amongst an element of the younger generation within my family. I'm confident some of my colleagues felt similarly inside their own groups. It's not so much what had been said, or even demanded, but more the sense of visible frustration when I've made decisions that have displeased. Of course, I speak specifically of my eldest son Ahmed."

"Up until now I've had nothing concrete upon which to base my suspicions, save the fact I'm cognizant of times when information that should have come across my desk didn't."

"You said up until now?"

"Yes Nicholas, either wittingly or unwittingly, you set a trap for Ahmed yesterday by asking about Rahmat Beras. Everything I told you yesterday, I believed to be true. Today, not so much. After Ahmed denied the existence of an ongoing relationship with Beras over recent years, I sent Jabir to do some digging. I believe he's been up most of the night."

I nodded. "Perhaps he shouldn't be driving today."

From the front seat, Jabir raised a reassuring arm. He was clearly listening to every word.

"Fifteen years in the Royal Saudi Armed Forces before coming into my employ has certainly toughened you up, has it not, my friend?"

A nod from the man behind the wheel.

"Anyway, back to the point. Under my instruction, Jabir has spent many hours examining documents from our communications center. It's easier when the staff is off duty. Jabir has access to all our networks. Even my son's private encrypted network. I'm sure Ahmed has no idea we have such access because I've never had cause to use it... until now."

"The thrust of the matter is, Jabir discovered these documents."

Faez nodded at his bodyguard.

Jabir reached into his jacket pocket and produced a wad of white paper. He passed it to his boss in the rear seat. Faez unfolded the papers and handed them to me.

"Please read."

I skimmed through them. The first group were copies of emails between Ahmed Faez and Rahmat Beras. There was nothing particularly damning in them. The exchanges seemed mostly personal, two old friends catching up. The critical point was the dates. The emails showed communication at regular intervals over the last seven years. That proved that Ahmed had lied to his father.

"It's concerning that your son lied to you regarding being in touch with Beras, sir. But there is nothing damning in the

214

content unless I've missed something."

"No Nicholas, you've missed nothing, but please read on."

The second set of documents appeared to be transcripts, presumably from speech to text software, their content entirely different.

They began years earlier.

AF: "Have you made the arrangements?"

RB: "Yes, I'll be elected to the board next month. The donations have been beneficial."

AF: "Good, then you can set to work as instructed."

Twelve months ago.

AF: "Your plan has been received and shall be funded. Proceed."

RB: "Thank you. The decision is a wise one."

AF: "The details of how you achieve the goals are not important, but please communicate the results of each action."

RB: "Of course."

A few weeks ago.

RB: "The Reardon pipeline has been devastated. Soon the blame will fall on the naïve fools at Crimson Wave."

AF: "Has the environmental damage been impactful?"

RB: "As much as required. And let me say, we've taken out some personal insurance to ensure Jones' silence."

A few days ago.

RB: "The North Sea has gone as well as Guyana."

AF: "Then you're ready to proceed with the final part of your plan?"

RB: "We will be shortly. There has been a surprise complication. They'll be dealt with. Our actions will have a global impact. And your wallets will bulge."

AF: "Don't tell me. It's important there is no trail leading back here."

RB: "There will be none."

AF "I'll report your progress back to the group this week."

I stopped reading and looked up at Faez. His eyes burned with intensity.

"The group," I said.

"Yes, Nicholas. You see, we have a problem."

Chapter 35

Kalid Faez allowed a couple of minutes to pass before he next spoke. The rhythm of the busy Riyadh traffic became a calming influence.

"Nicholas, you'll need to forgive my cloak and dagger approach. This information was too important to be spoken of in my office. If there is such subversion within my company, and my family, everywhere may have ears."

"What about this car?"

"Given what I've found out in the last twenty-four hours, it would not surprise me to find my own vehicle is, what's the CIA term?… bugged. Also, my chauffer is not as trusted as Jabir. I'm certain Ahmed will not have arranged any monitoring on this vehicle."

"Why?"

"Because it's his. I borrowed it without him knowing."

Minute by minute I gained new respect for Kalid Amir Faez's covert abilities.

"Identifying this renegade group is crucial. You mentioned other families may be involved?" I said.

"I'm almost certain. In families of average wealth, youthful rebellion involves little that is of great consequence. When you control the abundant riches of the major Saudi oil dynasties, the perspective changes. Several families are uncomfortable with the push for increased revenue from their juniors. Why do the young not see that with age comes a wisdom that tempers greed?"

Faez put up his hand to silence me before I could respond.

"There is another factor that leads me to believe that there is more than one family involved."

"What's that?" I asked.

"Ahmed is too stupid to be the brains behind such a scheme. This type of action requires thought, aggression, and dominance. In our patriarchal society, others follow the strongest and smartest man. I'm almost ashamed to say that will not be my son."

"It's possible that Beras is the mastermind and your son's group only contribute the finances," I proposed.

"Yes, that may well be the case. You will need to find that out, Nicholas."

"I'm aware Ahmed stated he'd report back to the group this week, and I appreciate your confidence in me, Mr. Faez. But it appears that I only have the wedding celebration to try to identify who is part of this clique, never mind exactly what they're planning," I said.

"I can assure you that our social circles in Saudi Arabia are extremely strict. Ahmed will only confer with peers from other leading families. Of that, I'm sure. I'm equally certain that despite their youth, they would never risk meeting and perhaps being overheard at such a large event. They would need a more personal environment."

"I've been over the schedule for the festivities. I can't see you've allowed any downtime for such a group to meet surreptitiously," I replied.

"There is such an occasion, Nicholas. The Katb Al-kitab is the actual ceremony where Zafina and her betrothed will be wed in simple Muslim custom, and it takes place tonight. No one except a very tight circle of people are invited. There will be a sheik, a few close friends, some of whom act as witnesses, and immediate family members. The setting will be on my own private island, which is only a quick flight away. Tomorrow is the Walma, where we celebrate the marriage with all our friends. It is a huge party to which many, including Jim Reardon are invited."

Faez stopped mid-sentence. A stony look of realization crossed his features.

"Nicholas, at the Katb Al-kitab tonight, the people who are likely to make up this breakaway group might be present."

"Perfect. Can you get me in?"

"No," replied Faez.

I sat there, stunned.

"What I mean is, the list is so small and exclusive that any outsider would be immediately noticed. Besides a trusted few, my staff on the island have been sent away. We can't even say you're involved in security."

A great opportunity to gather the intel I needed seemed to be fading from my grasp.

"Is there no way at all?"

"I'm afraid the only stranger present will be Miss Cetia Forez. She is our special guest performer and is performing a single acoustic song as part of the ceremony. Considering she's probably the most famous pop singer in the world, I don't think you'll be able to masquerade as her," Faez chuckled.

Perhaps not, but I had an idea.

Ten minutes later, we pulled up at Cape Canaveral. The Al Faisaliah Hotel stood like a rocket ship tethered to its launching tower awaiting take off. The building's symmetrical shape narrowed from a broad base to a sharp tip hundreds of feet into the sky. Parklands surrounded the structure with more conventional buildings, still part of the hotel complex, nearby.

The other white Rolls Royce Phantom had pulled in ahead of ours. Greatrex and Reardon were stepping out.

"Inside is the Prince Sultan's Grand Hall. The premier wedding venue in Riyadh," announced Kalid Amir Faez.

After Jabir had opened his door, Faez took the lead.

"Follow me gentlemen. I will take you to meet our special guest. Nicholas already knows who she is. I think you will be suitably impressed."

I smiled in acknowledgement.

Greatrex raised an eyebrow.

Jabir guided us across the Hotel's impressive lobby through to the doors of the Grand Hall. The space took luxury to yet another level. An array of lights glittered across the curved roof. Gold and blue ceiling drapes ran the length of the vast space suggesting a level of royal grandeur. A sea of tables, already laid with crystal and silver, gleamed against the white tablecloths laced with gold trim. In the center of each table stood a large circular silver pot and an enormous bouquet of flowers. Some distance away, on the main stage, there was enough musical gear to equip a decent size concert. A few techs and musicians looked busy, presumably finalizing the set up before a sound check.

Faez strode to the stage, taking the lead once again.

Avoiding all the pitfalls of leads, cases and equipment, Faez ushered us up to the stage wings. A slender female figure in an expensive-looking track suit, her back turned, appeared to be talking intensely with one of the techs. She had a cream fabric shawl, color coordinated with her suit, covering her head. As she swung around, the dark brown curly strands of her hair protruded from each side of the scarf. Beauty framed in beauty.

Faez stood proudly tall.

"Mr. Jim Reardon, Mr. Jack Greatrex and Mr. Nicholas Sharp, I'd like you to meet the wonderful and extremely popular Miss Cetia Forez."

Reardon was frozen, his mouth agape.

Cetia Forez smiled back at him. "Mr. Reardon, Mr. Greatrex."

She shook their hands before turning to me.

"How are you, Nicholas? It's been too long."

"Hi Tia," I responded.

It was Faez's turn to drop his jaw. "You know Mr. Sharp, Miss Forez?"

"I most certainly do. Would you like to explain Nicholas, or shall I?"

I stepped in. "I've been fortunate enough to play piano on a few of Tia's tracks and done a couple of live shows with her."

"Not only that, but Nicholas contributed to the writing of 'My Heart is in You', a song I believe you all may be familiar with." Cetia smiled as she spoke.

"That was an enormous hit across America," said Reardon.

"And in Saudi Arabia," added Faez.

Greatrex chuckled in the background. He hadn't met Tia, but he knew of my connection with her. I enjoyed playing with her. She had incredible vocal talent, but I'd found the song writing by committee a little more difficult. It wasn't my way, which is why I didn't pursue it. The royalty checks, however, were appreciated.

"So, what brings you here, Nicholas?" the singer asked.

Awkward moment.

Sensing my hesitation, Faez stepped in.

"Nicholas is a friend of my family," he said. "He has done us and our friends several favors through the years, so he is here, along with Jack, as my guest."

Tia grinned. "You know, I've heard a few rumors about some of Nicholas Sharp's 'favors'". She held her hands in the air to make quotation marks. "The industry does like to talk."

Time for a change of subject.

"Tia, I believe you're performing at the Walma, the big celebration tomorrow?"

Cetia smiled. "Yes, and I'm looking forward to it so very much."

Professional to the end. I imagined she was also looking forward to the million dollar plus performance fee that would be accompanying it.

Nicholas Sharp, cynic.

"Ms. Forez, I've let the cat out of the bag and revealed to Nicholas that you'll be playing a song at the Katb Al-kitab tonight. In fact, we should be off shortly. I believe our aircraft is waiting."

Greatrex and Reardon appeared confused. Understandably.

"Tia, what song are you performing at the ceremony this evening?"

"Funny you should ask, Nicholas. The bride and groom have chosen 'My Heart is in You'."

My mind ticked over like a computer. This could get

awkward.

"Tia, who's your keys player?"

"That would be me," came a gruff voice from behind. "Nicholas Sharp, I saw you walk in. Freakin' great to see you, sunshine."

I swung around. A tall man, dark skin and a gray beard offered his hand. Bobby Hopkins was one of the greatest contemporary pianists and keyboard players in LA. He'd been somewhat of a mentor to me when I was starting out in my post-Marine career.

"Bobby." A handshake and a hug.

As good as it was to see my old friend, I sensed my recently connived plan slipping through my fingers. I couldn't ask to step in to replace such a fine musician.

Bobby turned to Tia. "We're having some technical difficulties here, Tia. Nothing we can't resolve, but it's an elaborate keys set up, so I really should be here. Did I just overhear Mr. Faez say we're about to leave for tonight's ceremony on the island?"

"I'm reading your mind Bobby," Tia responded. "Nicholas, I'm sure it would be a real treat for the bride and groom to have the song's co-writer perform it with me tonight. What do you say, Mr. Faez?"

"That would be a wonderful turn of events," Faez responded.

Tia turned back to me. "Nicholas?"

"I'd be honored," I replied, with a courteous bow.

Sometime shit just comes together.

Chapter 36

The thing about luxury is that after a while, it begins to feel normal.

Climbing the stairs to Kalid Amir Faez's Gulfstream G800 stuck a familiar chord. We'd traveled to Saudi Arabia in Jim Readon's jet. Same brand, same model. In fact, I eyeballed it over the tarmac, easily identifiable by Reardon's company logo. Surely everyone should have one of these.

"Will your son and daughter be joining us on the flight?" I asked Faez as he showed Cetia Forez to her luxury seat across a marble coffee table from his own.

"No, Nicholas. Ahmed and Zafina will be taking my second jet a little later."

"Ahh, so we get the comfy ride," I joked.

"By no means," he replied. "The second plane is identical to this one. I don't like to be inconvenienced if one aircraft has service requirements when I need use of it."

By my calculation, that added up to around one hundred and forty million dollars' worth of convenience.

"Of course," I responded, taking my seat at the rear of the cabin. We'd left Greatrex and Reardon, heading back to the Ritz Carlton. I knew they'd be keenly awaiting my report in the morning. When I'd suggested to Faez that we detour to the hotel to pick up some clothes for me, he stated that a complete attire, including all personal requirements, would be waiting at our destination.

Our destination.

Neither Faez, nor Jabir had indicated exactly where the oil baron's private island was located. I hummed the Beatles 'Magical Mystery Tour' in my head as the plane sped down the runway, figuring I'd find out soon enough.

Less than an hour of pampered luxury later, we touched down at Prince Abdul Mohsin Bin Abdulaziz International Airport in Yanbu, on the western coast of Saudi Arabia.

"Best be quick, my friends. My private helicopter will take us direct to the island," announced Faez.

I didn't ask how many of those he owned.

As the upmarket chopper swept a lazy arc across the sky, the sun radiated a golden hue over the calm waters below. What had been a dot on the horizon was rapidly taking the form of a single land mass, like a green and brown ship against the tranquil blue of the sea.

"The island of Maladh," announced Faez, leaning out from his seat and staring out the window. "This is the ancestral home of my family, or at least the modern ancestral home," he smiled.

"It's a long journey for a simple ceremony that could have been held in Riyadh," I commented.

"Perhaps so, Nicholas, but life is made of memories. When we land, I believe you'll see why we've come."

I nodded. Tia smiled graciously.

An hour later, I sat ensconced in an oversized gloss white

painted chair with cushions that felt as though they were stuffed with clouds. The Red Sea glimmered like sparkling champagne as the sun set nestled into the horizon. The view from the patio fifty yards above the waterline was mesmerizing.

The calm environment seemed at odds with the purpose of my visit.

I heard footsteps behind me - Faez. He'd donned new robes and a more ornate igal around his gleaming white ghutra. He sat down opposite me.

"What do you think, Nicholas?"

"I'm beyond words, Mr. Faez."

"To me, this island is the most beautiful jewel in the world, and the surrounding sea, its gallant guardian. My departed wife and I had our Katb Al-kitab here. It is appropriate that Zafina continues the tradition."

"Your home is magnificent, sir, and the view is overwhelming," I suggested. Faez had given me a brief tour of the stone and whitewashed concrete mansion. The gardens, the majestic rooms, the grandeur made Tracy Island seem like a log cabin on a rock.

"Maladh is Arabic for haven. And this place has been a haven for my family for a long, long time. We unearthed our first oil field on the mainland in this district. The Al Madinah Province has always been our home. It has sheltered us, allowed us to work hard and in the end made us extremely wealthy." Faez swept an arm across the view as he spoke. "It is fitting that my daughter pays homage to the past and takes her vows here."

The oil tycoon paused for a moment, as we both savored the last rays of the setting sun.

"Up until recently, the Red Sea has been a secret paradise, largely hidden from the rest of the world, Nicholas. But I fear that is changing. Our Crown Prince is encouraging development. He wants to welcome the tourists, and their money, into our country and our economy. I see his point, but I also see the risks. We're entering a new era of synthetic islands, modernization, and significant economic activity. That includes a laser focus on this majestic region. I know those in charge are aware of the environmental vulnerabilities. They are safeguarding the natural order as best they can, but still there is danger."

I remained silent.

"I suppose my passion and connection for this region is one of the reasons I've never encouraged offshore oil exploration. A lone catastrophe may well inflict irreparable damage. Are you aware that not far from here there are some extremely large offshore fields?"

"But not yours?"

"No, Nicholas, not mine."

"If I didn't know better, I'd say you speak like an environmentalist yourself, sir."

"Environmentalist, no. But perhaps to some extent, a conservationist. I have little time for fools tied to trees, but I do appreciation the world Allah has given us."

"Does your son share your passion?"

"Ahmed spent his youth here, although he wasted more of it socializing with girls than finding solace in nature. I'm not thinking for a second that his involvement in this shameful scheme is due to his love of the wild. Make no mistake, it's about money. Nothing more, nothing less."

"That brings us to the task at hand, Mr. Faez."

227

"Yes, it does." Faez glanced over his shoulder, back toward the house. "Ms. Forez is in her room resting. She plans to meet you for a rehearsal in the main hall in one hour. There will be a Steinway Grand piano for you to perform on."

Of course there will.

"My son, daughter, and some of their close friends should arrive about the time you are rehearsing. With regard to your presence here, they'll know nothing more than you are Ms. Forez's accompanist. Here is a list of people arriving with them."

Faez reached into his robe, pulled out a sheet of paper and passed it to me. I gave it a cursory glance. I'd study it later.

"What's the order of proceedings?"

"The ceremony begins at 8 p.m. Before that time, everyone will be preparing themselves - showering, dressing, etc. By 9 p.m. it will be over. There is a one-hour window for some food, treats, congratulations and a brief social interaction before 10 p.m. I have insisted that everyone retire to their rooms early. Tomorrow is a big day, and we leave the island at 6 a.m."

I looked Faez in the eye.

"Forgive my impertinence, sir, but these are not children, and this is not a school camp. Will everybody do as you've asked?"

"A week ago, my answer would have been 'without hesitation', Nicholas. As I've said, our culture is patriarchal, my word is law. However, after our recent discoveries, I'm uncertain. I believe that is where you 'kick in', as they say."

"Yes, Mr. Faez, that is exactly when I will 'kick in'."

My gut felt uneasy. Eavesdropping on a bunch of rich kids in daddy's big house didn't seem that difficult. But when

228

you considered the damage these people had already caused, their relationship with Rahmat Beras and Compass Black, the malicious nature of their activities, and the lives threatened and lost, I couldn't be certain that 'kicking in' wouldn't involve me 'checking out'.

Chapter 37

The huge chandeliers hung from the ceiling as though they were casting Allah's light across the room. Columns laced with gold leaf were embedded into the walls, exploding in a maze of bling and opulence.

I sat behind a white Steinway concert-size grand piano, its vast lid raised, open to the room. Next to me, Cetia Forez stood ready, hands clenched, smile glued to her face.

In the middle of the room, clad in simple robes, sat the Islamic cleric, his features serious and intense. Before him Kalid Amir Faez's daughter, Zafina, smiled, her strong chin and intensely dark eyes radiating a mystic charm. Her stunning white dress cascaded to the tiled floor. Next to her perched a tall man in stone-colored garments with a jet-black beard. He appeared content, eager. I knew him to be Abid Badawi, the son of an extremely wealthy oil and gas baron and Zafina's betrothed.

The dozen or so guests sat behind them, the women with head coverings, the men in traditional attire. From the back, Jabir observed the ceremony. The hint of a smile suggested some pride and happiness, but the stealth in the movement of his eyes belied a professional at work. Next to Jabir, another figure appeared just as watchful. He wore similar robes to the others, but somehow they didn't seem to sit naturally on his shoulders. After studying Faez's list, I had a fair idea who most people in the room were, but I couldn't identify this second man. That worried me.

The ceremony progressed according to Muslim tradition. Although I'd not been to a Muslim wedding before, I understood the rituals. Toward the end, family members read the Surah Al-Fatiha to bless the marriage. Then, in silence, the contract was signed.

With traditional proceedings over, came the nod to modernism. Everyone turned in their seats to face Cetia and me. That was my cue.

The song began with a gentle rippling piano, simple chords but with an elegant movement. Several people smiled in recognition. I increased the intensity, expanding the dynamics as I swelled the final introductory moment. Just before Tia's entrance, I quashed the volume, allowing the last chord to fade into an echoed silence.

Then Cetia Forez showed everyone in the room why she was a singer of international renown.

Her voice edged into the verse, breathy but intense. People leaned forward, captivated by her spell, wanting to engross themselves in her being. The next four minutes became a dance of emotion and intensity as Tia carried the listeners deep into her soul. A tear rolled down Zafina's cheek. This was a moment she'd remember forever.

Then it was over.

Considering the size of the audience, the applause resonated loudly across the room, the warmth of the reception evident. Cetia Forez took a bow. I bowed my head toward the keyboard, not wanting to distract.

Zafina and Abid led everyone out of the room, the cleric and Kalid Amir Faez following. They both appeared content with the proceedings, although Faez seemed slightly agitated, wringing his hands together a little too tightly.

It was time for treats and, if Faez had his way, a brief celebration.

Cetia and I wandered down the long, expansive corridors, passing archways on both sides leading off to who knows where.

"That was something else, Tia. If there was a show to steal, you just stole it," I said.

"You are kind Nicholas. I think we make a good team. Let's work together soon."

"It would be my pleasure," I responded.

As we arrived at her room, Tia grasped the doorknob. Before turning it, she swirled around to face me.

"Nicholas, I don't know why you're here, but my intuition tells me you are facing some danger." She smiled or rather radiated. "Please be careful. I'd hate for anything to happen to one of my favorite musicians."

With that, she pecked me on the cheek and stepped into her quarters. The lady was a class act.

After a few more steps, I exited through a doorway on the opposite side. Like everything else in this vast palace, my room contained enough luxury and bling to satiate any appetite for extravagance. I relaxed into one of the deep green velvet armchairs. Now that I'd eyeballed everyone, it was time to plan. I wondered how things would play out after bedtime.

Shortly before 11 p.m., I eased my door open and edged my

way back along the corridor. Faez had provided me with a plan of the building and pointed out the possible locations for a clandestine meeting. The lights had been dimmed. Whatever staff Faez allowed to stay were obviously following their boss' instructions to the letter.

I noted no light under Tia's door as I slipped past. A few minutes later, I stood outside the massive double doors that led to the hall where the ceremony had taken place. I eased one open. Darkness. I closed it and moved on.

The silence was palpable, only broken by my own footsteps, which I tried to mute. At each location Faez had suggested, I stopped and listened before easing open the appropriate door. Like a ghost town, I saw only shadow and darkness, yet I felt intruded upon, watched.

Despite much consideration, I had no specific expectation of what I might find. It seemed possible I'd find a small group, talking, planning. I hoped to get a chance to listen. Ideally, I'd manage to corner one of the group members alone, possibly Ahmed. Perhaps I'd be able to intimidate some truth out of them.

Fear incites honesty, but it can also breed deception.

Ahead of me, a stone stairway, about ten feet wide, led downstairs to the bowels of the building. If I planned to host a secret meeting, I figured that may be the spot to choose. I descended the stairs, pressing all my weight onto the balls of my feet. Stealth.

At the bottom of the staircase, I paused to listen. Ever so faintly, the drone of a human voice ebbed through the stony silence. I was close. About fifteen yards along, the passage swung sharply to the right. I stopped at the corner and craned my head around. The voice now seemed louder, and it had a friend.

Halfway down the corridor, a faint glow lit the tiles in front of a large double door. This would be it. I scanned the space, watching for a guard or lookout. Nothing, but there was plenty of darkness offering concealment to anyone wanting to go unnoticed.

Silently, I slunk from shadow to shadow, easing my way along.

A short time later, my back pressed against the wall, I scrutinized the shadows. Still nothing. From my new position, the voices seemed louder. The conversation was intense, but incomprehensible. Clearly, I'd need to be directly outside the doorway. Risky, but I had no choice. I patted my pocket. I was unarmed, but my cell phone provided some reassurance. I had both Faez and Jabir's numbers on speed dial in case things went pear-shaped.

Several seconds and ten steps later, I pressed my ear to the door. What had been the murmur of male voices now became distinguishable. Then one voice rose above the others, speaking with authority and direction. The others faded to silence; possibly respect. Surprisingly, the voice giving the orders belonged to a woman.

Zafina Faez.

"There is nothing that requires us to slow down or postpone our plans. We knew there would be challenges and we've prepared for them. Your reluctance is unimpressive. Both Rahmat and our chairman will be displeased. We will approve the next stage, and that is the end of the matter."

My head spun, a kaleidoscope of misinformation. How could

we have missed this? How could Faez have underestimated his daughter's acumen and intentions? Pressed by my weight of thought, I nearly failed to notice the sound of footsteps from within the room heading toward me. I'd only just slipped back into the shadows when the door swung open.

I counted eight people leaving the room. Zafina Faez led the way. Everyone else was male, each one recognizable from the earlier ceremony. The last figure through the doorway stopped. He surveyed the corridor before turning back to close the door. In the glow emanating from the chamber, his features were clear.

Ahmed Faez.

Opportunity had arrived.

I'd considered how to approach this meeting and had decided a subtle approach would serve me best. In the darkness of the corridor, I changed my mind.

Stepping out of the shadows, I raised my forearm and slammed it into Ahmed's throat, pushing him up against the wall. With the pressure I brought to bear, he couldn't speak or, more to the point, yell out. We waited in that position with Ahmed struggling to break free for fifteen seconds as the last figure in the group rounded the bend in the corridor. An inch between our faces, I smelled his fear. His bulging eyes read like an open book.

As the footsteps receded into the distance, I released my arm and slapped Ahmed hard across the face. Not enough to knock him out, but enough to let him see who was in charge.

"Listen to me Ahmed, it's over. Too many people know about your relationship with Rahmat Beras, including your father. I intend to stop you, your sister and your rich-kid friends before more lives are lost. Do you comprehend that,

235

Ahmed? Do you get it?" The aggression in my words seemed to cut into him like a blade.

"No, no, you have it all wrong, Mr. Sharp. I know who you are, and I'm aware you have a relationship with my father, but you are so wrong. You don't understand," he pleaded.

I'd expected more anger, but you can never predict cowards.

"Then you explain it to me, Ahmed. Tell me why Deagan Jones' boy was kidnapped, tell me why your men in Compass Black came after me, tell be why you blew…"

"No, I didn't do any of that. I will explain."

"You may not have done those things yourself, but you authorized them, sanctioned them. Your father has proof, and I've seen you here."

As I spoke, I grabbed his robe and twisted it around his neck. I needed him to talk now. Later, he'd use his money to buy his way out. I wasn't going to leave him that option.

Ahmed attempted to speak, his voice strained and laboring.

"Please, you must listen. The plan, *Iyku Balw*… I've only just found out… my father… twenty-four…"

The gunshot rang out like a cannon. I flinched for a fraction of a second before noticing the red spot appear between Ahmed Faez's eyes. It welled in depth, weeping a crimson stain across the young man's cheeks. Slowly Kalid Amir Faez's only son slid down the wall onto his father's expensive tiled floor.

A second shot penetrated the stonework just where Ahmed had been standing, sending shards of stone in all directions, including my face. I didn't need another warning. I dove for the shadows, rolling away from the light of the door as I hit the floor. Another shot echoed down the hall. The tiles near my right ear shattered, piercing my neck.

I kept rolling.

With no weapon at hand and my cell phone now a mythical protection, I slithered as far into the darkness as I could. This wouldn't end well… at least for me.

More shots thundered down the passageway. Although protected to a degree by the shadows, Ahmed's killer would eventually get lucky, and a bullet would find me. It was a simple process of elimination.

Suddenly, out of nowhere, the volume of gunfire doubled in intensity. It was as if there was a second gunman.

Whatever slim chance I'd had, just evaporated.

The cacophony of noise rose. I pressed myself onto the floor, attempting to slide my way toward the bend in the corridor. If I didn't cop a direct hit, a ricochet was bound to get me.

I glanced backward toward the meeting room, still casting a light across the passageway. A moving figure in a white robe stole across the doorway. He'd been stalking the shadows of the opposite wall, but the glow momentarily lit up his features.

Jabir.

At least now, the good guys had a weapon. My hope disintegrated as Jabir raised his weapon, pointed it directly at me, and fired.

Shit.

The round missed. I slithered further along the hallway, waiting for the next shot. Nothing made sense. If Jabir was shooting at me, who was the other guy with the gun? Which one of them had shot Ahmed Faez?

The rounds grew closer, tiles smashed around me like a porcelain battlefield. I'd just decided to stand up and bolt for it when a shot rang out inches from my ear. I looked up to see another swirling white robe in the shadows. A firm hand gripped my arm and yanked me forward. The man in the robe fired a second round over my shoulder and down the corridor.

As I stumbled under his grip, the figure half turned to me. "Come on, Mr. Sharp, we've got to get you the hell out of here."

Chapter 38

We sprinted down the passageway and scrambled up the stone steps to the ground floor. Bullets ricocheted around us, but the darkness offered some protection. There would be time to figure out exactly what had just happened, but right now, survival was more important.

"There's a helicopter on the pad. I can fly it, but we won't make it without some cover. It may well be an opportunity for you to put your renowned skills as a marksman into practice, Mr. Sharp."

As he spoke, my new friend fired off another couple of rounds, attempting to keep some distance between Jabir and us.

"Not a problem," I replied, "but I'm not leaving this island without Cetia Forez."

Still running and breathing hard, the robed man responded.

"That's been taken care of. Ms. Forez left the island forty minutes ago."

Who the hell was this guy?

We broke through a pair of large double doors onto the rear patio that led to the landing pad. As the doors closed behind us, the pane in one of them exploded, spraying glass all over our backs.

Jabir was too close.

We scrambled down a final flight of steps to the pad. The same helicopter that Tia and I had shared a ride with Faez on the way over stood stationary. Fortunately, it also stood unguarded.

"Give me your gun," I yelled, "then go get the damn thing started. I'll keep Faez's man at bay until we're ready to leave. We don't need him taking potshots at the helo before we get off the ground."

I preferred giving orders to receiving them.

My companion scampered off to the chopper. I turned my attention to Jabir. As I pivoted, the wall beside me sprayed stone particles into the air. This was becoming habit forming.

I got one round off before diving behind the wall. When I stuck my head up, another round landed dangerously close. Jabir appeared at the top of the steps. Although it was dark, this area remained reasonably well lit by spotlights. For a split-second Jabir glanced in my direction, assessing the success of his last shot. He then turned his weapon towards the chopper.

I didn't wait. Despite the light revealing only a fraction of his torso, I fired. The thing about firing an unfamiliar weapon is the necessity to account for its foibles. My shot veered wide. Half expecting a negative result, I fired second and third shots in quick succession.

The red splotch on Jabir's shoulder spread rapidly, even before he dropped his weapon. That was all I needed. As I dashed for the chopper, the blades slowly began to spin. I yanked open the passenger door and climbed in just as the bird started lifting off.

Twenty feet off the ground, I looked down. Jabir was made of tough stuff. He'd picked up the gun with his other hand

and continued to fire. As we rose, I heaved the window ajar and got off two shots. I heard his round tear into the metal above my head as I saw mine hit his thigh. He went down again.

My satisfaction was short-lived as the chopper's engine began to cough and splutter.

"Your friend has done some damage. I don't know whether he's hit the engine, the fuel line or something else," said the robed man. "Either way, I'm not putting her down unless she falls out of the sky."

It dawned on me that for the second occasion in recent weeks, I'd hitched a helicopter ride under a barrage of firepower. It was a habit I intended to break.

My pilot struggled with the controls as the pitch of the engine oscillated wildly. Whenever we appeared to gain some height, we'd lose it almost immediately. All too aware that there was a conversation to be had, now was not the time. Whoever this guy was, he'd just done me an enormous favor.

Eventually, the helo settled down.

"I'm pretty sure the main damage is to the fuel line. According to the gauge, we're going through way too much gas. If the Gods stay on our side, I reckon we'll make Yanbu."

"Whose Gods?" I asked.

We flew into the darkness.

"So, you are?"

"Fair question Mr. Sharp. My name is Trent Crais. I'm a special agent from HSI."

"HSI?" I asked.

"Homeland Security Investigations. I work out of the Dhahran office."

"I'm thinking you weren't on that island as one of the Faez

241

family's wedding guests."

"That's a yes and no. I was invited by Ahmed Faez. We've been in touch for a while. Ahmed indicated he was in fear of his life, hence my presence. Sadly, I failed to protect him. That will stick in my gut for a long time."

"Did Kalid Amir Faez know who you were, and that you'd be there?" I asked.

"Ahmed had told his father he'd arranged his own security. The old man wasn't pleased."

"That would explain the look on his face when he saw you after the ceremony."

"Yeah, Ahmed had been instructed to bring no outsiders."

"How did you get Cetia off the island?"

"One of our agency choppers. We spun a yarn that she needed to return to Riyadh due to some technical problems with the upcoming show."

"Faez knew?"

"Kind of, she told him as she was leaving. He wasn't keen, but he didn't try to stop her."

"Okay," I said. "Let's take a step back. There's a lot going on in my head right now. Nothing seems to be panning out as I expected, including both your presence and the fact that the good guy's bodyguard killed the good guy's son and then attempted to kill me."

"I guess it depends on your definition of 'good guy.'"

I figured we were ten minutes out from an unpredictable reception in Yanbu, so I needed as much information out of this man as I could get, as fast as I could get it.

"You said you'd been talking to Ahmed Faez. What were you talking about?"

"He approached us. HSI keeps tabs on the oil and gas

business. It's in our country's interest. Ahmed thought there were some unusual discrepancies within the family company. When he'd brought it up with his father, he'd been dismissed."

"What kind of discrepancies?"

"Money going where it shouldn't. Mostly into the bank account of one Rahmat Beras. He didn't understand. Beras had been an old college chum of Ahmed's, but they hadn't talked in years."

"Interesting take on the situation," I replied. "Did Ahmed tell you if he'd discussed the situation with anyone else within the organization?"

"He'd spoken with his sister. Apparently, she basically shut him down as well. She said there would be reasonable explanations for everything, and they'd look at it all later."

"He didn't accept that?"

"He did… until the assault on the Reardon oil line. Then he came to us."

"What made him think that the attack was related to his family's company?" I inquired.

"One of the discrepancies he discovered was encrypted receipts totaling several million dollars. They were scattered between companies whose expertise involved underwater demolition."

"A company whose entire energy holdings are based around onshore oil production should have no need for that type of expertise. So, when he found out about the Reardon attack, he did the sums?"

"That appears to be the case."

I drew a deep breath. Greatrex, Reardon and I had this completely ass about.

I turned to Crais. "So, when Jack Greatrex, Jim Reardon

and I came on the scene, what were your thoughts? Did you think of giving us a heads up?"

"We thought about it. In fact, it was discussed at higher levels within Homeland than I have access to. They decided to let it play out and see what a rogue outsider could uncover."

"The result being, a man who appears to be an innocent informant is dead, an international singing star is whisked away in the middle of the night to avoid an incident, and I'm nearly killed. You're not really a compassionate lot, are you?"

"Hold your horses for one second." For the first time, Trent Crais' voice held an angry edge. "I didn't make those decisions, and to be honest, I didn't agree with them. Too many people were becoming exposed. Remember, I'm the asshole that dragged you out of this alive."

"Point taken, and thank you."

"My pleasure. These days I spend too much time behind a desk. I'm gutted we lost Ahmed Faez, but to be frank, I didn't mind getting a chance to get out and about and play cowboy. What we have to do, Mr. Sharp, Nicholas, is make it through this. I'm thinking they're not just going to let you fly off into the distance."

"Then I'd better get busy," I replied, pulling my cell out of my pocket and pressing dial.

"Jack."

"Nicholas, what's happening? We've had no word from you."

"Jack, there's a lot to tell you, but not now. Grab Reardon and that jet of his and fly to Prince Abdul Mohsin Bin Abdulaziz Airport in Yanbu."

"Now?"

"Yes now. Things are about to become very hot for us in

Riyadh, in fact, anywhere in Saudi Arabia."

"What have you done, Nicholas?"

"I haven't done anything yet, but I'm sure as hell going to."

I paused for a moment. My trust in Jack Greatrex was eternal and unlimited, but Jim Reardon was another matter. Reardon had led Greatrex and me straight into the hornet's nest. Whether this was accidental or intentional was the billion-dollar question. My gut said Reardon was all right, but I'd figured Kahlid Amir Faez to be on the right side of this too.

"Jack, keep an eye on Reardon. I think he's okay, but we need to be certain."

"What about Ahmed Faez? Has he fessed up to his plans?"

"That's the thing. It wasn't his plan at all, it never was. His sister Zafina is working the room here and judging from the last hour of my life, I believe Faez senior is backing the whole operation, and right now he doesn't like me much. Essentially... we've been played."

Chapter 39

Special Agent Crais received permission to touch down in the private jet area of the airport. Touchdown was probably an exaggeration. Our wheels slammed down onto the tarmac with such force I thought the undercarriage would break apart.

"Sorry about that. I'm a bit rusty."

We climbed out. The stench of diesel filled my nostrils. I glanced up. A steady flow of liquid flowed out from the tank near the rotor.

"Aviation turbine fuel," announced Crais as he appeared next to me. "That leak is ferocious. We should get out of here."

"No," I responded. "Let's do the opposite. Call the airport emergency services. Get them over here."

"There'll be questions," said Crais.

"I don't care about the questions," I responded. "I reckon we've got about ninety minutes to kill here before our ride arrives. What better way to do it than in the company of police and fire personnel?"

"You make a good point."

"What about your people, the HSI crew? What can they do to help?"

"Not that much, I'm afraid," replied Crais. "There's not a lot of us in Saudi. Our function here is primarily to monitor, investigate, and report. We're not equipped for covert operations at a moment's notice. The fact we got Ms. Forez out in a hurry was difficult enough to arrange."

Crais spoke into his cell, reporting our condition. Almost instantly, sirens wailed, and lights flashed through the darkness as rescue teams sped to our aid.

"Where is Cetia?"

"She's been taken out of the country. We've also made arrangements for her band and tech crew to be lifted out of Riyadh."

"So, you're not taking any chances?"

"Lesson learned," replied Crais, his eyebrows furrowed in concern.

The next hour rushed by as we responded to a barrage of questions from several uniformed emergency services people.

"Where were you?"

"Was the tank full when you took off?"

"What is your business in Saudi Arabia?"

Foam was poured over the top of the helicopter in a bid to suppress the possibility of fire. Probably wise; there were some pretty expensive aircraft in the neighborhood.

"How do you believe the leak originated?"

"A bird strike," replied Crais.

Bit by bit, the urgency of the situation diminished as the crews realized a potential blaze had been averted. We'd been held a safe distance back from the chopper but were still in clear view of it.

I glanced at my watch.

"If Greatrex and Reardon got their act together quickly,

247

they should be arriving sometime in the next thirty minutes," I said to Crais.

"I've gotta say I'll be a happier man when we get you and your friends out of the country," he replied. "Kalid Amir Faez will have a big reach, especially in this region. The Faez family is local royalty."

"We've just got to drag this out a little longer," I suggested.

No sooner had the words left my mouth than a short, slightly unkempt Saudi officer in a crumpled shirt appear at our sides. His hair looked like it hadn't seen a comb in a month.

"Mr. Crais, Mr. Sharp?"

"Yes," we both responded.

"My name is Hafeez, Airport Police Investigations."

Crais raised an eyebrow.

"You two seem to have been fortunate to escape this situation unscathed," Officer Hafeez observed.

"Yes, we were," I answered.

He continued.

"Bird strikes are quite rare in these parts, although they are more frequent when taking off and landing. My officers tell me that you had just taken off from the island of Maladh when the incident happened?"

"That's correct," said Crais.

"It didn't occur to you to perform an emergency landing back on the island immediately?"

"We were confident of making the mainland," replied Crais.

Hafeez looked over at the helicopter.

"They must have been pretty big birds," he said.

"What makes you say that?" I asked.

"Well, I imagine it would take a strong beast, perhaps even

248

raptor size, to carry a weapon that could make those bullet holes."

Great. The 'Columbo' of the Yanbu International Airport Police.

I glanced back at the helicopter. Now that the danger had passed, the foam suppressant was slowly falling away, gradually exposing the perforations to an eagle eye.

"Gentleman, there are many aspects to this situation that appear abnormal. For instance, you're departing from an island owned by Kalid Amir Faez, in his helicopter, yet neither of you are employees of either Mr. Faez or his company."

I thought it wise to remain silent.

"There are bullet holes in the tank and on the fuselage of the aircraft, yet you claim to have been struck by birds. I think it is best that we have a conversation back in my office. I've put in a phone call to Kalid Amir Faez, I'm sure he'll be able to clarify the situation."

The officer motioned an arm towards two young and attentive airport police officers standing nearby.

"No," said Trent Crais.

"I beg your pardon."

"With due respect, Officer Hafeez, that will not be happening," Crais insisted.

For a moment, Officer Hafeez looked slightly dumbfounded. As tattered as he appeared, he probably wasn't used to his commands being disobeyed.

"I'm afraid this is not an offer, Mr. Crais, it's a directive."

Both men locked gazes, assessing the situation.

"Officer, I'm about to reach into my pocket to retrieve some identification. If I try to grab anything else, your men over there can shoot me dead where I stand. All right?"

Hafeez glanced over at his men and nodded. They both tensed and placed a hand on their service weapons. The policeman looked intrigued.

"Please do so carefully, Mr. Crais."

Crais reached into his jacket pocket and produced a wallet. It wasn't the one with his pilot's license in it that he'd shown the authorities when they first arrived. He pulled out a plastic identification card and held it up for Hafeez to see.

The policeman nodded to one of his men, who took the card from Crais. He passed it to Officer Hafeez before returning to guard duty next to his colleague.

A thick tension hung in the air.

Hafeez studied the card on both sides.

"US Homeland Security, Investigations. The situation grows increasingly complex," he said.

"It does," agreed Crais.

More silence.

"Could I suggest you and I take a short walk together, Officer Hafeez?" suggested Special Agent Crais.

"I believe that appropriate," agreed the policeman.

For a third time, he nodded to his two men, both of whom now focused their attention solely on me. Crais stepped forward and he and Hafeez strolled off across the floodlit tarmac side by side.

When they returned, neither man was smiling, but at least Trent Crais wasn't in handcuffs. Crais marched straight up to me while Hafeez walked over to speak to his men.

"I hope your friends are running on time," Crais began. "We have exactly thirty minutes to be out of here and, in your case, out of the county, before our world falls apart."

"How the hell did you manage that?"

"I pointed out to Officer Hafeez that keeping us here would lay a host of problems at his feet. Not only would there be the international ramifications of the issue with Homeland Security, but in fact all the damning evidence at his disposal is pointing toward the hero of the Al Madinah Province, Kalid Amir Faez."

"Forensics," I said.

"Exactly," replied Crais. "Once they start pulling bullets out of that aircraft, they'll find the ammunition came from a weapon belonging to Faez's own bodyguard. While there is a chance Faez may claim your friend Jabir was only protecting his boss, I doubt that Faez would want the authorities examining his activities too closely at the moment. Especially considering what is about to become public knowledge… the tragic death of his son."

"Particularly given that an autopsy would reveal the gun that killed Ahmed was the same weapon that fired on our helo. Good work."

Crais smiled.

"The deal was sealed when I mentioned that Faez would have demanded our arrest by now if he wanted to make a big fuss. I suggested the smart move would be to read between the lines and take the silence as a message from Faez that the big man preferred the whole affair just to go away. Hafeez is a clever operator. He comprehends the issues for all involved. Hence the thirty-minute window. After that, it's a different story."

"What about Hafeez's men?" I asked.

"He said they'd stay loyal to him and follow through as instructed, for the good of the province…and maybe a little bonus."

"Remind me never to underestimate you, Special Agent Crais."

"Just Trent, although some of my close friends do call me Cowboy."

"I'm beginning to see why," I replied.

Each second felt like a minute. Everything depended on how quickly Greatrex had contacted Reardon, and if Jim Reardon would respond not only to the request of making a dash across the country, but to do it with extreme haste. I tried to get the big fella on my cell, but there was no reply. That could mean he was out of range… or in the air.

Neither Crais nor I doubted that Officer Hafeez would be as good as his word. His two offsiders hadn't taken their eyes off us, hands still firmly planted on their weapons. Hafeez had retreated to his car, putting some attempt of distance between us and him. Life in a Saudi jail hung over our future like a guillotine waiting to drop.

Ten minutes before the deadline, one of the officers responded to a call on his radio. A minute later, both men turned and climbed into their boss's vehicle. They sped off back to the terminal.

Crais and I just looked at each other?

"What do they know that we don't?" I asked.

Crais shrugged his shoulders.

Right on cue, Jim Reardon's Gulfstream G800 taxied into view, the Reardon Oil logo glistening in the taxiway lights.

Thank God.

Almost immediately after the plane pulled to a stop, the door popped open assuming its alternate role as the aircraft's stairs. I figured there'd be no refueling with everyone under instructions just to get us out of there as fast as possible.

We scurried over to the bottom of the stairs. Greatrex stood in the doorway waving us on board.

We'd made it halfway up the stairway before things went to hell.

"Mr. Sharp, Special Agent Crais, please stop."

"Keep going, don't look around," I said to Crais. Whoever he is, if he wants us, he'll have to come and get us.

"Police, stop," the voice more urgent.

By the time we reached the doorway, Greatrex had disappeared. I spun to find a solidly built man, mid-forties, with no uniform, midway up the stairs waving an ID card. Crais and I kept moving. It would be harder to drag two people off an aircraft than shove them down some stairs.

About ten feet along the aisle, Crais ahead of me, I pivoted to face the intruder.

Three large men, dressed in black suits and dark shirts, gathered behind the first man.

Mr. Sharp, Special Agent Crais, I'm Tariq Yusuf of the General Intelligence Presidency. I'm afraid you'll need to return to the terminal building.

"That's all been sorted, Agent Yusuf. If you speak to your colleague, Officer Hafeez, he'll tell you we've been cleared to depart Saudi Arabia," I said.

"I can verify that," added Crais, holding up his own ID card.

"May I help you gentlemen?" came a voice from behind Crais. "I'm Jim Reardon and this is my plane."

I twisted to catch a look at Reardon. His jaw set firm, he appeared to be in his best boardroom 'I'll suffer no bullshit' frame of mind.

"We know who you are, Mr. Reardon, but I'm afraid your presence has no bearing on this matter," replied Yusuf, who then turned back to me. "Mr. Sharp, you seem to misunderstand. Officer Hafeez is in charge of the investigation team here at the airport. My agency reports directly to the King. Officer Hafeez's decision has been overruled."

Yusuf carried a smugness in his condescending smirk.

"Time is pressing Agent Yusuf. Can't you ask the questions you need to here?" I suggested.

"I'm sorry Mr. Sharp. That would be inappropriate. You and Special Agent Crais will need to come with us."

Behind me, Crais chipped in. "Agent Yusuf, may we examine your identity card please, and those of your colleagues? I'm more than happy for you to check my own credentials." Crais waved his ID card in the air.

"You can examine my credentials at your leisure in the terminal office," Yusuf insisted, the smirk replaced by an underlying frustration in his tone.

There is a moment in any confrontation where a professional can read another professional's body language. It's human nature - when preparing an assault, even the experienced tense up. That's exactly what I noted in the three men behind Tariq Yusuf. They retracted their arms closer to their bodies, splayed their finger as though ready to reach for a…

"Gun," I yelled, "down."

In the same instant, all three men drew their weapons, each choosing a pre-prepared target. The first man trained his weapon on me, the next on Crais, the final on Reardon.

We froze.

"It's a shame, Mr. Reardon. You truly didn't have to die

today, but Mr. Sharp and Special Agent Crais lacked the sense to leave gracefully. And by the way, Crais, your gut spoke the truth. I'm certainly no representative of the GIP. I believe Mr. Sharp has had dealings with my organization before."

"Don't tell me," I said, "Compass fucking Black."

"At your disservice," replied Yusuf, the smirk returned. "And we won't be proceeding to the terminal as you may well have gathered, although to be honest, terminal is still an appropriate description of where you are going. Now, where is Mr. Grea…"

Within the confines of the cabin, the shots were deafening. The man at the back of the group crumpled, the next one in line a second later. In a natural reaction, Yusuf swung around to his men just as Greatrex threw a pistol in my direction. I caught it and dived for the cover of the oversized seat next to me. The man behind Yusuf hadn't turned. He fired straight at me, but my sudden movement caused him to miss.

"Shit, I'm hit," yelled Crais, who'd been directly behind me.

I came out low, my head an inch from the floor. Yusuf had his gun out and aimed toward the front of the aircraft where Greatrex had been a moment earlier. I knew the big fella would be dodging around. Evasive maneuvers 101. No further grunt from behind told me the Compass Black operative had missed his mark. Yusuf should have looked down, expecting my move. He hadn't, so I shot him in the gut.

He doubled forward but didn't give up. The man behind him got a round off over Yusuf's head. The bullet hit the floor where I'd just been positioned. By then I'd reached the opposite side of the plane and come up behind a seat. The man didn't see it coming as my headshot took him down.

Yusuf remained standing, but only just. Clearly in extreme pain and leaning on the back of a seat, his gun hand trembled, but he was so close to Trent Crais that he couldn't miss.

"All of you drop your guns or the agent dies," he yelled.

If Greatrex and I dropped our weapons, we'd all die. The big fella would know that, too.

Crais lay struggling on the floor, clutching his bloodied side.

"All right, don't shoot. I'll drop it," I said, throwing my weapon on the seat, out of reach.

For the first time in the whole confrontation, I heard Greatrex's voice.

"Take it easy asshole, I'm putting mine down too."

I didn't turn around.

Yusuf stared down the aisle at Greatrex. The big fella would be making a show of dropping his gun. Dragging it out, the reluctant surrender. Clutching his gut with left hand, Yusuf rose straight, gun now aimed squarely at Greatrex, his smirk evident through grimaced teeth.

When the man behind Yusuf had gone down, he'd flung his weapon in the air. It rested on the floor just in front of Yusuf, out of my reach. I looked down at Trent Crais. He was barely conscious, but his eyes didn't leave the Compass Black leader. Suddenly, despite his own pain, he rolled onto his wounded side, grunting in agony.

"Holy shit."

Yusuf knew better than to be distracted. Now that I was disarmed, he retained his focus on Greatrex.

Crais grunted again, this time stretching himself out length-ways. I couldn't imagine the pain his movement caused. But it also allowed his foot to get close enough to the discarded weapon to kick it toward me.

A second later, Tariq Yusuf of Compass Black died, his beloved smirk morphing into a death mask.

Chapter 40

"We'd better get out of here."

I kneeled beside Trent Crais. He lay on his back on the floor between seats. Reardon had immediately gone to the washroom and grabbed some towels to slow the bleeding. He also returned with a first aid kit. I pressed the towels down on the HSI agent's wound.

"Can this thing fly?" asked Greatrex. "Bullets leave holes, you know."

"And not just in the fuselage," muttered Crais.

"I'll get the pilot to check the plane out… quickly," said Reardon. He'd coped with the extreme events of the last few minutes pretty well, holding his composure.

"How will the pilot react?" I asked. "There's been gunfire in the cabin, and now we have a few extra passengers."

"So far he's done the right thing," said Reardon. "Even pilots of private jets are trained to remain locked in the cockpit at any sign of disturbance in the cabin. I'm pretty sure he won't let us down. He's ex-US Air Force and seen quite a bit."

"What about the bodies?" asked Greatrex.

"I figure if we just throw them out the door here, we'll create issues with the authorities that will escalate matters," I replied. "We'll have to keep them onboard. Perhaps we can stow them out of sight in case we're inspected at the other end."

"Speaking of which, where is the other end?" asked Greatrex.

"Let's head back to Houston, the good old US of A. I've got a stack of news to tell you, but we should focus on getting off the ground first, while we can."

A short time later, the pilot had inspected the plane and given it a clean bill of health. The same couldn't be said for the four corpses stowed under the floor of the baggage compartment. To his credit, our pilot remained quiet, seeking Reardon's reassurance before completing his pre-flight check. Sometimes it took a veteran to recognize a veteran. Judging by his calm demeanor, the pilot had 'warrior' written all over him.

On closer inspection, Trent Crais' injury didn't seem as bad as I'd originally thought.

"How are you feeling, Cowboy?" I asked.

"It probably looks worse and feels worse than it is. Don't reckon I'm ready for the big range in the sky just yet."

Crais had elected to stick with us, turning down the offer of a visit to the local hospital as a needless complication. He was one tough operator.

Extremely relieved to be cleared for take-off, Reardon, Greatrex and I remained silent until we reached cruising altitude. We'd managed to get Crais semi-upright in the chair next to me. The bleeding had slowed considerably. Greatrex and Reardon sat opposite.

"So…" I began. "First up, I'd like you to meet Special Agent Trent Crais from Homeland Security Investigations. To put it simply, Trent just saved my ass. Now I have a story to tell you both, and it ends with us being the mugs in someone else's very elaborate game."

Thirty minutes after that, as the Gulfstream G800 purred through the night sky, Greatrex and Reardon were up to date.

"Unbelievable," observed Greatrex.

"The trouble is, Faez's story was too believable," I responded. "And we fell for it."

"I can't believe I didn't see through the man. I've known him, on and off, for years. I figured he was one of the few straight shooters in the business," said Jim Reardon.

"I guess it depends on who he's shooting at," I replied.

"I'm sorry I led you into this, Nicholas and Jack. You trusted Faez on my say so."

"No point in recriminations," I responded. "You were as fooled as we were. Now there's a lot to do, and a heap to figure out. And by the way, I haven't mentioned it, but I'm certain we're chasing a twenty-four-hour deadline."

"Holy crap," said Greatrex. "What makes you say that?"

"Ahmed Faez's final words, and I quote: *'Please, you must listen. The plan, Iyku Balw... I've only just found out...my father... twenty-four...'*."

"You're thinking he was going to say twenty-four hours? That's logical. But what in hell is Iyku Balw?" asked Greatrex.

"I can translate the words, but I can't tell you what they mean," said Crais. He'd been dozing, but obviously keeping an ear open to our conversation.

"Go on," I said, surprised he remained lucid.

Crais wriggled in his seat, trying to get more comfortable.

"I've picked up a fair bit of the local lingo in my time in Saudi. 'Iyku' is the term for 'echo', while 'balw' denotes the color blue. But don't ask me what in God's name that all means."

"Echo blue. Ideas, anyone?" I asked.

Unsurprisingly, stony silence.

"I have no clue what it means," said Reardon, "but I'm having a great deal of difficulty comprehending that Kalid Amir Faez would order the execution of his own son to keep some nefarious plan hidden. What sort of man would do that?"

"We can't be sure he did order Ahmed's murder," I replied. "There's a strong chance that Jabir took the initiative on his own. It probably depends on how far he'd been brought into the plan. If Ahmed's death was Jabir's gambit, it's feasible he planned to frame me."

"So, the justification for getting rid of you was not only because you knew there was an operation underway, but also because you were a witness to a murder?" asked Greatrex.

"That's one scenario," I replied. "The trouble is, even though we have a timeline, we don't have any real idea what this plan involves, nor where it will take place."

I turned back to Crais.

"You're probably thinking it's time for me to call in the troops," he said.

"I sure am Cowboy."

"Mr. Reardon, do you have Wi-Fi on this fancy stagecoach of yours?"

"Certainly."

Crais nodded toward to his left coat pocket. "Nicholas, can you grab my cell out of my jacket, please? I've got some calls to make."

We spread out across the cabin to give the agent some privacy.

Twenty minutes later, we repositioned ourselves around

Crais, awaiting the news.

"It's not great," he began. "Those good-for-nothing pen pushers who call the shots in my department tell me there's not enough evidence to act on. They'll monitor, undertake discreet investigations, and keep me informed."

"A dead man, an attempted murder, an injured government agent, a kidnapping and four corpses isn't enough evidence?" asked the big fella.

"My people say it's only our, well really, Nicholas' and my words on how this went down. You need to know I'd been basically put out to pasture in Dhahran. I'm not held in particularly high esteem by my colleagues."

"I figure there's more to it than that, Cowboy. The powers that be don't want to tackle a powerful Saudi oil baron without definitive proof of a crime against the US. Without doubt, it's all about the oil," I said.

"I'm afraid Nicholas is stating the truth," added Reardon. "Oil, particularly Saudi oil, speaks volumes."

"Well, that leaves us nowhere," said Greatrex.

"Not completely," began Crais. "We have some intel, and now that they're monitoring the players involved, I'm hoping we get more."

Crais coughed uncomfortably between sentences. A reminder that despite our patch-up job, he needed professional medical care as soon as possible.

"Okay," he continued, "so, the first thing we've uncovered is that Kalid Amir Faez's private jet took off from Prince Abdul Mohsin Bin Abdulaziz International Airport thirty minutes behind us."

"Do we know where they're headed? I assume they lodged a flight plan," I said.

"That's a negative. No word on destination, no flight plan. I imagine they lodged some local riyal or US dollars in the right hands instead."

"Who boarded the plane?" asked Greatrex.

"Definitely Faez, and our sources say his daughter Zafina accompanied him," replied the agent.

"Let's take a moment to think this through," I suggested. "For all we know, we're heading in completely the wrong direction. That said, we've got to get Cowboy here to a hospital anyway."

I saw little advantage in turning around or just dropping down to the next friendly airport.

"Jim, if you were going to wreak havoc on the offshore oil industry, what would be your prime target?"

Reardon considered the question, pausing to look out the plane window, as though the clouds would help him find the correct answer.

Eventually.

"There's no clear response to that. The biggest offshore fields are in the Persian Gulf. Their destruction would have the most significant economic effect on the industry. On the other hand, there are valuable fields all over the world. If you wanted your greatest impact to be felt in the United States, then the Gulf of Mexico would be your target. The Gulf fields produce around fifteen percent of the US's oil and after the Deepwater Horizon fiasco in 2010, the American sensibilities to oil spills are high."

"So, we're heading back toward Houston," said Greatrex. "At least that's at the front fence of the Gulf fields. If that's Faez and Rahmat Beras' chosen target, we'll be in the neighborhood."

"That's a big 'if,'" Crais added. "If they choose the Persian Gulf fields, we'll be on the other side of the world."

I looked at the three men. We were playing a guessing game in a situation where guessing wasn't good enough.

"There's one other significant factor," I began.

"The boy," said Greatrex.

"Exactly. Deagan Jones' son has his life on the line here. That's if they haven't already killed him after our incursion to Saudi Arabia," I responded.

Greatrex paused for a moment, then looked at me thoughtfully, his lips pursed.

"No, I don't think they've killed Joshua. They'll keep him alive until this is over, then they'll murder him without hesitation."

"So, where is he?" I asked.

"I'm almost certain that Rahmat Beras will keep Joshua Jones close at hand. In fact, whatever their plan is, I'm sure Beras will have Josh with him, in case it all goes wrong. The more I think about it, the more it rings true. I'd almost stake my life on it," said Greatrex.

The big fella's words were not spoken lightly, yet neither were mine.

"If that's the case, it's not your life we're placing at stake here, Jack. It's the life of a fourteen-year-old boy."

Ten minutes later, Trent Crais' cell buzzed.

"Yup, sure, I got it. Thanks."

He turned to us.

"Kalid Amir Faez owns a super-sized, high-spec, private yacht. And it's just been sighted in port preparing to depart."

"Which port?" I asked.

264

The agent stared at me momentarily.
"Havana, Cuba."

Chapter 41

RAHMAT BERAS

Rahmat Beras looked into the night sky. His plane may not have been quite as 'state-of-the-art' as Kalid Amir Faez's, but it did the job. Beras slithered his lean body back in his seat and sipped a Cîroc vodka. It seemed the Russians couldn't do anything right these days. They didn't even make the best vodka anymore.

Beras reflected on his relationship with Kalid Amir Faez. At the beginning, he'd needed the old man's support to break out of the middle class cycle he'd been born into. Making friends with Ahmed Faez at Harvard had been a considered strategy. He knew Ahmed came from oil money and that the boy's financial future was secured. Beras wanted to be part of that. He found the friendship easy. Ahmed was a likable guy, but it quickly became evident he didn't have the driven ambition to grow his family's fortune. Still, they'd enjoyed a measure of fun together, sharing some high-quality recreational drugs… and some high-quality girls.

The father, Kalid, was a different beast. Beras immediately hit it off with the old man when he'd joined Ahmed on holidays back in the Middle East. Many evenings Beras sat with the elder Faez on the patio overlooking the Red Sea on the family's island, Maladh. Beras shared his plans of using the lucrative healthcare industry not to heal the sick, but to rake in billions. Faez senior had been impressed and the offer of financial backing followed.

Beras wondered if Kalid Amir Faez saw qualities in him that he wished he'd seen in his son.

The result, of course, was that Rahmat Beras now held considerable wealth, along with the power that accompanied it. At times, Beras surprised himself with his own relentless ambition. No matter the amount of riches and influence he accrued, he wanted more.

The relationship with Faez senior continued long after Beras moved on from Ahmed. Beras was a strategist and a thinker, always ahead of the game, consistently finding ways to accumulate wealth.

When Kalid Amir Faez's wife, Niesha, died, Beras noted a darkness that seemed to stain the old man's soul. His enormous fortune hadn't been enough to fight the disease. That kind of failure, and loss, could damage a man who's grown accustomed to things always going his way. Beras noticed that Faez began making decisions that weren't completely rational. He wanted revenge on the Western world that had promised so much, at least medically, yet delivered so little.

Faez's faith in Rahmat Beras became absolute when he used his power to ensure the doctors treating Faez's wife would never practice again. Of course, Beras knew they were innocent of any wrongdoing, but the medicos became collateral damage to Beras' long-term strategy. For him, any cost to others was the price of doing business.

Beras grew to embrace the need to expand his horizons

beyond the healthcare industry. The energy business held the power of the future in its hands. Oil was at the core of that sector and Kalid Amir Faez was one of the most powerful oil men on the planet. The kind of money Faez dealt with was only a dream, even for the wealthy Rahmat Beras.

Beras wanted in.

When Beras had explained his plan to the old man, sitting on his patio, watching the sun set over the blue waters, he was surprised at the elder's enthusiasm. Niesha loved the island and the beauty of the surrounding sea. She had implored Amir never to embrace offshore exploration because of the environmental risks. They'd no need to, she said. Their wealth was already more than the family could ever spend.

Amir acquiesced to his wife's wishes.

After her death, when Beras presented his plan, Faez saw it as a way to halt offshore drilling permanently. It was clear to him that with Russia struggling in their ability to supply the west with resources, the strategy would add untold wealth to the family's bottom line. He was aware there would be damage, but it would be short term. Neisha would have been pleased.

'*What about these environmentalists?*'   he'd asked Beras. '*They're well organized nowadays. They are also abundantly resourced. Many large corporations are backing them. They are a force to be reckoned with.*'

Then Beras told him about his scheme to infiltrate Crimson Wave, the highest profile of all the activist groups. He would buy his way to their destruction.

'*Rahmat, you are a most dangerously brilliant man. I'm glad we are on the same side.*'

The plane would begin its descent shortly. Beras glanced

over at the boy. He looked restless and defeated, just as his father would be when this was over. What hope would some crackpot environmentalist and his kid have against the resources he'd mustered? The Compass Black man, James Muldoon, sat beside the youngster. Beras wouldn't be overjoyed to end such a young life, but it was simply business after all.

"Gentlemen, if you would put on your seatbelts, it would be appreciated. We'll be landing shortly," boomed the voice over the intercom.

Beras, Muldoon, the boy and the several other Compass Black operatives on board complied. Within the hour, they'd all be joining Kalid Amir Faez on his luxury yacht. Beras was unsure of the old man's state of mind. His son's death had probably hit him hard. Still, it was for the best. That's why Beras had ordered the killing. Jabir had been told that if there was any sign that Ahmed would reveal their plans to Sharp or anybody else, that all concerned parties should be eliminated. The money Beras had paid Jabir over the last few years assured the latter's loyalty beyond question.

Beras had been surprised when Faez said he planned to join him for the climax of the operation. He'd assumed the old man would want to keep his distance. He supposed that with Ahmed's sudden death, which Jabir informed him was at Nicholas Sharp's hand, and the calling off of the wedding celebrations, the oil baron had wanted a personal stake in the proceedings.

Of course, neither he nor Faez could be everywhere, but this is where it would all begin.

Chapter 42

JOSHUA JONES

Joshua Jones was scared, really scared. He loved his father and admired him, but Josh was only a kid. He knew his dad fought against the odds all his life, and most times, beat them. In the navy, and in Crimson Wave, his father kept pushing and risked his own wellbeing over and over, all for the sake of doing the right thing. Josh so desperately wanted to be like him yet sitting on this plane surrounded by all these men, armed men, Josh didn't know what he could do.

At first, he'd figured the guy they called Muldoon was in charge. He seemed to be giving the orders when they'd been in Spain. Josh thought rescue was imminent when he heard shots fired. He figured his rescuers had arrived, but it wasn't to be. Muldoon and his people were too quick on their feet and got him out safely. Josh knew it had been Nicholas Sharp and his friend Greatrex that had attempted to free him. They were like his dad, relentless. As he looked out the window into the dark sky, Josh hoped Sharp had something else up his sleeve, anything at all.

From what Muldoon said to his men after the rescue attempt in Spain, Nicholas Sharp had caused a lot of damage, and they'd lost too many people. Muldoon was furious, raving on about Sharp killing his brother. Josh didn't understand why bad men did bad things and then complained about the consequences.

They weren't like his dad.

The new guy, the one they called Beras, wasn't like his dad either. He scared Josh, big time. He had cold gray eyes, brutal eyes, like the bullies he'd encountered at school, only on steroids. Nobody spoke back to Beras. When he issued orders, his voice was low, unemotional. While others seemed to get angry or frustrated, or perhaps like him, scared, Beras didn't flinch. He didn't seem to have emotion. Was that even possible? Josh worried about his dad and Nicholas Sharp. If they came to get him, Josh decided Beras would show no mercy. Perhaps they shouldn't come. Josh didn't want to die, but he didn't want his dad to die, either.

The plane flew on into the night.

For Josh, the fear lingered.

Chapter 43

ZAFINA FAEZ

Zafina stared into the night. They'd be landing shortly. The last twenty-four hours had been tumultuous. The wedding ceremony, the meeting, then the complications. Zafina was aware Ahmed didn't support their plans. He couldn't even really understand their strategy. She'd explained it to him and brought him along to the meeting so he could see for himself the backing she and her father had mustered. The group comprised the future. Young Saudis who would soon control the oil industry. They were energetic and brave. They saw what needed to be done, marveled at the plan, and came along for the ride. After all, it was in their best interests.

But Ahmed had been a fool. When he became fully aware of the agenda, he spoke up, trying to sway the others away from the plan. It was far too late for that, so Zafina put a stop to it.

When it all began, Zafina had been surprised that the group of testosterone-filled young men would follow a woman. She supposed the combination of their greed and the support of her father had gotten them across the line. Zafina was as strong as her brother was weak. She knew that, and her father knew that. Her strength and guile were the reasons her father asked her to represent the family in the matter.

Last night, things became complicated. Ahmed was killed. Jabir told them Nicholas Sharp was the shooter, and that he'd tried to stop Sharp. Jabir's wounds backed the story, yet Zafina remained uncertain. Aware that ultimately Rahmat Beras was the instigator and mastermind behind the project, she wouldn't have put it past him to arrange Ahmed's execution. Beras didn't tolerate weak links, and he appreciated Ahmed was not the man his father was. Her brother's death would remain a question mark.

Of course, with Ahmed's tragic demise, the wedding celebrations had to be postponed. Abid, her new husband, sympathized, although he didn't understand why Zafina had to rush off to destinations unknown with her father. But Zafina understood where she should be. Since being told of Ahmed's death, her father quickly transcended into a state of shocked silence, communicating at the most minimum levels. She needed to be with him. When he said he wanted to accompany Beras, Zafina recognized the need to be there as well, to ensure success. Too much remained at stake for mistakes or miscommunication to be tolerated.

Zafina understood that Beras wouldn't allow any missteps. She appreciated exactly who he was. They'd been lovers since his days at Harvard with Ahmed. It saddened her that their relationship would cease now she'd married. But business was business. It also saddened her that people had died for their plan to come to fruition, and yet more souls would be lost within the next twenty-four hours, but in their new world, death was the price of success.

Chapter 44

NICHOLAS SHARP

"It's the Gulf of Mexico," I said.

"If they're heading for Havana, damn right," agreed Greatrex.

"We have the where, but we're missing the what and how," said Crais.

"At least we're pointed in the right direction," said Reardon.

It was a relief for us all.

"I reckon we know the how," I began. "Trent, you mentioned that one of the discrepancies that Ahmed Faez uncovered was invoices from companies whose expertise involved underwater demolition."

"Correct."

"So, it's pretty clear that between those invoices and the practice run on your pipeline in Guyana, Jim, plus the assault in the North Sea, that their plan involves underwater sabotage. At least that's a start," I said.

Jim Reardon tilted forward in his seat.

"Nicholas, do you know how many miles of pipeline and how many rigs there are in the Gulf of Mexico?"

I shook my head.

"There are over four thousand oil platforms and more than twenty-six thousand miles of oil and gas pipelines on the seabed."

"Crap," said Greatrex.

"Then knowing the how is meaningless," I began. "Unless we can pinpoint an exact location, we're basically pissing into the wind. We can't just take a boat out into the Gulf and look for suspicious activity. Talk about a needle in the haystack."

"I don't want to rain on your already sodden parade, but there is one thing you haven't considered," said Reardon.

We gazed at the oilman.

"Invoices for millions of dollars of explosives can either buy you a lot of bang, or several separate bangs. Perhaps there are numerous locations. How could we cover that?"

"We can't," I responded. "But what you're suggesting might explain a nagging doubt. I understood the trial run in the waters off Guyana. It's only around the corner geographically, and conditions would be similar to the Gulf. But the strike in the North Sea? It's an entirely dissimilar environment."

"Shit," said Greatrex. "It's not only the Gulf. They're going to attack other geographic locations as well."

We silently considered the prospect for a moment.

"There's always the chance the North Sea assault is unrelated to Faez and Beras' plans," said Crais.

"Do you believe that for a second?" I asked.

"No, but I thought I'd put it on the table," he replied.

I scrutinized the men next to and across from me. The lax shoulders and downward cast eyes told of despondency.

"It's been one step forward, two steps back from the start," I said. "At some point we're going to have to grab the ball and run with it. By the time we land in Houston, we'll have less than twelve hours before any action we take won't matter at all, either to the pipelines or to Joshua Jones."

"Are your people still refusing to act?" Greatrex asked Crais.

"Our evidence trail hasn't changed, so neither has their decision," he replied. "Needless to say, I don't agree with them."

"All right," I said. We'll keep gathering intel from Trent's connections, but won't expect anything else from them, at least for now. I reckon we need to change our perspective and start looking at this from a different angle, and I know just how to do that. Excuse me."

I stood up, walked to the front of the cabin, and placed the phone call I should have made way earlier.

Chapter 45

"We're going in at Scholes International at Galveston," announced Reardon. "The pilot tells me landing will be okay, but he'll have to lighten some weight to meet the take-off margins. That won't be our concern. Scholes has a dual advantage. We'll be closer to the water than Houston and there'll be less scrutiny at a smaller airport."

"Considering our uninvited passengers, that's probably a wise move," Greatrex responded.

"I've also arranged for members of my security team to meet us," said Reardon. "They'll help dispose of the bodies and we'll have more hands available if we need them. By the way, the pilot informs me there's some weather setting in. It may get a little bumpy."

All arrangements in place, and after being bounced around like a feather in the wind, we touched down forty-five minutes later. The pilot taxied to a prearranged spot as far from the terminal as possible. When the door opened, six of Reardon's men were there to meet us, standing in the pouring rain. We waited while they did what they had to do.

I took advantage of the brief down time for a final briefing.

"Trent, thank you for your help, but your job is now to go with a couple of Reardon's team and access the medical attention you need."

"It kills me to agree," he responded, "but then again, it might kill me not to. But I will stay in contact with my people and keep you up to date with any new intel."

"Appreciated," I replied. Shifting my focus to Greatrex and Reardon, I said, "Now we've got to head out on the water. Whatever happens will happen there. Jim, this could get hairy. If you don't want to join us, we'll fully understand."

Reardon regarded me with alien-like bewilderment.

"And miss out on the fun, not a chance. Besides, I figure you could use some oil expertise on hand."

"To state the obvious, our biggest issue is understanding precisely what is going to go down in the next twelve hours," I said.

"I'd give anything to know exactly what 'Echo Blue' means. If it's an operations name, it may have the potential to provide useful direction."

"Perhaps I can help with that."

The deep voice resonated down the aircraft cabin. We all spun around.

"Deagan, I'm glad you could come," I said.

Jones strode towards us and sat down.

"How the hell?" began Greatrex. "I thought you were in FBI custody."

"I was," Deagan smiled. "But apparently Nicholas's friend, a certain General Colin Devlin-Waters, has a fair bit of influence with our federal brothers. I was released an hour ago."

"Your phone call," said Greatrex, smiling.

I nodded.

"Do you know where Josh is?" asked Jones.

"No Deagan, not for sure. I'm sorry. We're still hopeful of finding Josh, but a lot has to come together for us to have a chance. You just mentioned helping with the 'Echo Blue' tag?"

"Yup, I don't know if it's related, but Crimson Wave has a series of code names for potential operations all around the world. It was so we could react quickly to any given environmental incident without being monitored."

"Was Echo Blue one of the code names?" asked Greatrex.

Jones pursed his lips.

"Not strictly, and I've got to tell you this may not be good. We used the term 'echo' attached to any operation that we felt was likely to be replicated in different locations. We'd use it if whaling fleets left numerous ports in different countries simultaneously, and it would have been used if there were nuclear accidents or oil spills in several locations."

"What about the blue part of it?" I asked, afraid of the answer I might hear.

"Look, I'm not sure, but if I were a gambling man, I would say the tag signifies multiple events, all connected to the same matter, in this case, ruptures in undersea pipelines, hence the blue part, are on the verge of happening in numerous distinct locations simultaneously."

"Around the Gulf?" asked Reardon.

"No, Jim, we would have regarded the Gulf as one location in terms of resourcing a response. I suspect Rahmat Beras, in his own demented way, is utilizing our own coding to implicate Crimson Wave. Perhaps he thinks if anyone uncovered the code name, it might be tracked back to us, who knows. It would certainly amuse the smug bastard. I'm fairly sure these ruptures, explosions, call them what you like,

279

are about to take place in oil fields all around the globe."

"Fuck."

Greatrex spoke for all.

"Then we have no chance," said Reardon. The words hung like a death sentence.

"Yeah, we do," I announced. "If Faez and his daughter are flying to Cuba to catch their boat, it will be because they're heading into the Gulf. They're not stupid enough to attack America from her own soil. If they're here, it means their plan begins here. If we stop them, we might stop the whole damn thing."

Thoughtful silence.

"I've got a decent size launch on standby," said Reardon.

"No Jim, we can do better than that," Jones responded. "I've made a call, and I've got a boat and crew. The right boat and the right crew. They're waiting less than a mile from here."

"Well, you are the captain," I replied. "Time is our enemy, gentlemen. Let's get moving."

I turned my attention to Special Agent Trent Caris of the HSI.

"This is where we part ways, Cowboy…"

He wasn't listening. Cell phone to his ear, he was yelling into the device.

"I don't give a rat's ass what you think, you fucking desk jockey. Get your people off their asses and have teams in position ready to act in every offshore oil field on the damn planet…yes, I said every single one, from the Persian Gulf to the North Sea… don't talk to me about strained resources you mother fucker, for once, do what the man in the field is telling you… ask whoever the hell you like, but just do it now."

Crais seemed to take a deep breath before speaking quietly into his cell. "Asshole, do you remember how it looked when people found out we had intelligence about 9/11 and didn't act? Well, once more, this is your moment, and if you don't do as I say, chances are it will be your final moment in government service."

He hung up and threw down the phone.

"Another pen pusher who doesn't get it?" I inquired.

"No, that was the director of the agency in Washington. I may have just resigned."

Chapter 46

We stood in the shelter of a freight warehouse on the dock around the corner from Galveston's main passenger terminal. The rain belted down mercilessly, while the wind howled and screeched through the alleyways between the buildings.

"Great night for a sail," said Greatrex.

"If it's bumpy for us, it'll be worse for Faez coming across from Havana," I replied.

The 'boat' that Deagan Jones had arranged was more like a small ship. I judged it to be around one hundred and seventy feet long. Under the wharf lights, she appeared to have an extensive flat rear deck leading to a bridge about two-thirds of the way along. A raised foredeck extended to the bow. She was painted top deck to waterline in a black, white, and gray camouflage pattern.

Through the deluge, she looked menacing.

"The Torrent," announced Jones, the pride in his voice evident. "She's state-of-the-art, does in excess of thirty knots, can handle almost any weather, and has quite a few tricks up her sleeve. She was designed and built especially for Crimson Wave along with her sistership, 'The Flood Tide'. We keep one in the northern hemisphere and the other in the south. The whalers had gained an operational edge on us. Now, with

282

these two beauties, we're back in with a chance."

"She looks expensive," said Greatrex.

"Over ten million US dollars each. The positive side of having some strong corporate relationships is organizations such as ours have access to more cash resources. In fact, you're standing next to one of our major donors."

Jim Reardon smiled but remained silent.

"Anyway, enough ogling," continued Jones. "We need to make way. Lord knows we're lucky she's spent the last three weeks in Galveston doing some fundraising."

We marched forward as Jones led us out into the rain toward the ship's gangway. A tall figure in wet weather gear appeared as we stepped up onto the deck.

"Nicholas Sharp, Jack Greatrex, this is Captain Vanessa Travers. Vanessa is the Torrent's regular skipper. Vanessa, I believe you've met Jim Reardon."

"Mr. Reardon, nice to see you again," the captain replied, her voice bellowing over the roar of the weather. After shaking hands, she led us up a metal stairway to the bridge. "Be careful gentlemen, in these conditions, everything is slippery."

Entering the bridge, the atmosphere changed instantly. The rain still lashed the enormous windows, but we couldn't hear it. The light had been dimmed so the abundance of electronic screens and dials glowed in the semi-darkness. Two large, padded chairs faced toward the bow, one in the center, the other on the port side. Anyone sitting in the center chair would have an array of controls at their fingertips, including an elaborate toggle set up at the end of the right arm. The days of a traditional ship's helm were long gone. At the rear of the bridge stood an identical chair facing the stern.

Travers caught me staring at it.

"Much of what we do involves close contact with other vessels. There are times I need to control the ship while maintaining a rearward view. Especially if we're required to ward the interlopers off with the water cannon."

"Water cannon?" I responded.

Jones smiled. "I told you the Torrent had a few surprises."

"How soon can we shove off, Captain?" I asked.

"Our crew has begun the process already. We're running a skeleton team, just the bare minimum. Deagan indicated there may be some risk involved in this mission. Everyone is here because they want to be here, and I declined several volunteers who were surplus to requirements," she said.

That revealed something about the quality of the Crimson Wave team.

Travers then turned to Deagan.

"I want to be clear about the command structure here, Deagan. I am in charge of the ship, and if I believe the vessel is in any danger, I alone will make the decision to respond accordingly. In all other matters, I'll bow to your knowledge of the situation and your experiences as a ship's master. Are we in agreement?"

Jones smiled. "Of course, Vanessa, and I appreciate your trust."

It seemed that despite Deagan Jones' ousting from Crimson Wave's boardroom, he maintained a loyal group of followers.

My cell chirped.

"Trent, how are you doing?"

"Just fine but being fussed over way too much. I've got an update."

"Shoot."

An hour ago, Kalid Amir Faez and his daughter were seen boarding a chopper, apparently taking them to their yacht, *Niesha,* which had departed from port a few hours earlier. They didn't depart Havana immediately. It appears they waited for some additional passengers. A short while later, a man matching Rahmat Beras' description boarded the chopper. He was accompanied by several men. Our agent on the ground suspected them to be bodyguards, but I'm thinking they probably belonged to your Compass Black group."

"Seems likely."

"The men traveled in a separate helicopter. They were joined by a teenage boy around fourteen or fifteen, blond hair…"

"Joshua Jones."

As I said the name, Deagan Jones spun to face me. I raised a palm.

Crais continued. "True to form Nicholas, this information came through way later than it should have. It appears Faez's yacht left the harbor in Havana approximately four hours ago."

"Thanks, Cowboy, we'll get moving. Let me know if you hear more."

I hung up.

Deagan Jones gazed at me expectantly.

"As of an hour ago, Josh was alive and flying out to Faez's boat. That's probably more good news than bad, Deagan," I said.

Jones grasped a nearby railing for support and took a deep breath before he spoke.

"Knowing that my boy is all right is more relief than I can express, Nicholas. But the fact he's surrounded by that pack of scumbags is frightening. We need to stop these people."

Jones looked around the cabin, at Travers, Reardon, Greatrex and me. The stakes were high, especially for Deagan Jones.

"Deagan," I began, "we'll find them, get your boy back, and then kill them."

Travers broke the ensuing silence.

"From what Deagan told me on the phone plus the information you just gave us, we must move quickly. The journey from Cuba will take hours, but they may not need to reach the US coast."

Reardon interrupted. "I've been thinking about it. Most of the oil platforms in the Gulf are over the continental shelf on the northern side, our side. Logically, most of the pipelines are laid on the seafloor in that area as well. But to activate any devices remotely, Beras and Faez may only need to go to the shelf's edge."

"That's around one hundred miles from here. The journey will take us at least four hours in this weather. If the boat you wish to intercept left Havana four hours ago, they will reach the shelf in anything between four to six hours. How fast is their boat?"

"We have no idea," I responded, "but Faez has virtually unlimited resources. I expect his boat will be fast, very fast."

"That means we'll both approach the shelf's perimeter at around the same time," the skipper replied. "Of course, the problem is that you don't know exactly where along the edge of the shelf they're heading. That's hundreds of miles to cover."

"Plot a course from here to Havana," I said. "I'm thinking and hoping they'll do the same in reverse. Then we'll just have to figure something out."

Travers shook her head. "It's not much. In fact, it's less than not much to go on."

"But it's all we've got Captain," said Greatrex.

"So, we better make it all we need," I added.

Travers shrugged her shoulders. "Prepare yourselves for a rough ride, gentlemen. The seas are growing, and we won't be compromising on speed. I hope none of you get seasick."

With that, she turned, sat in the captain's chair, and began barking orders into her radio microphone.

I gazed across the frothing water. A rough ride indeed.

Chapter 47

Two hours into the journey, it was clear the weather was worsening. Huge, thick waves crashed across the Torrent's bow, sending cascades of white foam and water across the bridge windows. The movement underfoot was akin to standing in an elevator consistently traveling up and down. One minute we gazed into the foreboding darkness of the night sky, the next moment the turbulent sea rose up, threatening the next deluge of water.

"Can she take this?" I asked Jones.

"Not a problem," he responded. "This vessel was built to withstand this and a whole lot more. I'm more concerned about the oil platforms out here."

"Surely their built to withstand almost anything?" I inquired.

"Yes and no," Reardon responded. He clutched onto Jones' chair. The oilman clearly wasn't enjoying himself. "In 2005, the Gulf copped a one-two punch of hurricanes Katrina and Rita. One hundred and fifteen platforms were destroyed, another fifty-two badly damaged. The blowback from that was enormous. The API released a whole new set of safety standards, as yet untested."

"We're not getting into hurricane level conditions so far,"

Travers interrupted, "but this weather is way worse than forecast."

An idea flashed into my mind. I should have thought of it earlier.

"Jim, in hurricane conditions, don't you people shut the wells down and monitor any potential damage?"

"We do," Reardon replied. As he spoke, the ship lurched violently to port, before gradually righting itself. Reardon's face paled as he held on for dear life.

"Sorry about that," said Travers. "Rogue wave, didn't see it coming.

"You were saying Jim," I urged.

"Yup, we normally close things down well in advance. The trouble is a shut-down costs us a fortune, so we're disinclined to go down too early," he replied.

"What about in these conditions?" asked Greatrex. He'd been sitting in the rear-facing skipper's seat. For an ex-marine, he didn't much like boats.

Reardon continued. "We're verging on borderline now. I reckon if the weather deteriorates further, our people will start taking action."

I looked Reardon square in the eyes.

"Do it now, get them on the phone and do it," I urged.

"Even in the current circumstances, that's a big call, Nicholas."

"It's no call at all, Jim. If my hunch is correct, you'll be unable to do it. You won't lose a cent... yet."

Reardon glanced at me questioningly. I could almost see the calculator behind his eyes ticking away.

"You're thinking if we shut down now, we can mitigate whatever Beras and Faez have in mind," he said.

"I'm thinking it, but not believing it for a second," I responded.

Now everyone looked at me as though I'd lost my mind.

Greatrex broke the silence. "I've gotta tell you folks, when Nicholas loses the plot, it's usually because he's found another one."

The sound of the storm echoed through the bridge.

"All right Nicholas, I'll direct them to shut down Reardon 8." Reardon reached for his cell phone, before stabbing at the pad. "No signal."

Travers passed over her headset and microphone. "Give me the number. I'll patch you through."

Twenty minutes later, the order had been given. As the ship plowed through the ever-rising waves, we awaited the result.

The radio buzzed. Travers had reclaimed headphones, so she could hear the call above the storm.

"It's for you," she said, passing the headset and mic back to Reardon.

Reardon listened, speaking only occasionally. "Yeah… what?… Did you make another attempt?… Give six and seven a go, if they don't work, try the others…" He hung up. "The system isn't responding. We're trying some other rigs. You knew this would happen, Nicholas?"

"I should have known earlier, not that it would have made that much difference."

Five minutes later, Reardon received a second call. "Right… shit… wait for instructions."

Hanging up again, he shook his head.

"Every shut-down system on each one of our platforms is down. That's impossible."

Another giant wave crashed over the bridge as we considered his words. The hull shuddered in defiance.

"Shit," said Greatrex. "Is it too late to say I can't make the trip?"

"At least now we know the full extent of what we're dealing with. Jim, you mentioned that when the Reardon 3 pipeline was attacked, the back-up systems failed for a while, but then you got them going. Correct?"

"Yup."

"We should have seen this coming. Your whole system across all your platforms has been hacked. I'd bet that it's identical on all other platforms for every company operating in the Gulf and, to be frank, most likely in many of the other offshore fields."

"That's huge," said Jones. "The sheer size of the task and the implications are immense."

I nodded. "Jim, can you get back on the line and start contacting your opposite numbers? Ask them to check and hopefully begin rectifying their systems. Jack, call Trent Crais and fill him in. He'll persuade people to talk to other fields."

"Consider it done," he replied.

"What about you and me, Nicholas? asked Jones."

"You and I are going to figure out how the hell we stop Beras and Faez if and when we find them. Because if we don't, there is nothing standing between them and the biggest environmental catastrophe the planet has ever seen."

Chapter 48

An hour slipped by. The waves pounded harder, visibility was non-existent, and the deck beneath us rose and fell with shattering intensity.

All the bad news was in. Every platform and company that had been contacted reported their emergency response systems down. Whereas most ships that had the opportunity had tried to escape the storm by either returning to port or outrunning it, Faez's yacht hadn't been sighted anywhere. Clearly, Faez's boat, *Niesha*, remained at sea. The only positive aspect was that the system failures across the world's offshore fields had energized the appropriate agencies into action. People started listening to Special Agent Trent Crais. Of course, it was too late for the cavalry. No help could reach us before the deadline passed. As regards the front line of defense, we were on our own.

Apart from a quick call to the General to see what aid he could muster; our only option was to wait until contact was made with Faez's ship.

If and when we caught *Niesha*, Jones and I hadn't fully agreed on our approach. But I respected his knowledge of the sea and the experience of his interactions with other unfriendly vessels in open waters.

So, we waited.

Every time a vessel came up on Travers' radar, she ID'd it electronically using the Automatic Identification System, as well as calling it up to confirm. Fortunately, because of the storm, there weren't that many ships in the neighborhood.

"I've got an unidentified craft on the radar," the skipper shouted. "There's no AIS read. They might have disabled the system, but the ship is definitely there."

We gathered around. Travers pointed to a dot on her screen.

"She's twenty-two miles southeast of us, traveling at approximately thirty-five knots. That's insane in this weather. If we turn and attempt to catch her now, we won't make it before she's inside what you're calling the detonation zone, not even if we run at full power."

I glanced over to Deagan Jones. There was no scenario we'd entertained that provided a solution.

"Even if we do chase her," continued Travers, "if it's not *Niesha,* but simply a vessel whose system is down, we've ventured off our line for no reason."

So much at stake and so damn helpless.

Yet Deagan Jones had more to lose.

"I know how to ID her," said Jones. "We'll do it like we do with the whalers." He turned and looked out the rear bridge window, pointing to a canvas covered blob lashed down on the rear deck. "We'll send the reconnaissance chopper."

"Not a chance," Travers responded. "Even if you got the bird off the boat, which in this weather is beyond unlikely, there is no way in the world you could land back on deck."

"I won't have to."

We all gaped at the environmentalist.

"What are you thinking, Deagan?" I asked.

293

"I'll get the chopper into the air. It's tricky but doable. Once I identify the ship, I'll return and dump the bird into the water beside the Torrent. You can pick me up."

Vanessa Travers looked like she might have a coronary.

"Are you stark raving insane? Stopping the engines and retrieving a man overboard in these seas presents an impossible danger, to you, to us, and to this vessel. It's not going to happen."

I stepped in.

"Captain Travers, is there a chance, any chance, that Deagan's plan might work?"

"Two percent at best," she almost spat the words out.

"Does anyone have any alternative solutions to present?"

Stony silence.

"I'm going to do it, whether you decide to pick me up or not," Jones announced.

I turned to the skipper. "If we don't act, and Rahmat Beras and Kalid Amir Faez succeed, the ramifications are unimaginable." I glanced across at Jones before continuing. "For Deagan, your friend and mentor, the consequences are far worse. His boy is on that boat. What choice does he have? What choice do we have?"

Travers stared out into the storm as the pounding waves smashed over the foredeck. She looked lost in thought. I assumed, like any good leader, she was considering all options.

Only there weren't any.

She swung around in her chair. "Deagan Jones, you're out of your mind, but we'll do it."

Chapter 49

Two steps out of the sanctuary of the bridge and Jones, Greatrex, Reardon and I were soaked. Attired in full wet weather gear, our task needed to be performed efficiently and quickly. Some of the Crimson Wave team had offered assistance, but we declined. At least for now, this was our fight.

After descending the stairway, Greatrex and I moved down the starboard side of the boat, while Jones and Reardon took the port. Each step required sliding our hands along the safety rail. If the movement of the ship felt insecure up on the bridge, it seemed downright murderous on the deck.

Slowly, we made it down to the stern. The small helicopter perched chained to the pad and covered with a tarpaulin. Each time the ship slid down a wave, a thick wall of water towered above us. As the swell moved under the hull, the wall of water disappeared, replaced by a wet blackness.

Jones told us the steps to follow. We yanked the tarp off the helo. It flapped in the strong wind, almost pulling Reardon over the rails. Fortunately, he had the sense to let it go. Greatrex and I hauled it in and tied it to the rail.

Jones climbed into the helicopter and began the starting procedure. The rotors flexed in the gale, but we'd been told to ignore all distractions and focus on our task. I sensed the ship turn as Travers headed the vessel into the wind, attempting to use the cabin infrastructure as protection during take-off.

As the engine coughed into life, the three of us bent down, our hands clutching the tie downs that secured the bird to the pad. In this weather, if we released too soon, the helo would go skidding off the deck, taking Jones with it. If we released them too late, the bird could tip, with the same result.

I gazed up at the lunatic in the pilot seat. If by some miracle he got off without issue, there was no guarantee the chopper would stay in the air. If it did, Jones was in for one hell of a ride. The landing didn't bear thinking about.

The vessel continued to heave up and down. Jones planned to synchronize his take off with the top of the swell. Although it meant exposure to a stronger wind, the chances of being taken down by a wave crashing over the aircraft decreased. A brief glance toward the stern and the dark foaming waters beyond betrayed the desperation of the situation.

Suddenly, the stern was flung upward. The beat of the helo's engine quickened. Jones looked down and gave me the thumbs up. I did the same to Greatrex and Reardon and we all flicked the safety release on the tie-downs together, pulling them back clear of the skids.

At first, nothing happened. Then the engine raced, and the bird jumped up. A second later, it slammed back down on the deck. Instantly, the helo started sliding backward, down the deck toward the stern. Jones revved harder, the motor screaming in the wind. The chopper rose again. This time, she kept ascending.

Six feet into the air and the bird pointed dangerously upward as the wind caught its underbelly. The angle pushed the tail rotor down towards the deck. A brief metal on metal sound screeched while sparks radiated around the tail. The three of us clambered back toward the nearest handrails, waiting for the helo to come crashing down onto the deck.

Then suddenly it was gone. The bird swept off the stern but thankfully into the air. I just picked up a distant whir as the aircraft's lights headed off into the storm.

Travers was right. Deagan Jones was out of his mind.

Chapter 50

DEAGAN JONES

Deagan Jones peered through the chopper's windscreen, although he didn't know why he bothered; the blackness was akin to an impenetrable wall. The bird bounced around like a ping-pong ball. There was no pattern to the movement, so Jones could only be reactionary. Nothing would be predictable on this flight.

The MD 500 was a solid machine. Jones knew that because he had picked it himself. He'd exhausted just about every model available before choosing the MD. Its Allison 250-C30 turboshaft engine provided the performance under pressure that the Crimson Wave reconnaissance pilots needed. Of course, the chopper wasn't designed to fly in these conditions, nor would Compass Black expect it.

Jones was aware that his chances of surviving the flight were minimal at best, but as Sharp had pointed out, there was too much at stake and no alternative. Despite Jones' dread at the thought of the possible environmental consequences if Beras and Faez succeeded in their plan, that fear paled compared to the possibility of losing Josh.

Parenthood.

Jones wrestled with the collective, correcting the bird's flight path every few seconds. He maintained sufficient altitude to avoid the largest cresting waves but had to stay at a low enough level to spot Faez's ship if he happened to come across it. In this visibility, that was a big if.

As a pilot, he'd been trained to trust his instruments. His experience also taught him to trust his gut. So be it.

The journey wouldn't take Jones long. Normally the MD 500 could make around one hundred and fifty knots, but in these conditions against such a strong headwind, who the hell knew?

Jones' plan was to reach his designated location at twenty-two miles southeast of the Torrent, and then begin searching in ever-increasing circles. If '*Niesha*' was running without lights, there would be no hope of spotting her. Even if she was lit up like a fairground, the chances remained slim.

No matter what, Jones would press on.

The bird dipped and swerved, at times almost flying sideways, but he kept peering through the screen as the rain lashed the glass, the wipers almost useless. His eyes scanned the blackness, willing '*Niesha*' to appear.

She just had to.

Chapter 51

RAHMAT BERAS

Rahmat Beras pressed back into the overstuffed armchair and surveyed the *Neisha's* luxurious lounge. Beras considered himself well off, but compared to Kalid Amir Faez, he was a pauper. Even as the ship crashed through the monster waves outside, the sense of isolation within the room was astounding. Yes, the carpeted floor rose and fell beneath them, but the ship's roll was minimal. Faez assured him the *Neisha* had been fitted with every possible stabilizing system. The ship's dual Rolls Royce MT30 marine gas turbine engines powered the hundred-and sixty-foot craft across the swells with a minimum of fuss.

Beras sipped on his vodka. They were now in international waters. Saudi alcohol laws didn't apply here, so the Faez family allowed their visitors certain flexibility.

"My captain informs me we should be on location within the hour," announced Faez, who sat opposite him.

"Was it really necessary for us to be here?" asked Zafina Faez. She lounged on a long sofa yet seemed less comfortable than her companions.

"From my point of view, there was no need at all, Zafina,

but your father insisted on coming," Beras responded.

The older man glanced at his daughter before turning to Beras.

"A great deal has happened in the last twenty-four hours. The death of my beloved Ahmed has caused me to have more, as the Americans say, 'skin in the game'. As you know it had been my intention that we be in the midst of your wedding celebration at this moment, my dear. Now, my reviewed objective is to be on site when our plan is activated. I also require assurances that my son's murderer, and the man who wounded my trusted friend, Jabir, will be eliminated."

Zafina nodded her head.

"Nicholas Sharp and his allies have been the unpredictable thorns in our sides," Beras responded. "We anticipated Deagan Jones' reaction, and of course have that well under control. As you know, his boy is in our custody downstairs."

"So how will you take care of Sharp?" asked the older man.

"The Compass Black team has been tasked with his removal immediately after our plan has been executed. One of their leaders, Muldoon, also has 'skin in the game'. Sharp and Jones killed his brother."

"That will ensure their thoroughness," said Zafina.

The two men nodded.

"And what of the boy?" asked Faez senior.

"With respect, it's best you don't ask that question," Beras responded.

Faez nodded.

"You're certain we should proceed with the attack on the Gulf fields first, before initiating the others?" Faez asked.

"Yes." Beras had explained this to Faez before, but he understood the old man's need for reassurance. "We...

you, have invested many millions of dollars, not just in the enormous quantities of TNT and the appropriate detonation mechanisms, but also in the manpower to place our devices where they will do the most damage. We don't want to waste that effort if there is an unforeseen malfunction in our schedule."

"But your testing on the Reardon rig and in the North Sea was thorough." Said Faez.

Beras nodded. "It was extremely thorough, including the hacking into their prevention and response systems. We have some of the best minds in the world guiding that aspect of the plan. But the bottom line is this: if something does go wrong here, in the Gulf, we can regroup, make the required alterations and proceed. On the other hand, if as expected, everything runs to plan, I'll give the order and the remaining five largest offshore oil fields around the globe will suffer the same catastrophe at the same moment. Please forgive my caution, Kalid, but my intention is to ensure success."

"I know we've spoken of this before, Rahmat, but you are certain of the result?" asked Zafina.

"Without doubt. The ensuing environmental crisis will be of such severity that the industry shall be regarded as inherently dangerous to the planet. Offshore production and exploration will be dissolved."

As Beras spoke, he gauged the conviction in the other two's eyes. Without doubt, they were with him one hundred percent of the way.

"And remember, to make sure that is the case, I now have a significant voice within the most influential of all the environmental advocacy groups, Crimson Wave. And, of course, after the offshore industry collapses, your wealth will increase immeasurably."

"As will yours, Rahmat," Faez replied.

"And Deagan Jones?" asked Zafina.

"Dead men can't speak," Beras responded bluntly.

"You have a most strategic and clinical approach to business, Rahmat. I recognized that from our first meeting when you were a young man. As I've said before, I'm glad we are on the same side."

"And always will be, sir," Beras responded deferentially.

A phone next to Faez's chair rang sharply.

"Yes… all right… await further instruction."

The old man hung up the phone, turning to Rahmat Beras.

"That was the captain. As unexpected as it would seem in this weather, a helicopter has been detected circling in the skies overhead."

Momentarily startled by the news, Beras quickly regained his composure.

"It will be dealt with."

Chapter 52

DEAGAN JONES

Astounded that he remained airborne, Deagan Jones hung on for dear life. The MD 500 had been tossed around like a child's toy. Twice he'd lost so much height, so quickly, he thought he was done, but the little helo kept going, in conditions far beyond its ratings.

He'd reached his destination ten minutes previously yet saw no lights on the water. That didn't surprise him. He couldn't really see anything at all. He scanned the vicinity immediately surrounding his given coordinates for a short time before beginning his circular sweeps of the area. Given the absence of any real visibility, Jones decided to descend to one hundred feet above the surface. The lack of altitude made flying extremely hazardous. There was no room for error.

Eventually, a dim glow appeared on his starboard side. He edged the bird toward it. As he got closer, the single light turned into several lights, their formation denoting the lines of a ship.

Jones climbed higher and soared over the top of the vessel. From what he could see, the ship matched the description of

Faez's yacht, but he'd need confirmation if Travers and Sharp were to concentrate all their efforts in this direction. He eased the helo into a small, erratic arc before pushing downward. He had to confirm the name on the stern.

Now, dancing across the wave tops, he made a pass behind the ship. There it was, 'Neisha' in large red letters on the white hull. Jones had just pulled on the collective to gain some altitude when the first bullet sent a spider crack across his left window. Despite the danger of performing such a maneuver at a low height, he flipped the bird onto her side, exposing the undercarriage to the fire. Two quick metallic thuds sounded under his feet.

Jones needed altitude and distance, and he needed it fast.

As he rose, he flicked the radio on. *"Torrent, this is Waterbird. Neisha has been sighted. I repeat, Neisha has been sighted. She's heading northeast at a speed in excess of thirty knots."* He then gave his location. No response came through his headset.

Another metallic clink at his feet caused him to re-prioritize his energies from the radio to flying the aircraft. Thirty seconds more and he'd be out of range. The storm continued to rage; Jones persisted in his fight for control of the bird. He prayed the Torrent received his message and would make chase.

One minute later, Jones breathed a sigh of relief. He was now a safe distance away from the ship and began an arc back toward the Torrent.

Then he saw it.

A flame. Burning just above sea level and rising, Jones immediately understood the ramifications. The flame belonged to some kind of SAM, Surface to Air Missile, and it was clearly headed straight toward him. Holy shit! How well were these people armed?

Jones had zero chance of outrunning the missile, and his helo didn't have a built-in defense system. Crimson Wave had never considered it necessary. He pushed the bird into a steep, almost vertical climb, just as he had above the Iwokrama rainforest several weeks earlier. This time, however, the circumstances were completely different.

The MD 500 rose. Jones looked over his shoulder. The flaring missile was gaining ground. His little helo was being shoved to and fro in the wind but kept ascending. Abruptly, the motor coughed, then coughed again. The third splutter ended in silence. Dead engine. Within seconds the helo somersaulted back on itself, spiraling toward the ocean below. Jones knew the engine would still be hot, providing the SAM with a heat signal to follow, but he hoped the sudden change in temperature may confuse it for a few seconds.

Jones saw the missile climb higher, but as his aircraft descended, the SAM seemed to hesitate momentarily before continuing its ascent. Jones fought hard, attempting to restart his machine. At this point, it was a race between which would kill him first, the missile or the ocean below.

Abruptly, the engine spluttered to life. The bird was falling fast as Jones struggled to regain control. The foam topped waves grew closer, too damn close. Above him, the missile had now turned back toward its target.

With one last tug, the bird flipped over. Control was his. Virtually skipping across the waves, Jones headed west, toward the Torrent. Above him, he noted the SAM heading directly at him only seconds behind.

With the spray from the surface occasionally splashing his wind shield, Jones' eyes darted between the surface and the missile above him. He couldn't afford to lose track of either. He counted down until contact, six...five...four...three...two... Jones shoved hard on his right pedal and pulled the collective sharply. The bird swung up and to the right, in the same instant, the missile, only inches from his rotor, plunged into the sea.

The immediate threat vanquished, Jones added a safe margin of height and headed toward the Torrent. In his ears, his headset crackled. He recognized Travers' voice.

"Waterbird, message received, sighting confirmed. Please return to base."

Jones chuckled to himself. What in God's name did they think he was trying to do?

Twenty minutes later the Torrent's lights appeared in his windscreen. Jones felt relief and apprehension. He swung the bird low over the ship's rear deck. Although lit up like a Christmas tree, it wouldn't do Jones any good. The large 'H' marking the helipad rose and fell like a cork simultaneously rolling at forty-five-degree angles on alternating sides. The ship didn't have a bear-trap, the mechanism that could bring navy and rescue choppers onto a moving deck in a storm. He'd have to ditch. Despite what's he'd said to the others before he left, the idea didn't thrill him.

"Torrent to Waterbird. Do you wish to attempt a deck landing?"

"Water bird to Torrent. Negative."

"Torrent to Waterbird. What is your approach plan?"

"Waterbird to Torrent. I'm going to ditch her, port side, amidships."

"Torrent to Waterbird. Going wet, port side, amidships, approach received. Retrieval team will be standing by, and Waterbird... good

307

luck."

Jones knew he was sure as hell going to need it.

He decided to approach at wave level and virtually slide down over a crest and dump the bird in the trough between waves. The swell should then bring him back up to a height where he'd be more easily retrievable to the ship's crew. Ditching on the lee side of the vessel, the ship's hull would offer some protection. The trick was making it out of the chopper. He patted the left-hand side of his MOLLE vest, assured that the SEA, Survival Egress Air system, was safely secured. He wouldn't access it until after impact.

For a minute or two Jones hovered the bird just behind the ship's stern, to verify an on-deck landing was out of the question. He knew all eyes on the bridge would be trained on him and noted two figures clad in wet weather gear on the port side, a net rolled up at their feet. They looked up expectantly.

This was the moment. He let two extremely large waves pass by underneath and then angled the helo down the third wave, its skids almost skiing across the surface. He hit the bottom of the trough with a thump that jolted him forward in his seat, testing the resilience of his harness.

The bird stopped dead, the view from the screen instantly turning to the deep murky green of the ocean. Relieved to still be conscious, Jones reached for the SEA's mouthpiece and placed it between his lips with his left hand, breathing sharply to activate the airflow. He shoved his right hand between his legs, clutching the seat, the rodeo position. As an experienced pilot, he knew what would come next. The helicopter immediately rotated upside down. With no wings to stabilize the aircraft, the weight of the engine above the cabin suddenly became an anchor, dragging the bird down.

As soon as the helo became fully inverted, Jones swapped his left hand with his right. The left held him in position in his seat. This was not the time to become disorientated. Reaching his right hand toward the cabin door, he rotated the release leaver and shoved hard.

Nothing.

Already the outside water pressure was too strong. Jones needed to let water into the cabin to equalize the pressure. He understood that each second wasted carried him further toward the ocean floor. He reached forward, opening every available vent, then, without losing his grip, he placed his feet against the door and shoved again.

Nothing.

He repeated the process. A small gap appeared around the door, allowing a trickle of water in. Jones drew his legs back and heaved again. This time the trickle became a rush as the helo's cabin saturated with seawater. As the water filled his sinuses, challenging his orientation even more, Jones pushed against the door one last time. It opened wide enough to allow him to struggle through the opening.

Nothing prepared him for the tumultuous violence of the ocean.

Jones swam for what he thought was the surface, but the currents buffeted him around, rolling him over in a three-sixty-degree somersault. Still, he pressed upward, hoping he was headed in the right direction. He felt his limbs weaken. Although not a young man, Jones was fit and strong, but the power of the ocean depleted his strength with every stroke. He pressed on until it became debilitating.

His thoughts drifted to Josh. He hoped Sharp would find a way to rescue the boy, because it looked like he wouldn't…

Suddenly, the deep green turned white. A second later, the foamy froth flew through the air, slapping at his face.

Jones realized he was still in a precarious situation. If the ship wasn't close by, he wouldn't have the strength to reach it. Suddenly, the swell surged beneath him, lifting him high enough to see the ship stood less than ten yards distant.

A chance.

He swam like there was no tomorrow. Abruptly, the Torrent disappeared as a wave smashed over Jones' head, thrusting him downward. He rallied against the force with the last of his strength. Five long seconds later, he was again surrounded by air and the foaming rage on the surface.

Jones looked toward the ship. A figure clung to a net on the side of the hull, its hand reaching out toward him.

Out of nowhere, a wall of water crashed over him, its breaking force sending him into a downward spiral once more.

Jones looked for the hand.

It was gone.

Chapter 53

NICHOLAS SHARP

My fingers curled firmly around the coarse netting. I reached out toward the figure in the water. He remained too far away. Pushing my legs through the net, hard against the ship's metal hull, I reached further. The wind and the ocean thrashed at me like a hail of saltwater bullets. My hand was an inch from Jones. I had him... and then I didn't.

As a huge onslaught of seawater overcame the two of us, Jones disappeared beneath the surface. I waited ten long seconds, hanging on desperately.

"He's not coming up, Jack."

Greatrex perched on the netting immediately above me, his strong hand gripping my wrist. Added security.

Another five seconds passed.

"Don't do it Nicholas." I could barely hear the big fella's voice above the howling wind.

Two more seconds.

"Don't..."

I shook myself free from Greatrex's grasp and launched myself into the water.

Nicholas Sharp, man with a death wish.

The brutality of the sea exceeded any expectation I may have had. The force pounded me back against the ship's hull before yanking me away just as brutally. I had no say in it at all. I dove below the surface, the roar of the wind evaporating behind me.

The chopper was long gone, cast down into the depths, but I could make out a small glow twenty feet blow me. I struck out toward it. I was pushed and turned, yet slowly closed the distance. I'd only have one shot at this before the air in my lungs expired.

A few seconds later, Jones' figure appeared through the murkiness. The guiding safety light attached to his belt glowing a little brighter. I grabbed his arm, but he didn't react. His body lay limp in the water, swaying gently. In a final desperate bid, I propelled myself downward, finally wrapping my arms around his waist. I looked up. The surface seemed an eternity away.

I kicked hard, praying, struggling, and hoping.

We broke through together; into the same thrashing violence I'd left less than two minutes earlier.

By the grace of somebody's God, Greatrex loomed above us, his giant paw reaching down.

"Take Jones, I'm okay," I yelled.

Thankful for the big fella's strength, I felt Deagan Jones' body yanked from my grip. I followed, clutching at the net. One hand following the other, I started pulling myself out of the water, but my strength was failing. Above me, Greatrex struggled to get the deadweight of Jones' body more than halfway up the hull. Then two pairs of arms reached out from above and finished the job.

Greatrex turned and hauled me up the last few feet, probably saving my life.

By the time we both crawled onto the deck, Jim Reardon was giving Jones the last of the rescue breaths before pumping his chest. A Torrent crew member kneeled beside him. Reardon repeated the process. Thirty compressions to two breaths three times.

The rain and wind continued its assault. The ship rolled violently beneath our feet, but no one seemed to notice. An emptiness swelled inside me as Deagan Jones lay motionless before us. After all he'd done...

Suddenly Jones' body convulsed. The convulsion turned to a desperate cough before water spewed out of his mouth.

Maybe the prayers worked.

Chapter 54

"I've done some calculations. There's no chance of catching them in time. That's one hell of a fast boat we're chasing," announced Travers.

It wasn't the news we wanted to hear.

"What if we change course to intercept them?" asked Greatrex.

"I'm working on that, but I still don't think we'd make it before they're in a position to activate," she responded.

We waited while the skipper finished plotting her chart.

"No chance," she finally announced, looking up from the screen. "No matter which course we take, it won't be an intersection at all. Faez's ship would pass the point of interception well before the Torrent unless we slow them down."

"Then we need to slow them down," I responded, "but how?"

Thirty minutes had passed since we'd retrieved Deagan Jones from the water. He sat in the second chair, clothes changed but still wrapped in a blanket. He'd regained a little of his color, but regularly burst into coughing fits.

"I know how to do it," he announced. "It used to be part of my trade."

After he described his plan, we all remained silent. No one

wanted to mention the elephant in the room.

"Deagan, you've done enough. Your actions over the last hour have been nothing short of heroic. But to be honest, you're in no state to leap into action again," said Reardon.

"This is my area of expertise. Nobody else onboard has been trained, and don't forget, that's my son on Faez's ship."

It was the moment for some brazen honesty.

"Deagan, I'm going to be straight up here," I began. "We would be out of the game completely if you hadn't done what you did, and Joshua would be beyond any help we could offer. You have got us this far. It's time for us to complete the job, or at least try."

"I need to go," he insisted.

"No Deagan. You need not to go," I responded. "Look at you, you're struggling to breathe, you're exhausted and, to be honest, you'd be a liability."

Nicholas Sharp, cruel bastard.

"But…"

"No," I repeated. "Give Jack and I a crash course in what is required and let us get on with it."

"Nicholas is right Deagan," said Reardon. "His plan will offer Josh his greatest chance and I believe somewhere deep inside you know that."

We waited.

Jones sighed, coughed, and then sighed again.

"All right, but I must tell you, even Crimson Wave's most experienced crew only pull this off one in five times. You're going to have to play your best game."

"Hmph," Greatrex responded. "Is there any other?"

315

"You sure you've got this?" asked Jones.

"We've got it," I responded.

Jones radioed a command back to the bridge and the twenty-foot Humber high performance rigid inflatable boat that Greatrex and I perched on, swung out over the waves. As the craft veered out, flailing violently in the wind, I started the two ninety-horsepower Mercury engines hanging off its stern. The engines roared to life. I raised my hand, signaling for the craft to be lowered. Three feet above a cresting wave, the davit locks released, splashing us onto the foaming surface. We immediately surged forward. Fifteen seconds later, we'd cleared the lee of the Torrent and bounced wildly across the swell.

RIBs were designed for just this purpose; they were strong, fast attack boats. Greatrex and I had both been trained in small craft handling in the Marines. We were rusty, but some skills lurked beneath the surface, hopefully enough to keep us above the surface.

I skippered and Greatrex clutched the metal frame beside me. If you weren't hanging on, you weren't staying on board.

"I sure love a relaxing cruise," said the big fella.

"Then I'll book you on one," I replied.

We both knew it would be tough enough to find the *Neisha*, never mind achieving our objective.

Surprisingly, it wasn't too long before Faez's ship's lights appeared out of the darkness.

"I hope they're pointing their SAMs toward the sky and monitoring their radar for larger vessels. It'll take a fair amount of luck for us to get close," I yelled into the wind.

Greatrex nodded.

I headed directly for the ship's stern. My plan was to run

along the lee side. They wouldn't hear our motor in the storm, although after the interaction with Jones in the helo, they'd be on alert. Just as I was about to round the stern, I noticed two men standing on the starboard deck, the lee side. One held an automatic weapon, the other a shoulder launcher for a man-portable SAM.

There'd be no protected approach for us.

We advanced from the stern along the port side, risking the danger of being wedged between the powerful swells and the ship's solid hull. Greatrex kept his eyes glued for hostiles on the deck. So far, so good. The spray was blinding as the RIB lurched from wave to wave.

At midpoint, I shouted to Greatrex. "Thirty seconds, get ready."

"On it."

Greatrex moved to the rear of the boat, quickly grabbing the rails that extended over the top of the outboards. A plastic crate sat roped onto to the starboard side. It contained a thick sea line with a flotation device attached to one end.

"Get ready…"

"Now."

Greatrex dropped the float overboard as we ran up beside the *Neisha*, holding tight into her hull. The line paid out rapidly, the float keeping it close to the surface. Faez's ship moved quickly, but we nudged up to a point parallel with her bow. Now in totally unprotected water and wrestling with the *Neisha's* bow wave, the RIB bucked like a rodeo horse. I fought with the wheel to keep her on track. As we passed the ship's bow, I swung the wheel to starboard. Our boat swung directly in front of the larger vessel, her nose within touching distance.

We'd almost made it clear when the *Neisha's* bow caught us. The stern of our boat kicked up in the air, tipping us onto a dangerously precarious angle.

"Hold on, and keep it coming," I yelled.

Greatrex hadn't flinched.

After a scary moment, the RIB righted itself and we swept down the starboard side of the vessel. The line had slipped under *Neisha*'s hull.

At the midway point I shouted, "let it go."

Greatrex shoved the rest of the rope overboard. I veered to port, wanting to leave the glow of *Neisha's* deck lights before the men at the stern noticed us. Crossing broadside to the waves, we raced off into the darkness.

Once out of sight, I turned and ran parallel to the ship. We waited.

According to Deagan Jones, the maneuver we'd just performed was the classic prop foul technique Crimson Wave used to either slow or stop the whaling boats in the Antarctic Ocean. You only knew you'd succeeded if the opposing vessel slowed or stopped.

Neisha pressed on through the waves.

"I think we blew it," I shouted to Greatrex, who still stood at the stern holding the grab rail.

"Looks like it. Can't see any sign of her slow…"

As the big fella spoke, the swell surged under *Neisha's stern, causing her to rise in the sea*. The bow dipped before the ship began to level out.

"Is that…"

"She's stopped dead in the water," shouted Greatrex. "Any moment she'll start reversing, trying to clear the props.

That was the cue.

Our real work was about to begin.

Chapter 55

RAHMAT BERAS

Beras sensed the frustration grow within him. Control seemed to be slipping from his grip. It wasn't a sensation he was accustomed to. How could those Compass Black fools have failed to take down an unarmed civilian helicopter. Especially considering the armaments he'd supplied them with? They were meant to be the best operatives in the world. The next couple of hours may well put that to the test.

He stood on the *Neisha*'s bridge beside Faez's captain. He faced off against Muldoon.

"Why didn't you send our own helicopter up to chase the intruder down?" He asked the mercenary.

Muldoon looked drawn and tired, his face showing lines Beras hadn't noticed before.

"Conditions precluded the use of the helo," Muldoon responded.

"Clearly not for the pilot who likely identified this vessel."

"No," replied Muldoon, chastised.

"Someone out there will now be attempting to chase us down. Are your men prepared for any eventuality?"

"Absolutely Mr. Beras. We are well armed. I've got guards

posted on the lee side of the ship where any attempt at boarding would have to originate and our radar is tracking all ships in the area. No one is close enough to impact our plans."

Beras had been mildly reassured, but they'd come too far to let anyone stop them - although Nicholas Sharp did appear to have an unforeseen level of tenacity. He exited the bridge, making his way back down towards the lounge. The deck rolled under his feet. Damn this storm.

Kalid Amir Faez sat in the same comfortable seat where Beras had left him.

"Is everything under control, my friend?" the oilman asked.

"Certainly. Muldoon's men were unable to take the helo down, but it really doesn't matter. With our speed, no one can match us. We'll be gone long before they could catch us, and there will be no evidence of our involvement."

"Excellent."

"There may be a problem," Zafina Faez spoke as she strode into the room.

Zafina moved with graceful intensity, her eyes like a dark mystery. She had always beguiled Beras. For him, she was a singular weak point, but now that she had married, it was no longer an issue.

"We've just received word. Deagan Jones has been released from FBI custody," she continued.

"How did that happen?" asked the older Faez.

"Apparently, some sort of unexpected political interference," the woman replied.

The old man frowned, turning his gaze toward Beras.

"This is not good news, Rahmat. You said it had been taken care of, and that Jones had been removed from the picture."

"No, it is not good news," Beras responded. "Zafina, please stay close to the boy downstairs. I don't see how Jones could possibly interfere with our work out here, but the boy's presence has always been our insurance."

Zafina nodded.

The old man continued expressing his dissatisfaction.

"Are there any other unexpected factors we need to consider, Rahmat?"

At that moment, the deck beneath them shifted, the stern rising as quickly as the bow fell. The sense of propelled motion ceased.

Kalid Amir Faez gazed at his protégé, his contempt unconcealed. Beras turned and bolted toward the bridge.

Chapter 56

NICHOLAS SHARP

"Bring her up on the port side, slightly aft of the bridge," I yelled. "We'll be extremely exposed to the weather, but it's the last place they'll expect to be boarded from. The crew should be focused on the issues at the stern."

"It's not the crew I'm worried about," shouted the big fella.

Greatrex had taken control of the craft, replacing me at the center console. I squatted at the bow, holding on to a grab handle with one hand and a grappling hook in the other. My pocket contained the Colt M1911 pistol Travers had provided from the Torrent's small armory. I also had several spare rounds, but not enough to win a prolonged firefight. If that scenario eventuated, the cause was lost. My backpack, tightly secured around my waist and shoulders, held some other surprises.

Greatrex brought us straight in on a ninety-degree angle to the ship, the darkness and the spray, our camouflage. In these seas, no sane person would consider such a boarding if the vessel was moving. Even stationary, it was touch and go.

Twenty feet out, I tensed, at ten feet my muscles screwed tight, at three feet I threw the grappling hook upward. With an audible clunk, it straddled the rail. I tested the line with a strong yank and then began my ascent. The moment my foot left the RIB, Greatrex pulled away. He had to vanish into the dark for now.

In the movies, ascending a vertical rope looks easy, the reality is it's not. I felt the pain in every muscle in my arms and legs as I hauled myself upward. When the ship sank into a trough, the roped arced away from the hull, leaving me dangling in mid-air. When she rose, my body was slammed unforgivingly against the metal vessel.

Inch by inch, I strained and hauled until my eyes were level with the deck. After surveying the area, I hoisted myself up and climbed over the rail. I reeled in the rope, scurried to the nearest shadow, and waited.

No yelling, no alarm. So far, so good.

With so many armed men on board, stealth was the only option. I had two tasks. The first to find Joshua Jones and remove him from the ship. The second was to leave the contents of my backpack in appropriate positions around the vessel. The Torrent didn't carry explosives, but Jim Reardon had managed to procure some at no notice.

To achieve either task would take opportunity and luck.

I decided to begin with the charges. Aware that I'd have no chance to access the engine room or the fuel tanks, I decided to be strategic with my placement and hope a chain reaction would ensure the ship was completely disabled if not destroyed. There would be no innocent individuals present on this vessel, except for Joshua, so everyone was an adversary.

Through the wind, I heard voices coming from the stern. Stopping unexpectedly in the water would have caused an element of chaos.

That was part of the plan.

The decks were well lit, as was the stairway leading to the bridge. I glanced around before making a dash for the space under the stairs. The deck was wet and slippery and spray from the waves smashed against the ship's infrastructure before draining away. I made my hideaway, but only just.

"Mr. Faez will not be happy about this, captain. I suggest you get it fixed."

I pressed myself into the shadows and watched a pair of feet descend the metal steps. A tall man of lithe and fit appearance stepped down onto the deck. His suit and shoes, although quickly becoming sodden, looked expensive. Rahmat Beras? I'd seen pictures of him, but the view from my position was limited.

Another set of feet appeared. I pressed hard against the alcove wall. The second man followed the first.

"If we want this sorted, we'll need to oversee it ourselves."

James Muldoon. I recognized the voice.

Every instinct in me begged to take Muldoon out then and there, but it would serve no purpose and only jeopardize Johsua's safety further. I remained in the shadows.

The two men headed toward the stern. I took the opportunity to climb the wet stairs, keeping my head low so no one staring out through the bridge windows might spot me. On the next deck, behind the wheelhouse, I spotted a floatation ring secured to the wall. Perfect. I shed my backpack, reached in, and withdrew a roll of four sticks of Gelatin Nitroglycerin Dynamite. It was a bit 'old world'. I would have preferred the more stable C4, but the oil industry still used dynamite for blasting through hard rock, and it was all Jim Reardon could get his hand on in a hurry. I placed the roll between the ring and the cabin wall and set the attached timer.

One down, five to go.

Again, listening for the sound of voices or footsteps and hearing none, I ventured back towards the bow, clinging to any available shadow. I moved on to place the second charge.

Twenty minutes and a couple of close calls later, I'd completed my first objective. The charges were placed semi-haphazardly, but it would suffice. The next task would be more challenging. I needed to locate Josh and remove him from the boat.

I had no idea where to begin. Faez's ship was enormous. It would take several hours to search it thoroughly, even if there were no hostiles on board. I put myself in Beras' position. Where would I keep the boy, so he was secure but close enough at hand in case I needed him quickly? On a vessel this size, I figured either the crew's quarters or the staterooms. The staterooms would be easier to access, so I'd try them first.

Easy to say, harder to do.

Staying below the enclosed railing that encircled the second deck of the ship, I crawled along under the windows until I located an entrance point to the interior. I needed to avoid the stern at all costs. That's where the action would be. Fifteen yards along, I found what I required. The door wasn't locked. There'd be no reason to secure it. I pulled the Colt out of my pocket, yanked on the door's lever, and opened it.

In a George Clooney moment, I'd suddenly stepped from the *Perfect Storm's* Grand Banks of Newfoundland, into *Oceans 11* at the Las Vegas Bellagio. The wind, spray and noise was instantly surpassed by the most ostentatious luxury imaginable. Again, I was reminded of Kalid Amir Faez's immeasurable wealth. I didn't really know which direction to go, but I assumed the staterooms would be upstairs. Rich people always seemed to like to live upstairs.

No sooner had I begun making my way toward the bow than I heard voices. Two males chatting. I spotted an alcove halfway along the passageway. I bolted for it and sunk myself into a corner. If whoever passed glanced to their right, I was done. Seconds later, two men in white uniforms strolled past. Crew. I caught a snippet of their conversation.

"With the money the old man is paying us all for this, we'll be set for life."

"I don't give a damn what they're planning. In fact, they could blow up New York for all I care. Just pay me the cash."

Both men laughed.

There were no innocents aboard this ship.

Fortunately, neither man looked in my direction.

I continued my way along the corridor. I rounded a corner to the left, entering an even more luxurious mezzanine area. Possibly where the staterooms began. I didn't know how many suites the *Neisha* contained, so I just started trying doors as quietly and inconspicuously as possible.

Seven minutes later, I'd had no success. Around the next corner, a wide staircase, paneled with huge mirrors and gold beading, appeared. Perhaps there would be more state rooms upstairs.

I took the stairs three at a time, my feet almost soundless on the plush carpet. Gun in hand, I stepped into the mezzanine on the third deck.

Mistake.

Ten feet up the corridor that led off the mezzanine stood

two men. They were dressed head to toe in black. Both had MOLLE vests with all the appropriate gadgets and, more to the point, both held Kalashnikov automatic weapons.

I jumped back into the concealment of the stairwell, but every fiber in my being told me I was too late.

The first Compass Black operative rounded into the stairway within seconds. I was prepared. The butt of my gun struck him sharply across the face as my knee connected with his groin. He groaned as he fell to the floor.

It didn't go so well with the second guy.

After witnessing what happened to his comrade, he paused, probably waiting for me to move. I thought about doing the same, but then realized he could call for backup with a radio. My decision was between going in high or low. I chose high.

It was the wrong choice.

The second man came round the corner, crouching down below my waist level. When he saw me, he began to raise his weapon. I immediately lunged forward tugging it from his hands. The gun slid down the corridor. My opponent yanked at my ankles while charging at my torso with the weight of his body, sending me barreling down the stairs. I hit the midway landing and thumped my head against the wall paneling. My attacker pulled a knife from his vest before leaping down toward me. His footing was sound, and he moved like lightning.

With his knife headed for my throat, I attempted to roll to the left. My face immediately smashed into some more paneling. I hadn't realized I lay trapped in a corner. The blade was now less than a foot from its target. I reached up with both hands, grabbing at the man's wrist. I couldn't stop the attack, but maybe I could alter its course. As I wrapped my arms around his forearm, I shoved to the right. The sharp metal sliced through the air, glancing across my cheek before lodging into the wood an inch from my ear.

I sensed the blood seep down my face. In reaction, my attacker balled his right fist and slammed it into my eye. Vision blurred; I kicked out but found no target. The man's next blow hit me in the kidney. I gagged in pain but still managed to reach down and make another grab at his wrist. This time from underneath, just as he pulled back. Reaching over with my other hand, I used all my strength to push his arm upward and to the left. Momentarily, the guy looked confused, as though not comprehending my strategy. A second later, as the knife, still stuck in the paneling, sliced into his fleshy forearm, he understood completely.

Blood spurted across his arm and my face.

I followed through with a backhand blow across his head combined with a knee striking up at his chin. He pulled back but didn't retreat.

The window of opportunity was small. I raised both arms and yanked at the knife handle. Seeing my attempt, the man launched himself toward me. As he did, the weapon loosened. The Compass Black man was almost on me when I swung the blade in a close arc, slicing through his throat.

The flow of blood was immense, as was my relief.

Stealth no longer remained an option. I ran back up the stairs and along the hallway. If the two Compass Black operatives had been guarding a doorway, I figured there must be something on the other side they didn't want anyone to see. I flung the door open.

The room was empty.

Chapter 57

JOSHUA JONES

If Josh had been scared on the plane, he was petrified now. The floor beneath him shifting continuously did nothing to quell his anxiety. He'd been out to sea with his father several times, but never in weather like this.

He wondered what his dad would do if he were in the same situation. Josh figured he'd probably find a way to escape. His dad was like that. Inventive. But no matter which way he looked at it, Josh couldn't see a way out of this. How does a kid flee a ship in a storm while being guarded by armed mercenaries?

Simple answer. He didn't.

Suddenly, the men outside began yelling. Josh leaped from the bed and ran to the door. He couldn't hear much, some grunting and perhaps some scuffling. Was this his chance?

Probably not, but Josh Jones decided to give it a go. That's what his dad would have done.

The boy waited, the sounds outside growing more muted. Maybe it was just a false alarm. Or maybe an opportunity.

Josh resolved to go for it. He flung the door open. Nobody was there, but he heard grunts and bangs from the staircase down the corridor. Closing the door quietly behind him, he padded off along the passageway in the opposite direction. As he rounded the first right-hand turn, making him invisible to any pursuer, relief overwhelmed him.

He ran forward. There must be a way.

Chapter 58

NICHOLAS SHARP

The room was empty. Whatever the Compass Black team had been guarding was now gone. I scanned the area for evidence of anyone who had been present. Nothing appeared evident from the bedroom. I moved slowly toward the bathroom. Cautiously, I stuck my head through the doorway. Again, empty.

There must be something. I allowed myself a two-minute search, but I only needed one. Wedged halfway underneath the lamp base beside the bed was a swap card. A portrait shaped picture of a football player, ball in hand. But it wasn't an American football. I flipped it over. I read through the brief biog of the player, a star of the Cork City Football Club in the League of Ireland Premier Division.

League of Ireland, where Deagan Jones' boy had been kidnapped.

I placed the palm of my hand on the bedcover. Still warm. Joshua Jones had been in this room, and every fiber of my being told me he'd only just left.

I bolted out the door.

The sole scenario was Josh turning right. Going left would

have led him to me and the Compass Black men. I scrambled after him. Despite my lack of familiarity with the ship's layout, it was apparent that this passage led to the stern, which was in precisely the wrong direction.

I ran faster.

After rounding two turns, I glimpsed a figure turning right about thirty feet ahead of me.

"Josh, it's Sharp, Josh."

He either didn't hear me or was so scared he didn't want to stop.

I sprinted ahead.

When I reached the same corner and turned into the next corridor, it was empty.

Shit.

The ship was only so long, eventually Josh would run out of room. A minute later, that's exactly what happened.

I turned the final bend into a vast foyer area centered around a grand stairway leading down to the outer deck... at the stern of the vessel.

Joshua Jones stood at the top of the stairs, looking down.

"Josh, stop. It's Nicholas, don't go down there."

The boy looked up at me. Josh's face showed a mixture of relief and panic.

"Nicholas, thank..."

Out of a corridor on the opposite side, a figure suddenly appeared. Zafina Faez. She held a decent size pistol in her hand and was pointing it at the boy.

"Josh, I've been looking for you," she said, not sounding the least bit motherly.

She then glanced at me.

"Don't even think about it, Sharp. The boy would be dead

before you could act."

All the relief drained from Josh's face, leaving only a grim mask of terror.

"It'll be all right Josh," I said.

"It will be all right Sharp, but not for you." As Zafina spoke, she edged toward the stairway.

"We're going to leave you now, Sharp. If you'd care to join us, I'm sure our Compass Black team will be delighted to welcome you."

Before I could react, the woman took one final step towards the petrified boy and shoved him down the stairs. She followed, disappearing after him.

Sometimes life just doesn't present you with choices.

I leaped forward, jumped the rail and plummeted down the stairwell. I did my best to keep my gun hand level, but as I landed, my right leg buckled. By the time I rose to my feet, the situation was alarmingly evident.

Zafina Faez stood at the stern, leaning against the railing. She had her left arm around Josh Jones' waist. She pressed the barrel of her pistol against Josh's temple with her right.

"Amazing, I really thought you'd make a break for it," she yelled above the howling storm.

Wind lashed her face while the ship rode the huge swells. Behind her, a wall of deep water rose before morphing into the dark night sky. But it wasn't what I saw at the back of the woman that concerned me. On each side of her stood two Compass Black mercenaries, feet apart in the shooter's stance, aiming their Kalashnikov automatic rifles at me.

"I suggest you take the boy inside, Ms. Faez," shouted the operative on the far right. James Muldoon. "Now Sharp, surely even a 'gung-ho' fool like you can see that you haven't got a chance here," he continued. "Drop your weapon."

"Don't move an inch Zafina," I said, my gun aimed at her chest.

Behind her, the swell rose above the stern once more. Nobody else noticed.

"Sharp, you have one second to live," yelled Muldoon.

"An American fool hero like you won't shoot a woman, Nicholas Sharp," yelled Zafina. She smiled as she spoke, confident of her invulnerability.

So, I shot her.

The next moment was a blur of chaos.

The man beside Muldoon tumbled down as a round penetrated the back of his head. I dived left just as a hail of bullets ripped into the wall where I'd been standing. As I hit the deck, I took out the Compass Black operative on the far left. Clean shot to the chest. The guy beside him crumpled simultaneously. But that wasn't my work.

Muldoon took cover behind a marble pillar that supported an upper deck. He craned his head, searching for the other shooter. Two rounds splintering the column sent him back into hiding.

I rushed forward, grabbing Josh by the arm as he gazed down at Zafina's crumpled form.

"We're out of here, mate," I yelled as I guided him along the deck toward the bow.

"Keep your head down."

Bullets shattered the glass around us as we pushed on.

"How…"

"I don't have time to explain. Just keep moving," I shouted.

Greatrex and I had known that if shit went down, it was likely to happen on the stern of the ship. As arranged, he

335

maintained position in the RIB a couple of swells behind *Neisha*, stalking the bigger vessel while remaining in the darkness. In the howling of the storm, his engines would go unnoticed. I figured he'd seen what was going down and acted accordingly. Greatrex may not be in love with the sea, but he was one hell of a boatman. Controlling the RIB while making those shots was impressive.

"Keep pushing forward Josh. It's our only chance," I said.

I knew the events that would unfold behind us. The remaining Compass Black operatives would be swarming over the boat. Without distraction, they'd find us quickly, and I held no doubt about our fate if they did.

Greatrex would be the distraction. The plan was for him to appear out of the darkness, shoot up the decks of Faez's ship and depart rapidly. Guerrilla warfare. It had been a successful tactic against the American forces in Vietnam. This was our version of it.

Gun shots sounded through the night air. They came in bursts and from different directions. While it was good for Josh and me, Greatrex's luck couldn't hold up for ever.

"We're currently on the port side. Our extraction point is the starboard side, just aft of the bow." I shouted to the boy. "We've got to make it there."

The big fella was clearly keeping the Compass Black operatives busy. We made it to the bow unhindered.

Barely able to stand upright on the rolling deck, we rounded the bow. The question remained, could Greatrex manipulate sufficient clear time to rendezvous here undetected? We only needed a few seconds to get the boy off the ship.

I grabbed Josh, pushing him under the overhang of the ship's helipad. The space was just enough for both of us.

But I never made it.

Standing up to check if Greatrex was within sight, I suddenly lunged forward as if hit by a train. My face smashed against the metal deck rail as I crashed down. A boot hammered into my ribs, then another stomped on my neck. The pain jolted through my body like electricity.

I rolled onto my back, looking up at the figure towering over me.

James Muldoon.

Without hesitation, he flipped his rifle over and drove the handle into my gut. I gagged, searching for a breath.

The snarl on his face, his skin drawn tight, and teeth exposed like a hyena, spoke the intensity of his hatred.

"It's over Sharp, and to be honest, it wasn't that hard. All I had to do was think like you. A cold-blooded killer. We both know that's who you really are. While the others were firing blind into the night, I channeled you, and here we are."

He stabbed me again with his rifle butt, clearly reveling in my pain.

I tried to talk, but the words came out as disconnected splutters.

"Kill me... if you want... but for God's sake, let the boy go... what's he to you?"

"Hero to the damn end, aren't we? Of course, I'm going to kill you, and yes, the boy means nothing to me except a paycheck and the joy of the knowing that the man who killed my brother will die understanding he failed to protect a child."

I turned my head sideways, my cheek pressing against the cold deck. My pistol lay five feet away. It may as well have been five miles.

Muldoon noticed my glance and laughed.

"A sniper without a gun. Now, just pathetically mortal."

"You're a prick Muldoon."

"And you're a dead man."

He flipped his gun again, pointing it directly at my forehead.

"Goodbye, Mr. Sharp."

I didn't close my eyes, but I wanted to. Muldoon's hand squeezed on the trigger, and the shot resonated. But the round went wide as the operative lost his balance when his legs were pulled from under him.

Josh.

No invitation required. I pounded my fist into Muldoon's cheek as he toppled over me. His grunt told me I had more work to do. Raising myself to my knees, I punched him hard in the gut, a bit of his own medicine. The grunt morphed into a gasp.

We struggled over his weapon, each of us gripping it desperately with both hands, a fight of strength and willpower. Suddenly, a light flashed, reflecting off the edge of the chopper pad beside us. I heard the roar of outboard engines. Greatrex.

"Josh, jump. Do it now."

As I wrestled with Muldoon, I could only afford a quick glance at the boy. He stood transfixed.

"Josh, now. This is your one chance."

He seemed to snap out of it.

"What about you…"

"Just go."

He went.

As the boy disappeared over the side, I hoped Greatrex was there to catch him. The receding sound of the RIB's engines gave me hope.

Muldoon gritted his teeth like a wild animal, his sole focus on retaining control of his weapon. I did the same. It could go either way.

Out of the shadows along the deck, voices yelled. Shit. More Compass Black men. Even if I win, I lose.

I looked up, to see them scampering down the gangway. They were only ten yards away. I tugged harder on the rifle. So did Muldoon.

Although perched above him, I had no advantage, but I had a better view. I caught sight of his men. He couldn't. I also saw my pistol lying two feet from Muldoon's head. One chance.

In a single movement, I released my grip on the rifle. It retracted straight back into his face. Leaning over him, I reached out and grabbed at the pistol. It slid away on the deck, but only a couple of inches. Muldoon began to smile under me, sensing victory.

I strained further. Suddenly, the pistol was within my clasp. Muldoon was swinging the Kalashnikov around. With my free hand, I pressed it against his chest as I raised the pistol. His men, now only five yards distant, hadn't fired for risk of hitting their boss.

I fired.

Straight between the eyes.

Nicholas Sharp, cold-blooded killer.

I looked up. The Compass Black men were only two yards away. I got off a quick couple of shots in their direction and dived over the ship's rail.

Three seconds later and for the second time that night, I felt the violent, freezing, swirling water overtake me as I sank beneath the surface.

Chapter 59

RAHMAT BERAS

"Sharp is dead. We're uncertain of the boy's fate, but it doesn't matter."

The older man leaned forward in his seat.

"A little while ago, Rahmat, you said the boy was important in keeping Deagan Jones under control. Now you say it doesn't matter."

"We have the starboard engine running again. We are proceeding, on plan, but slightly behind our schedule," Beras responded.

"There seem to be a lot of mishaps, Rahmat," said Faez. The older man glared into the younger's eyes. "You seem uneasy. Is there something you're not telling me?"

Beras looked down, aware there was no way around this.

"Talk," Faez insisted.

"I am so sorry. Nicholas Sharp killed Zafina."

The old man crumpled before Beras' eyes. His skin crinkled, his shoulders sagged, and his eyelids shut so tightly, Beras wondered if Faez would ever open them again.

Eventually, the old man looked up. Never before had Beras encountered such a hateful gaze.

"Are you certain Sharp is dead?"

"No doubt, Muldoon's men saw him go overboard. There was no boat below."

"Then proceed."

Chapter 60

"Because I knew you'd do something stupid like just going over the edge."

Jack Greatrex stared at me, a smug grin on his face.

Safely on the bridge of the *Torrent* with Deagan Jones, Joshua, Jim Reardon, and Vanessa Travers looking on, I wondered how the big fella had managed to pluck me out of the Gulf of Mexico after I'd spent twenty minutes flailing around, drinking too much seawater, and eventually resigning myself to my watery fate.

"We wreaked some havoc during another round of the ship before our final attempt to find you. You'd drifted a few hundred yards west. It's not really me you need to thank Nicholas, it's Josh. He spotted you," said Greatrex.

I studied the boy, sitting huddled close to his father. The lad had been through a lot, way too much for a kid of his age.

"You certainly are you father's son, Josh. Not only finding me in that whirlpool but attacking James Muldoon like that. You're a brave guy."

"He was a prick," said the boy.

"Yes, indeed he was," I laughed.

"I hate to break up this reunion," Travers interrupted, but we're just coming up on the *Neisha*. They've slowed considerably, but they're almost in the target range required to activate their plan."

I looked at my watch. It had stopped, clearly not as waterproof as advertised.

"What's the time Travers?"

"Eight minutes until the explosives you left on board Faez's boat are due to detonate."

"Are we far enough away to be safe?" asked Reardon.

"Affirmative," replied the captain. "But I thought you'd like to witness her go for yourselves."

"Affirmative," I responded, smiling, and then coughed my guts out.

A few minutes later we were running parallel to Faez's ship, around a mile to the west.

"Three minutes," said Greatrex.

I was convinced that everybody onboard that ship was guilty. From what I saw, everyone knew what they'd come to do, or at least that it involved murder. Faez and Beras' campaign had already taken too many lives. I thought back to Teddy Best, the fisherman, Pedro, and Deagan Jones' trusted friend, Soloman Triak.

No, there were no innocents on that vessel.

"One minute," the big fella continued his commentary.

Sixty seconds later, the bridge's radio spluttered to life.

'Crimson Wave, Torrent, this is private vessel Neisha. Please respond.'

Travers looked at me questioningly, eyebrows arched. I nodded.

'Neisha, this is Torrent.'

'To whom am I speaking?'

'This is Captain Vanessa Travers, master of the Torrent. Please

343

state your business.'

'I am Rahmat Beras, currently in charge of the private vessel Neisha. I assume there are several interested parties listening in to this transmission. Jim Reardon, Jack Greatrex, possibly even Deagan Jones.'

'I repeat, please state your business.'

'Let me begin by not offering you my commiserations on the death of Nicholas Sharp. You will also have noticed by now that the explosive devices Sharp left on this vessel have not detonated. That is because they are sitting in front of me on our bridge, timers disarmed. That fool, Sharp, died for nothing.'

'Not for nothing Beras, he saved my son.'

'Ah, Deagan, you do seem to keep popping up. Well, the illusion that Sharp saved your boy is at best, temporary, I'm afraid. If one of you takes a look through your binoculars, you'll see two of my men setting up a MANPAD. That's right. A portable missile system that I'm led to believe will have no difficulty in sending your vessel to the ocean floor. You have cost the Faez family a great deal. Now you will pay with your lives.'

'Not going to happen, Beras,' I interrupted.

'Who is this?'

'A voice from the grave.'

'Sharp? Impossible.'

I didn't respond. This would come down to seconds. I hoped my appearance would cause Beras enough confusion to buy us a few more of those precious seconds.

There was a small, locked cupboard on the bridge. From our earlier experience, I knew it held firearms, including the pistols Greatrex and I had used earlier. It also contained a rifle. Travers had explained it was for use against a possible piracy attack.

I looked at Travers while pointing to the cupboard. She threw me the keys. With my thumb and fingers, I signaled to the others to keep Beras talking… if they could.

"If you're going to kill us, at least tell us what your damn plan is, man,'" said Jones, grabbing the microphone.

I pulled the rifle out of the cabinet and checked it. It was a Bergara B-14 HMR, a reasonably straight forward and effective weapon. Throwing the strap over my shoulder, I slammed open the starboard door and sprinted outside to the bridge deck. The wind and waves hadn't abated, making the conditions for any kind of accurate shot almost impossible.

I needed more height and a flatter base to try what I had in mind. I glanced up to see the monkey island, the deck on top of the bridge cabin, which held the radar and other marine toys. I climbed up onto the guard rail. What would have been a reasonably easy maneuver in calm weather seemed impossibly dangerous as the ship weaved and tossed its way through the storm.

What the hell, I was dead already.

I clambered higher, my shoes losing grip twice, resulting in my body flailing in the wind like a flag as I gripped the edge of the roof. Eventually, I swung myself up onto the monkey island. There was no rail, so I slid across the smooth surface and wrapped an arm around the radar base.

"It's worse than we thought, Nicholas. They're planning on taking out a heap of platforms as well as the pipelines. Plus, their MANPAD is almost prepped."

After listening to Beras' spiel, Greatrex had ventured out, binoculars in hand. The confusion caused by my resurrection may have bought time with Beras, but clearly not with his weapons guy.

"How long?" I shouted down.

"Fifteen seconds at most."

I yanked the rifle off my back and thrust it forward. Lying flat on the deck, I had a clear view of the Compass Black operative propping the missile launcher on his shoulder, a colleague standing behind him for backup.

"Ten seconds, Nicholas."

I began to squeeze the rifle's trigger when my target disappeared.

The *Torrent* had risen up on a swell as Faez's ship rolled down.

Damn.

"Five seconds, Nicholas."

All I could do was wait... and count.

Four... three... two...

Suddenly, the missile launcher sprung back into view.

"Nicholas, he's about to fire."

Without pausing to inhale, I squeezed the trigger.

Glued to my site, I saw the shooter take a violent step backward before falling. As he tumbled, he must have released the missile, because it soared straight up in the air, at right angles to the sea. The projectile would have needed to be manually armed after it locked on the *Torrent*, so we were safe. Even if the SAM returned to hit the *Neisha* directly, it wouldn't explode. Shame really.

But the thought of it gave me an idea.

"You got him, Nicholas. Come on down."

"Not happening Jack."

If the status quo didn't change immediately, Beras and his people would still reach their target range, fulfill their mission, and many innocent lives would be sacrificed. Everything we'd been through would have been for nothing.

That couldn't be allowed.

"Tell Travers to maintain this course." I yelled.

"Roger, maintain course."

I swung the barrel of the rifle toward *Neisha*'s bridge. It was fortunate that glass surrounded every ship's bridge, providing a substantial view out.

It also provided a substantial view in.

RAHMAT BERAS

Beras sat on the bridge chair, eyes glued to the *Torrent*, waiting for the flare of the missile that would send her under.

Nothing.

He turned his binoculars to the port deck of his own ship, just in time to see his operative stumble, and the SAM released straight into the air.

How the hell had that happened?

He swung the binoculars back to the *Torrent*. A large figure stood on the bridge deck, looking upward and to his rear. Beras followed his gaze.

Sharp.

Flat on the roof, rifle in hand. The fool. Didn't he get it? He may have taken down one operative, but Beras had plenty more men and several spare missiles for the launcher. It would only be a matter of a few minutes and the *Torrent* would cease to exist.

For a few seconds, he stood in the window, staring across the space between the two ships. Then he sat back in the chair, secure in the knowledge that Sharp couldn't touch them.

NICHOLAS SHARP

I scanned the *Neisha's* bridge through the rifle's sight. I made out multiple figures; three, maybe four. I focused on a silhouette at the window. He sat on a chair, partly concealing the captain. Beras. Several packages lay on a shelf in front of him. Even at this distance, I recognized them.

The shot seemed impossible. The angle was steeper and the target much smaller than before. All I'd previously had to do was wound the Compass Black man somewhere on his torso and prevent him from firing. Now I had to hit a small package on a shelf a mile away in a moving sea with winds stronger than I could calculate.

I peered through the sight, toward the distant target, attempting to figure out how to make the shot. There were just too many variables. I tried to judge the rise and fall of both ships, but the ocean was an unpredictable force.

In the end, all I could do was commit… and pray.

I decided to fire on the peak of the third swell.

Rise. Check distance.

Fall. Wait.

Rise. Wind. Beyond measure, but I'd need to angle the shot radically upwind from the target.

Fall. Wait.

Rise. Breathe in. Steady the weapon as much as possible….

Squeeze the trigger.

A radio antenna above *Neisha*'s bridge snapped off before spiraling off into the wind.

Failure.

It wasn't all bad news. Now I had relativity. I brought the tip of the rifle down, moving it minutely to the left.

Fall. Wait.

Rise. Check... everything.

Fall. Wait.

Rise. I tensed, ready to fire. The bridge came into view. The figure I assumed to be Beras had risen from his seat and now stood, blocking my view of the package. The rain lashed my face, dowsing my eyes in a watery film.

Crap.

Fall. Wait.

Rise. The figure had moved back to his seat. The package sat clearly in my sight.

Now or never.

RAHMAT BERAS

A metallic scrape clattered on the bridge's roof, inconsequential.

Confident a satisfactory resolution was approaching, Beras allowed himself a moment to focus on their impending success. Staring out the ship's window to the swirling sea, his gaze momentarily dropped down to the package on the shelf in front of him.

"Shi..."

NICHOLAS SHARP

Fire.

The initial explosion blasted the bridge right off its infrastructure, turning the site into a whirlwind of flames. The power of Gelatin Nitroglycerin Dynamite. Secondary explosions ripped down through the decks like fireworks. I waited, sodden and exhausted, atop the Torrent's bridge, knowing the best was yet to come.

After a brief interval, there it was. A huge fireball rose into the sky as the vapors within *Neisha*'s massive fuel tanks exploded into nothingness.

Slowly, the burning wreck descended into the foaming swell.

So dead men can't talk.

Well, consider that a message from those you killed, motherfucker.

Epilogue

Five Weeks Later

"Sure as hell, it would have been a mess if you guys hadn't shown up."

Trent Crais appeared back to his normal self.

"You seem fine now, Trent. How do you feel?" I asked.

"Ready to save the world. Oh, hang on, we just did that," he chuckled. "It takes more than being on the wrong end of a firefight to keep this cowboy off his horse."

"Once a Texan, always a Texan," said Jim Reardon.

We sat backstage in a well-appointed VIP lounge at the Forum in LA. Cetia Forez had just performed to a sell-out crowd and had four more shows over the next week. Tia had been kind enough to invite me on stage to perform our song again. It had been a very different performance to the night at Kalid Amir Faez's hideaway on the island of Maladh. Who would have thought that within twenty-four hours of playing at the wedding, I'd be responsible for the death of the bride and her father?

"What's the turn up from the aftermath?" Greatrex asked Crais.

"Well, our people, along with every other agency in the country, and several from other nations, actually got their asses into gear. They've taken a number of Compass Black teams into custody and are in the process of dismantling and removing all the explosive devices at all locations, beginning with the platforms. And I can tell you there are a lot of them."

"Will they be able to locate them all?" asked Greatrex.

"Without the Faez family's financial support to bail them out, the Compass Black people caught on the ground started singing like the Texas Boys' Choir. They'll get them all," Crais replied.

"And how about you, Cowboy, after the spray you gave your boss, do you still have a job?" I inquired.

"There's the thing," the agent began. "It seems, at least in the agency's eyes, I'm the man of the moment. They offered me a promotion. I'm now in charge of our Houston office."

"Well, that's one for the good guys," said Deagan Jones. He and Josh had been invited by Tia to attend the show. She mentioned she had a special reason but didn't explain further.

"Are you looking forward to meeting a world-famous superstar, Josh?" asked Reardon.

"Well, yeah, kind of. I'd have preferred Dave Grohl, but she's pretty cool."

After what Josh had been through, I reckoned he was pretty cool.

Jones spoke. "You know, I wondered why Rahmat Beras got into bed with the Faez family at first. He was an incredibly wealthy and influential man in his own right. But I figured the scope and cost of their machinations required next level financing. I'm reluctant to admit it, but infiltrating Crimson Wave so he'd have a voice at the table in the response to what would have been the world's largest environmental catastrophe was a stroke of misguided genius."

"It's funny how wealth breeds greed," said Reardon.

Huge words coming from an oilman.

"So how about you, Deagan? Are you back in the driver's seat at Crimson Wave?" I asked.

"Big time," Josh replied proudly.

"Yes, it's worked out pretty well. Apparently, the fact we came so close to disaster, and I contributed to the solution has increased our influence… and our funding."

"What about you Nicholas? How do you feel about everything that went down? In the end, you saved the day," said Jones.

"That's the rubbish I've come to expect from you, Deagan," I replied, smiling. "You, more than anybody, know what a team effort this was. Just look around this room."

"Nice avoidance," Jones responded. "Yet you didn't answer my question."

I glanced up at Greatrex. He knew me well enough to appreciate those weren't the sort of questions I liked.

"Maybe we should move on," he suggested.

I raised the palm of my hand.

"No Jack, it's okay. After what Deagan has been through, he deserves a truthful answer. To be honest, Deagan, I hate this shit. Like all of us, I'll never fully understand what drives people to do what they do. I now accept that if I'm there, and can do something, I will."

I looked over to Greatrex.

"Correction, we will. But everything has a cost. I killed a woman. As old-fashioned as it sounds, I'll need to come to terms with that. When I took the shot that brought down the boat, I prayed that there were no innocents onboard. I was pretty sure, but who could be one hundred percent certain?"

"Perhaps I can help you with that," said Crais. "Amongst

those in the Faez organization that were interviewed by our guys was one of *Neisha*'s crew, a cook. He was supposed to be on board but called in sick the night before they left. Under some pressure, he informed us that the entire crew, and for the journey it was a minimal size, had not only signed disclaimers stating they would never speak of the events they would see, but each of them also accepted five hundred thousand US dollars into their bank accounts to ensure their silence."

Greatrex checked my reaction.

"One box ticked, Nicholas."

Deagan Jones studied me across the room, his stare penetrating.

"You're a rare bird, Nicholas Sharp. A hero who entertains regret. A fighting man who'd rather sit at a piano than fire a gun."

I looked him in the eye.

"Takes one to know one, Deagan."

Thankfully, the moment was interrupted by some shuffling and murmurs from the corridor. The door opened and a large security man strode in. He surveyed the space before opening the door wider and stepping to the side.

A second later, one of the most beautiful and talented women in the world strolled into the room. Cetia Forez's presence stopped the conversation cold.

"Tia," I said.

"Nicholas, as usual, you played like a virtuoso." The lady of the hour walked over to me, kissed my cheek and said, "Please introduce me. I don't believe I've met everyone here."

I did the intro thing. When Tia got to Josh, she reached for his hand, before leaning forward and pressing her lips to his cheek. His color flushed... Dave who?

When I introduced her to Deagan Jones, she also clasped his hand. "You are a hero of mine, Captain Jones. I've followed your work for years."

Jones smiled. He seemed taken aback.

"And you're probably wondering why you received such a mysterious invitation to my show," she added.

"The thought had crossed my mind, Ms. Forez."

"Tia," she corrected. "It is my intention, with one stipulation, to make a donation to Crimson Wave. I believe it should be quite substantial. All the proceeds from this week's five LA shows will go to your organization."

Crais whistled, impressed.

"You are kind, and I assure you, your generosity is greatly appreciated," Jones responded.

"So, Tia," I interrupted. "What is the condition?"

Tia laughed and turned toward me.

"I am going to be the one to unwrap the mystery of Nicholas Sharp. You shall take me out to supper tonight and tell me exactly what happened in Saudi Arabia and afterwards, including why I was whisked out of the county by secret government agents with no warning."

The lady smiled.

Everybody else gaped at me. No pressure here, just a few million towards a great cause.

Greatrex chuckling in the corner seemed to have trouble controlling himself.

Everything went quiet. The silence of expectation.

I shrugged my shoulders, snatched my car keys out of my pocket, and stood up.

"Grab your coat, girl... and your check book."

JACK GREATREX

Greatrex stood at the gate. For a moment, he closed his eyes. This would be difficult, but he had to do it. He took a deep breath, pushed the gate open, and strode up the path.

The door opened before he'd finished knocking.

"Jack."

"Amanda, thanks for seeing me."

"Don't be silly. It's inevitable I'll hear everything, and I'd rather hear it from you."

Greatrex followed Amanda Best inside.

They sat on a comfortable sofa, bodies angled sideways, facing each other. Amanda reached for Greatrex's hand.

"Please, leave nothing out. I need to understand."

Greatrex revealed the whole story. The lead up to the events in Guyana and all that happened subsequently. He explained the misconceived plot, the potential disaster and, of course, he spoke of those individuals responsible.

When he was done, the two shared a subdued silence.

After a time, Amanda gazed up at the big fella, tears slowly washing down her face.

"What about Pedro? Why did he leave Teddy at the mercy of the sea?" she asked.

"A couple of Compass Black operatives forced him at gunpoint. Later they made sure he'd never talk."

Another moment passed.

"Then Teddy died doing what he loved," she said.

"You mean diving?"

"No Jack, he gave his life for his greatest passion, rescuing the planet from the vandals who threaten it."

Greatrex reflected on the words before nodding.

"Yes, Amanda, that's exactly what he did."

A few minutes later, Greatrex closed the gate behind him. There were times he wondered if it was all worth it. The danger, the bloodshed. The belief. Then he thought of Teddy Best. A man who bartered his own mortality for the depth of his convictions.

Greatrex turned and walked down the road. With each step, his doubts dissipated into the air.

Afterword

Get your FREE electronic copy of the NICHOLAS SHARP origins Novella PLAY OUT, the latest news about new releases and some other exciting freebies along the way by joining my mailing list at my website: https://markmannock.com

Although you can begin reading the NICHOLAS SHARP THRILLER series at any point here is my suggested order of reading:

1. **KILLSONG** (NS thriller No. 1-*available on Amazon*)
2. **BLOOD NOTE** (A NS short story-*available exclusively to my mailing list members. I'll send you the link 7 days after sign-up*)
3. **LETHAL SCORE** (NS thriller No. 2-*available on Amazon*)
4. **HELL'S CHOIR** (NS thriller No. 3-*available on Amazon*)
5. **SILENT VOICE** (NS thriller No. 4-*available on Amazon*)
6. **COUNTERPOINT** (NS thriller No. 5-*available on Amazon*)
7. **ECHO BLUE** (NS thriller No. 6-*available on Amazon*)

PLAY OUT-an origins novella (*available exclusively to my* *mailing list members on sign-up*) can be read at any point. The story takes you back to when Nicholas Sharp left the U.S. Marines.

What readers are saying about the Nicholas Sharp Series:

"I had to keep reading to the end, could not put it away until I had finished."

"I love Lee Child and now have another author who is just as good."

"Jack Reacher's attitude... John Lennon's sensibilities."

"I really enjoyed the sniper-musician-reluctant warrior character..."

"I've read hundreds of books throughout the years and the pandemic has provided me with extra time to discover more reading treasures. Play Out (Nicholas Sharp Origins novella) is one of the best."

"Without a doubt this is a cracking novel... the story then keeps at you in leaps and bounds! Full of action all the way. Just brilliant!"

Checkout Mark's **Lachlan Byrn Thrillers**

1. **DIE AS YOU KILL** (LB thriller No. 1-*available on*

Amazon)

Reviews are life's blood to an author. If you've enjoyed ECHO BLUE please consider leaving a review on the book's Amazon page or on GOODREADS.

About the Author

Mark Mannock was born in Melbourne, Australia. He has had an extensive career in the music industry including supporting, recording with or writing for Tina Turner, Joni Mitchell, The Eurythmics, Irene Cara and David Hudson. His recorded work with Lia Scallon has twice been long-listed for Grammy Awards. As a composer/songwriter Mark's music has been used across the world in countless television and theatre contexts, including the 'American Survivor' TV series and 'Sleuth' playwright Anthony Shaffer's later productions.

Mark is presently writing the successful 'Nicholas Sharp' thriller series about a disillusioned former US sniper whose past plagues him as he makes his way in the contemporary music industry. Sharp is a man whose insatiable curiosity and embedded moral compass lead him to places he ought not go. The series is currently read in over 50 countries.

Mark also writes the exciting new Lachlan Byrn Thrillers. Is Byrn a vigilante or a serial killer? You decide!

Mark lives in Kettering, Tasmania with his family. His travels around the globe act as inspirations for his writing.

Mark enjoys hearing from his readers, so please feel free to contact him.

You can connect with me on:
- https://markmannock.com
- https://www.facebook.com/markmannockbooks

Subscribe to my newsletter:
- https://markmannock.com

Also by Mark Mannock

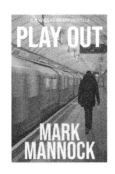

PLAY OUT
A Nicholas Sharp Origin Novella

Sign up to my mailing list and receive this book for free!

Set five years before **KILLSONG**
A Terrorist attack on the London Underground. Nicholas Sharp doesn't think so.

While on leave from Iraq, the U.S. Marine Sniper finds himself intervening when innocent lives are threatened. He walks away, but for Sharp it's never that easy. Something doesn't feel right. Twenty-four hours later everything is wrong.

The brief solace he finds in his beloved piano is shattered when Sharp becomes the attacker's next target. Step up or step away. Nicholas Sharp doesn't like to kill, but he sure as hell knows how to.

Somewhere between Clancy's *Jack Ryan* and Ludlum's *Jason Bourne*, Nicholas Sharp may be a flawed and reluctant hero, but you certainly want him on your side.

"I've read hundreds of books throughout the years and the pandemic has provided me with extra time to discover more reading treasures. Play Out is one of the best." **Goodreads Reviewer-5 STARS**

The Nicholas Sharp origins novella PLAY OUT is sent to you FREE when you join my mailing list at
https://markmannock.com

KILLSONG
Nicholas Sharp Thriller #1

Reluctant, determined, lethal. Nicholas Sharp is a killer musician... literally!

Nicholas Sharp knew there would be blood on his hands. It was just a question of how much.

The death of a child and her mother, or the loss of countless thousands. Sharp is ordered to choose, but the former Marine Sniper gave up following orders long ago.

Sharp's newfound refuge as a musician is suddenly blasted apart. While he is preparing to back well-known singer Robbie West on a USO tour of Iraq, a close friend and her daughter disappear.

Trapped in a deadly maze of colliding worlds and dark agendas as competing forces race to locate discarded biological weapons, Sharp is compelled to act.

One wrong decision, one misstep… and the consequences could be disastrous.

"I had to keep reading to the end, could not put it away until I had finished." **Amazon Reader- 5 STARS**

Available on Amazon:
http://www.amazon.com/dp/B08CT1FHF5
http://www.amazon.co.uk/dp/B08CT1FHF5
http://www.amazon.com.au/dp/B08CT1FHF5
https://www.amazon.ca/dp/B08CT1FHF5

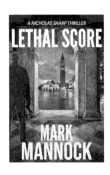

LETHAL SCORE
Nicholas Sharp Thriller #2

"A great book that has more twists and turns than you can imagine. Pick up and read at all costs." **Goodreads Reviewer 5 STARS**

You can't stop someone with nothing to lose...

Nicholas Sharp is on a tour through Europe, the concerts are sold out and the former Marine sniper turned musician is living in luxury thanks to promoter Antonio Ascardi.

Suddenly it all goes wrong. People are dying along the way and Sharp is blamed. Now a hunted man, accused of terrorist crimes across the continent, Nicholas Sharp must fight for his life and freedom.

Available on Amazon:

http://www.amazon.com/dp/B08CSYKG18
http://www.amazon.co.uk/dp/B08CSYKG18
http://www.amazon.com.au/dp/B08CSYKG18
https://www.amazon.ca/dp/B08CSYKG18

HELL'S CHOIR
Nicholas Sharp Thriller #3

A goodwill visit to Sudan, what could possibly go wrong?
Nicholas Sharp is performing as part of a political and cultural group representing the US. Suddenly caught up in the middle of a political coup, the leader of the American contingent goes missing and his security staff murdered.

Communication with the outside world is cut off. It falls to Sharp and Greatrex to track their missing leader down.

But then things get really complicated...

"The story then keeps at you in leaps and bounds! Full of action all the way. Just brilliant!" **Amazon Reader-5 STARS**

"Great read and a fun ride." **Amazon Reader-5 STARS**

Available on Amazon:
  http://www.amazon.com/dp/B08LRB8CWN
  http://www.amazon.co.uk/dp/B08LRB8CWN
  http://www.amazon.com.au/dp/B08LRB8CWN
  https://www.amazon.ca/dp/B08LRB8CWN

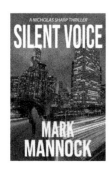

SILENT VOICE
Nicholas Sharp Thriller #4

It's dangerous to be right when the government is wrong...

Hunted down by their government's secret service, the members of protest band Kha Cring flee to Los Angeles to begin a new life. After an unexpected attack, the musicians' safe exile in LA is jeopardized. The desire to fight for their country's freedom undiminished, the band find their soaring popularity and politically messaged music no longer enough to protect them from the evil they escaped.

A deadlier weapon is needed. Nicholas Sharp.

In an instant things go terribly wrong as Sharp finds himself the focus of a network of international conspirators intent on wiping both he and the members of Kha Cring from the face of the planet.

Available on Amazon:

http://www.amazon.com/dp/B08W1V9FWS
http://www.amazon.co.uk/dp/B08W1V9FWS
http://www.amazon.com.au/dp/B08W1V9FWS
https://www.amazon.ca/dp/B08W1V9FWS

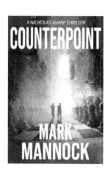

COUNTERPOINT
Nicholas Sharp Thriller #5

Looking in the mirror, he saw only death...

Pursued by one of the world's most efficient and ruthless assassins, Nicholas Sharp almost admires the deadly operator's meticulous talents, until the assassin starts coming after Sharp through his friends. Sharp's investigations reveal that the killer also has another target in sight: the US Secretary of Defense. Is there a dark connection?

Face to face with a past he'd considered banished from his memory, Nicholas Sharp questions not only his own moral compass but also his slim chance of survival.

Available on Amazon:
   http://www.amazon.com/dp/B0BVTVWZ6N
   http://www.amazon.co.uk/dp/B0BVTVWZ6N
   http://www.amazon.com.au/dp/B0BVTVWZ6N
   https://www.amazon.ca/dp/B0BVTVWZ6N

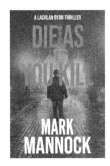

DIE AS YOU KILL
Lachlan Byrn Thriller #1
Assassin, vigilante or serial killer?
Vadim Aleyev, President of the Russian Federation is out of control. He's pushing his country, his people and the world to the brink of a catastrophic war.

Around the globe, world leaders are worried, yet no one seems prepared to act. Then one nation unleashes its most fearsome weapon: Lachlan Byrn.

Assassin, vigilante or serial killer? Byrn has a passion for his work that transcends the rules of engagement. He gets up close and personal with his victims… very close, very personal and he's exceptionally deadly.

As the clock ticks, can one man with a tenuous grip on his own sanity, achieve the unachievable?

Available on Amazon:

http://www.amazon.com/dp/B0CJ4PSW97
http://www.amazon.co.uk/dp/B0CJ4PSW97
http://www.amazon.com.au/dp/B0CJ4PSW97
https://www.amazon.ca/dp/B0CJ4PSW97

THE NICHOLAS SHARP THRILLERS BOX SET BOOKS 1-3

Nicholas Sharp is a killer musician... literally!

Nicholas Sharp is a disillusioned former US sniper fighting a troubled past and an uncertain future. Seeking solace in his work as a professional musician, Sharp is a man whose insatiable curiosity and embedded moral compass lead him into situations fraught with danger. Nicholas Sharp doesn't like to kill, but he sure as hell knows how to.

Somewhere between Tom Clancy's Jack Ryan and Robert Crais' Elvis Cole, Nicholas Sharp may be a flawed hero, but you definitely want him on your side.

Book 1: KILLSONG
  Book 2: LETHAL SCORE
  BOOK 3: HELL'S CHOIR

Available on Amazon:
  http://www.amazon.com/dp/B08NYLGW1G
  http://www.amazon.co.uk/dp/B08NYLGW1G
  http://www.amazon.com.au/dp/B08NYLGW1G
  https://www.amazon.ca/dp/B08NYLGW1G

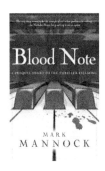

BLOOD NOTE

A Short Story Prequel to the Thriller KILLSONG *(should be read after KILLSONG-available FREE to mailing list subscribers 7 days after sign-up)*

Just turn around and walk away. That was all Nicholas Sharp had to do when the mysterious and intoxicating Elena approached him for help.

She knew far too much about him. The warning signs were all there.

Sharp didn't listen to them.

What followed for the former Marine Sniper turned musician, was a harrowing night of violence, deceit and intrigue.

When the sunrise ushered in a new day, Sharp thought it was all over…but it was really just beginning.

Printed in Great Britain
by Amazon

29070347R00219